White Plains

Rebecca Perkin

ISBN 9780995798427
Paperback Edition 2017
Published by Rebecca Perkin (www.rebeccaperkinauthor.com)
Cover design by Martin Meehan (www.martin-meehan.co.uk)

For Dad, who read with the best voices

and

For Jess, the greatest dog a girl could ask for

Prologue

June

'SAM, SAMUEL, WAKE UP. You've *got* to wake up.' The voice breaks through the darkness. Samuel groans. His eyelids feel so heavy he can barely open them.

'Ethan is that you?' he says.

'Yeah, Sam, it's me. You've got to open your eyes.'

His brother's voice sounds distant. He focuses all his energy on moving the tiny muscles in his eyelids, forcing them apart. He shrinks back as a myriad of light enters his pupils.

'What *is* that? What's all that noise?' Every part of his body is throbbing.

'We've got to get out,' Ethan says.

Samuel looks about him. They're in a cramped space, metal everywhere.

'The car … There was a crash,' he says, as rain lashes against the windows.

'Yeah,' Ethan replies. 'Come on, Sam, get with it. We've gotta get out.'

Samuel feels a tug across his chest, then hears the click as his brother releases his seatbelt.

'It's so hot, wha–, Ethan your head. You're bleeding.' The crimson liquid trickles out from his brother's dark hair and runs down his face.

'I know, it's alright. It doesn't hurt, much.'

'Oh God, Mum and Dad are gonna kill us. We only just got our license.'

'Don't worry about that now, you moron. I'm stuck, you've gotta get me out.' He pulls on his seatbelt. 'Anyway, it wasn't my fault. I dunno what happened, but it looks a mess out there.' Ethan tips his head back.

Samuel turns but his neck stiffens.

'Argh,' he moans, rubbing the tight muscles. He looks at the back windscreen; the glass has shattered and shards are everywhere. The wind is blowing in, whipping round the interior, bringing the rain with it. Out of the front window all he can see is steam, drifting up from the bonnet.

'It's my legs,' Ethan says. 'They're trapped under the wheel and my bloody seatbelt won't undo.'

Samuel looks at the back seats now pressing up against the front. He stares down at his brother's legs, but his feet are hidden.

'I'll get you out.'

His brother's pupils are large, his lips dry and his hair matted from blood and sweat. Samuel can feel the adrenaline start to work its way through his body. He wrestles with his brother's seatbelt.

'It's really stuck,' Ethan says. 'Where's your pen-knife?'

'It's in the boot.' Samuel yanks at the belt. 'I could maybe–'

'Just go get some help.'

Samuel glares at him.

'Who's older here?' Ethan persists.

'By three minutes. That hardly makes you a big brother.'

'Just do it, Samuel. *Please.*' Ethan drops his head. 'I think the tank's bust, I can smell petrol.' His words slur a little.

'You alright?'

'Yeah, I'm...' He inhales deeply. 'My chest's a little tight. And this is really starting to kill now.' He lifts his fingers to his head.

Samuel watches his brother's pupils dart about, seemingly unable to focus.

'Ethan? Ethan don't go to sleep. Maybe I should wait here until help comes.'

'No. No you've got to–' Ethan's eyes start to roll.

'Ethan! Ethan, come on, stay awake.' Samuel shakes his brother's arm, then pulls his eyelids open. He doesn't respond. Sitting back in his seat, Samuel shields his eyes from the headlights that are blinking, lighting up the night sky. He can feel the sweat seep from every part of him. His heart feels out of rhythm, like it doesn't know what to do and will burst out of his chest at any moment.

'Shit. *Please* Ethan, *please* don't do this to me.' Samuel checks his pockets. *Where is it?* He reaches down, scrabbling about on the floor, then he feels the solid object. 'There you are.' He picks his phone up and jabs his finger at the cracked screen, but nothing happens. The screen is black. He looks back to his brother, who isn't moving. 'Okay, I'm gonna go get someone. I'll be right back. Just, just hold on.'

He fumbles for the door handle. The cold metal is welcoming against his skin. He pushes but nothing happens.

'Come on.'

He leans his weight against the crushed door. Finally it creaks, then flies open. He dives out, falling onto the tarmac. His legs feel weak, as though all of his blood is being pumped elsewhere.

'I'll be right back,' he says, turning to Ethan. His brother is slumped in the chair, motionless, his head still bleeding.

'Help!' Samuel yells, struggling to his feet and running from the car. 'Someone help me!' He splashes through puddles, the rain beating down. There are crowds of people hovering on the hard shoulder and up the banks. A lorry is overturned, sprawled across both sides of the motorway. There are ambulances and police cars, but everyone appears too busy to help. He runs across the motorway to the other side of the road, where a crowd of people are huddled.

'Please, you have to help me. My brother, he's trapped in the car, back there.' Samuel points behind him. Two girls are sat down on the roadside. One is bleeding from her arm, the other her head.

'Sorry mate, my girlfriend's hurt,' a guy says. 'But there are some ambulance men over there. Firemen are on their way too.'

Samuel doesn't reply. His stomach growls but not from hunger, more like his last meal trying to force its way back up. He turns from the group and flicks his sodden hair from his face. His wet clothes cling to his skin and he blinks away the water that's collected on his eyelashes. A flashing strip of white catches his eye and he spots a man in a bright reflective jacket.

'Hey! Hey please, you've got to help me. My brother…' He runs out of breath, his chest tightening.

'You alright lad? Let me look at you,' the man says.

'I'm fine. It's my brother. You've got to help me. He can't get out. Please, come with me.' He grabs the guy's sleeve and pulls.

'He's just over here.' They clamber over the central reservation. He turns to check the man is still with him. 'His legs are trapped. And his seatbelt–' A huge bang fills the night sky, immediately followed by a rumble, which ripples across the metal landscape.

'Ethan!' Samuel spins back to the car. Smoke billows upwards and he can't see anything. He feels a tug from behind him.

'Wait lad! Wait!' The guy grips his arms, his hold too strong for Samuel to break free. The smoke stings his eyes and tickles at his throat.

'Ethan! Ethan, no!' Seconds later and the smoke swirls, outwards and upwards, thinning. Flames are now teasing their way up the sides of the car. Samuel twists, struggling to break free from the man's grasp. He can't see his brother, the blaze too fierce. Shouts and sirens surround him, but all he can hear is his heartbeat thudding in his ears.

Chapter One

Eleven months later

SAMUEL LISTENS FROM INSIDE HIS TENT. He's glad to be out of the cold rain. The tarpaulin feels damp on his back as he lies with his eyes closed and his arms folded loosely across his chest. The hairs on his arms stand to attention as a breeze enters a small gap in the tent's seam. *Bloody rain. When will you end?*

Moments later, as if in reply, the lashing rain subsides and the wind on the canvas slackens. Outside, a shadow flies past and as it goes, a fleeting chirp follows. Samuel jolts from the movement. The camp is fairly quiet, the weather keeping people inside. Only the distant shouts from the nearby army base filter through the storm. He looks up, focussing on the seam of the tent, gradually allowing his vision to blur. *I'm sorry Ethan, I'm sorry you're not here anymore ...* He pounds his fists into the ground, feeling the muddy earth beneath the tent. *Why do I talk to you? What good does it do? You can't hear me.* He squeezes his eyes tight in an attempt to clear his mind. All he has are memories, but even these are becoming more and more obscure; he worries that one day they'll be lost forever.

The rain continues to drip onto the roof of the tent. He listens as the drops gather and run down the canvas, filtering away. *Why did you have to leave me?* He shivers, then briskly rubs his arms.

A voice echoes outside. He ignores it, used to the murmurings of his friends from the camp. After a few seconds it comes again.

'Samuel! Samuel!'

'Ethan?' he shouts back. Since the crash, he's heard his brother's voice calling out to him hundreds of times, but usually when he's dreaming. He clambers onto his knees before leaving the tent, his legs too long for him to stand inside. His eyes take a moment to adjust to his surroundings. Stillness has settled in the forest.

'Ethan?' He knows it was probably his friends calling, but the familiar word still escapes him. As his voice carries into the night he feels the air around him chill. He senses movement just a few metres away and he squints, trying to get a better look. A branch snaps loudly behind him, echoing in the shadows. Spinning round he spies a silhouette dashing between two trees. Thudding footsteps pound into the soil, getting closer. Mud splatters, landing a short distance from his feet. Then, the impact comes. Falling through the air he feels time slowing down. The trees tower around him.

Through the branches a small twinkling light catches his eye. He tenses, waiting for the ground to come up and hit him. Instead his fall is broken by a pile of leaves. He sinks into them, grateful for the damp slushiness.

'Guys?' he calls out a moment later. 'Ed? George? Stop mucking about!'

Silence.

He scrambles to his feet, clenching his fists in front of him. The stampede of footsteps is now distant.

'Who's there?' he yells. No answer comes. The sound of human existence quietens, and forest life starts up again. The glimmering light still hovers among the branches. He blinks away the drizzling rain and moves towards it. As he does so the light grows and he can see the forest through the opening. The shimmering haze is almost too bright to look at, but he can see that the forest in it looks dry and sunny. He feels as though it's calling him towards it. He edges closer, squinting, trying to focus. Sweat forms under his clothes. A rush of air strikes his face. The forest, having only moments before been alive with a swarm of sounds, is now unearthly quiet.

'What the hell *is* that?' Samuel feels a tremble all around him. He tenses. 'Guys! Where are you? Come here, come look at this!' His words get drowned out by another rush of air. Tentatively he reaches out. A tingling heat runs through his fingers as he makes contact. He sees a blurred figure through the opening, then time seems to stand still and he's unable to move. The air feels as though it's been sucked from his lungs and from everything around him, creating an unnatural silence.

As quickly as everything stopped, it starts again. The forest is alive, the opening he'd been reaching out to suddenly rips apart, faster and faster, until big enough for him to step into. Sensing he can move again he pulls his arm back. He doesn't have time to think and before he realises it, the opening that had started as a slit, engulfs him. He looks back into the forest he's just been in, he has no time to do anything else, the hole swallows him up, contracting before shrinking altogether. He finds himself falling again, only this time it takes much longer for the ground to come up and hit him.

Chapter Two

'SITH, COME ON WHAT ARE YOU DOING?' Alexis calls to the wide-eyed boy who, at fourteen, two years younger than her, appears far less capable, his training seeming to have escaped him.

'I…I'm coming!' he replies, his thick curls flopping about his head as the horse under him trots towards her.

'What's the hold up?' Anka shouts to Alexis, dust scattering as his horse's hooves dig into the ground, obeying its rider.

'Just waiting for Sith. You keep going!' she replies, giving a sharp nod. 'Give him a chance,' she mutters, just as Sith pulls his horse up next to hers, struggling a little to control the beast that's far larger than him.

'What were you doing back there?' she asks.

'Nothing. It's just…I've done something…' Sith replies.

Alexis doesn't respond, but waits patiently for him to continue.

'There was this portal. I didn't realise it was a portal at first, it was small. I was going to close it. I thought Anka would be pleased, if I told him I'd closed it, but...'

'Sith stop rambling. What happened?'

'I, I got distracted. There were these people, and then this boy. He looked about your age. He started to walk towards me. I got scared and...'

'And what?'

'And I ran off. I think I left the gateway open. I'm sorry, I'm really sorry.'

'What!' Alexis hisses, looking round, making sure Anka hasn't heard Sith's confession. 'Who opened it? You know no portals should be open. We're not allowed to travel or watch at the moment, it's too dangerous.'

'I know. *Please* don't tell the Davadores.'

Alexis tugs gently on her horse's reins, bringing his head round, away from the direction of Anka.

'I won't,' she says. 'But this boy, did he come through the gateway?'

Sith looks at her, his brow so furrowed his eyebrows almost meet.

'I don't know.'

Alexis wrinkles her nose. 'The slight delay through the portal might mean we still have time to stop this. You go on, catch up with Anka and the others, I'll go back and try to close it. Whereabouts were you?'

'Just back there, through those trees. Alexis, I'm sorry, please don't be angry.'

Alexis looks at the boy, his young face so creased with worry.

'It's okay, I'm not angry. You didn't open it, but you should have known better and closed it when you had the chance. You know the Davadores' rules at the moment. Your training was cut short, but try to remember the training you've had. You have to be extra careful. We can't let *them* cause any more destruction, anywhere. Don't mention this to Anka.'

Sith looks down at the ground, his only reply a dispirited nod.

'Go, go on.' She watches him, his horse trotting off after the others who are now far ahead. 'Come on Brawn, let's go.' Her long auburn hair drapes over the horse's neck as she bends her head near to his ear. She pats his side and the horse conforms, trotting off in the opposite direction to the others.

'Whoa boy, steady now.' They enter the clearing to where Sith had pointed and Alexis swiftly dismounts Brawn. She tightens her grip on the strap of her crossbow, which is slung over her back.

'All looks quiet, hey boy? We might get away with it.' She strokes the horse, guiding him towards the portal that's still open in mid-air.

She falters, now close enough to the gateway she

can see the boy has already entered it. She holds her breath, knowing exactly what he must be feeling, his body frozen. She lifts her arm, her palm facing the gateway. A breeze skirts around her body and she allows the sounds to wash over her. A bird's feathers swish as it takes flight. The sound of insects burrowing in the dirt reaches her ears. Slowly the edges of the portal flicker, succumbing to her natural powers.

'*What am I doing?* I can't close it, he might not make it back. He'd be trapped.' She drops her arm, then with great speed takes cover behind some rocks. She stares into the boy's dark eyes. *Who are you?* The gap between them is closing, but the portal is still alive with electricity.

A splintering twig awakens her and she realises her foot has stepped forward of its own accord. The portal sparks as if forcing the boy through.

'Quick! Brawn get out the way!' Her words echo around the clearing as she soars up the nearest tree, just as the boy is propelled from the gateway.

She looks down at him, amazed that he made it through the portal without a guide. She can see he's hurt, how badly though is difficult to tell. His body looks strong, hopefully resilient. Having scaled the tree she's high enough to see around her for at least a few hundred yards. Averting her eyes for just a second, she scans the landscape, checking for any danger.

'I hope the Davadores haven't found out.'

The sun glistens on the tops of the trees, creating a sea of yellowy white everywhere. Looking back down she scours the clearing edge for Brawn, then spies him waiting patiently behind the cover of some trees. Her eyes fall back to the boy. *Sith was right, he can't be much older than me.* His dark brown hair looks ruffled and blood trickles from underneath it. His top is muddy and torn in places, but still clings a little to his shaped muscles. She drops her eyes to his feet, to his brightly coloured green and orange shoes. She stares for a few more seconds then begins her descent, knowing she must get him to safety, *they* could come along any minute.

Chapter Three

'ETHAN?' SAMUEL MURMURS, a wash of red in front of his eyes. 'Ethan?' He looks around the forest. Moments later the pain sets in, hitting him like a hammer striking his head. The blood pounds in his ears and the taste of iron suddenly enters his mouth, blood trickling down his face. He doesn't try to get up. He remembers where he is, the forest, not the car wreck.

What the hell happened? he thinks, as his eyelids close, the sunlight too bright. He brings a hand up slowly to his face to rub the bridge of his nose, then he squeezes his fingers into the corners of his eyes to try and ease the pain. Gradually he opens them, this time letting them adjust to the light. He tries hard to remember what happened, but his head feels foggy and confused.

'Ed? George! Where are you guys?' He struggles, trying to stand. Sharp pains course through his left arm as he pushes against the ground, managing to prop himself up into an awkward position.

'Argh,' he moans. *This is nothing, you've been through far worse pain than this, come on.* 'Arghhh.' The groan escapes him again as the pain shoots through his arm. As he checks for any cuts, a whisper floats past his ear. He stops, rigid, scanning the woodland. The bright flowers that surround the clearing remain still. There's a change in the air, though he can't work out what it is.

HIS HEAD DROOPS NEARER TO HIS CHEST, a feeling of lethargy washing over him. A rustling of leaves sound above and he slowly lifts his heavy head. He tries to ignore the fluttering in his stomach and he holds his breath as the noise gets louder. Something moves from branch to branch, farther down the tree.

'Hello! Ed, is that you? Stop mucking about.' No sooner does he speak, than the noise stops.

'Ed?' Fumbling on the grass next to him he searches for a rock, something, anything that could be used for protection.

Without warning something swoops down from the branches, landing near his feet. Instinctively he shrinks back and closes his eyes. Seconds pass but nothing happens. Peering through his eyelashes he can just make out a black shape, a few inches tall. He opens his eyes fully and standing in front of him is a small bird. The black shiny eyes stare inquisitively at him and his rainbow-coloured feathers twitch. Samuel laughs at how he'd been nervous only a few seconds before of this little creature.

'Hello. Where've you come from? I've not seen you around here,' Samuel says. He talks to the bird and the bird gawks back, bobbing his head every now and then.

After a minute or two the bird delicately starts to move on its spindly legs, tiptoeing around him. He stays still, not wanting to scare it away. The bird looks at the soles of his feet, then, as if it's decided that Samuel is no threat, it pecks against the rubber on his shoes. Realising it isn't food, the bird dances a little, moving its feet on the dry, dusty ground. Its head moves up and down, as its beak pecks at the soil. After a few moments, it finds some berries and seems quite happy to nibble at them, taking the smallest of bites. As it does so a shadow casts across the soil.

Samuel looks up.

'Oh. You made me jump,' he says, finding himself staring at a girl. Her long auburn hair falls down over her face. He squints, trying to see clearer in the beaming sun. Lifting his hand he shields the light from his eyes. She looks about his age. Beneath her hair her green eyes shine as she continues to stare at him, not saying a word. He gazes at her slim body and the brown leather straps that criss cross over her clothes. Two thick straps go across her chest, hugging into her plain vest top, which is clinging to her stomach. Thinner bands wrap around her wrists. His eyes continue down to her trousers, which are slightly baggy and sit low on her waist, only held up it seems by a thick brown belt. Attached to the belt is a leather pouch which hangs neatly on her left hip. Her boots are high up her calf and tied tight with thick laces. The last thing he notices, sitting against her pale skin, is a long leather necklace with a silver feather on the end. He feels the blood rush to his face as he stares at her collar bone and he quickly averts his eyes.

'Are you alright?' she asks.

He nods as she stares down at the bird that's still nibbling on the berries, quite contentedly. It looks up, apparently only just aware of her being there. In one swift movement it opens its brightly coloured wings, tiptoes on its feet and takes flight. It circles once around them then flies off, so quickly that all Samuel can see is a rainbow of colours.

'I think you frightened him,' Samuel says, wondering where the girl's from, not having seen her round any of the campsites.

'It was a she. And I didn't scare her.'

A few moments pass, but Samuel doesn't avert his eyes from the sky, hoping to catch a glimpse of the bird. Without warning the girl drops to her knees and grabs his arm.

'Ouch, what're you doing?' he cries, as she attempts to stretch it out.

'I think it's just bruised, maybe sprained.' She prods his arm. 'Your head is cut quite badly, how do you feel otherwise?'

He lifts a hand to touch his forehead, his hair matted from the blood.

'I'm okay, a little dizzy. I think I hit my head on a rock and passed out or something. Last thing I remember was the storm calming down. My mates aren't far, they're around here somewhere.' He looks about him. 'They were here just a minute ago, before…'

'I'm sure they are, but they won't be able to help you. I've got to get you home.'

'What?'

'I've got to get you home,' she repeats.

Samuel is confused by what she's saying. 'I feel weird.' He lightly rubs his head, trying to ease the fogginess. 'Something happened just now. I, I saw something.' He falters, not wanting to sound crazy. He stares up at her. 'It's okay, I can get back to them.'

'I think you're going to need a bit of help.'

Samuel looks away. 'I can manage, *really*.' He clenches his jaw.

'Come on we don't have much time. Can you get up?'

'I don't know. What do you mean we don't have time? Maybe I should call my friends.' He pats his jeans pockets, checking for his phone, but they're empty. 'It must have dropped out when I fell,' he mutters. He looks back up at her. 'Watch out!'

She ducks down and spins round, her long hair flicking through the air. She's so quick Samuel only notices the weapon in her hands once she's turned from him.

Chapter Four

'*BRAWN*, DON'T CREEP UP on me like that,' the girl says, rubbing the horse's nose.

'What's *that* for?' Samuel asks, staring at her crossbow.

She doesn't turn around, but murmurs something in the horse's ear.

'Is this your horse?' Samuel says, pushing his hands into the ground, trying desperately to stand, but not wanting her to see that he can't. 'He's big.'

'Yes, he's very gentle though. Come on, let's get you on your feet, quickly.' She bends next to him and places her hands under his arm, heaving him up. Her strength surprises him.

Samuel nods again towards the crossbow. 'Is that for some sort of camping activity?'

'I'm not camping, I live nearby.'

Samuel stares at her, not used to girls being quite so abrupt. His head feels heavy again, now he's standing. The girl looks about the forest, seemingly in a hurry.

'I didn't realise there were any houses near here. It

must be tucked away,' he says.

'Not really. I live in a village called Rythe; it's not too far.'

'Rythe? I've never heard of it.'

'It's quite small.'

Samuel pushes his jaw out, nodding slowly.

'I need you to stand over there for a minute,' she says. 'You'll be back with your friends in no time.'

'What are you talking about? I'm sure they're just through those trees.' He looks behind him. His hand suddenly feels wet and he stares down to find the horse's nose nuzzling his palm. The horse's coat is as black as a starless night sky, all except for one small part on his mane. This section is so blindingly white that it looks as though the black pigment has been stripped from each individual hair. Samuel stares into his eyes, their chocolate colour penetrating his. A flash of movement runs across the horse's iris and Samuel glances round him to see what it is, but there's nothing there. He looks back, waiting to see what will happen. A few seconds later dark shadows cloud the horse's eyes, then from out of nowhere Samuel watches as flames rise in them. The tenderness that they'd shown before is now gone and in its place is a blazing fire. Sensing the horse's distress, Samuel reaches his hand out towards him. As soon as he places his palm on Brawn's nose the flames in his eyes die down and within seconds they return to their original placid state.

'What *was* that?' he mumbles.

'He's been through a lot,' the girl replies. Samuel turns to her, not thinking she'd have heard him. 'I rescued him a few months ago. I think he's still nervous.'

Samuel runs his hand up the horse's nose. The horse lowers his head so Samuel can reach between his ears.

'But clearly not of you,' she adds.

Samuel smiles. 'My name's Samuel,' he says, turning to face her. 'Samuel Payne.'

The girl nods before replying. 'Alexis Hunt.'

'How old are you?' he asks.

'Sixteen. Why? How old are you?'

'Seventeen.'

She stares at him for a few seconds before turning away.

'I need to concentrate,' she mumbles. 'I've got to open another gateway.'

'Gateway?'

'Just stay quiet and let me focus.' She spreads her feet so they're hip-width apart, her boots pressing into the solid ground, then she lifts her arm in front of her.

'What are you doing?' he asks, just as a deep but distant sound reverberates in his ears. 'Do you hear that?'

Alexis whirls round to face him.

'I hear something,' he says again, as the thudding gets louder.

'Shhh, be quiet,' she replies, just as a low groan sails through the air. She drops to the ground and places her ear to the floor. A cloud of dusty earth puffs up around her.

'What are you doing?' Samuel asks.

'Shhh.'

Vibrations move through the ground into his feet.

'It's too late. They're coming,' she says, leaping up. 'We've got to leave, *now*.'

Chapter Five

ALEXIS DOESN'T LIKE THE RISING FEELING working its way up from her stomach and into her chest. She was so fixed on trying to open another gateway she hadn't heard the warning signs, but now she can feel the familiar heat on the back of her neck. Samuel mutters something but she ignores him, running towards Brawn and grabbing the reins. She swings herself up onto the horse effortlessly.

'Come on. Give me your hand.' She reaches down to him.

'I, I don't understand,' Samuel stammers, his rich dark eyes flicking from her to the horse. The drumming gets louder and she feels the ground shake. Samuel steps away from her and the horse, just as a deep roar bounces around the forest. He looks towards the trees and she follows his gaze. Leaves fall from their branches, the trembling now relentless. A swarm of growls fills the clearing, a clear response to the roar.

'What is that?' Samuel asks.

'You don't want to know.' She stretches her hand

farther. 'Come *on*.'

He looks at her, then back to the forest. Without saying a word he reaches out and she grabs his hand as he pushes from the ground. He lands in the saddle behind her with a grunt. Brawn doesn't wait a second longer, he veers around and gallops off in the opposite direction of the noise and the forest that once was safe.

'HOW ARE YOU FEELING BACK THERE?' Alexis asks, Samuel's grip now looser on her back. They've been travelling through the thick forest, Brawn at a constant canter; his extraordinary speed is something she's grateful for.

'I'm okay. What's going on? Who are we running from?' His breath is a little raspy.

'I'll explain when we're safe,' she replies. 'It's not too far.'

'What isn't?'

'Home. I must get back there.'

Samuel doesn't reply. She can feel his breath on her skin, his face close to her neck. Her eyes flit to the pouch on her belt, then back up at the path ahead.

'Come on boy, nearly there.' She feels the horse stretch, his legs taking long strides, his head down, focussed. She listens for the sound of hooves behind her, but there's nothing. She inhales, but no rancid smell fills her nostrils. *Please don't follow us. Please.*

'I FEEL REALLY DIZZY. I think I've got concussion,' Samuel murmurs. 'Maybe I should see a doctor.' Alexis can feel him swaying a little behind her.

'Not long, we're almost there,' she replies.

'I, I think I'm gonna be sick.' He leans away and she hears him cough.

'Samuel? Samuel?'

'Ethan, is that you?' he mumbles.

'No, Samuel, it's me, it's Alexis.'

She tugs his arms around her waist and tightens her grip. He leans his weight into her back.

'Come on Brawn, as fast as you can boy, we've got to get home,' she says.

Chapter Six

THE TREES ARE NOW SPARSE and the village is in sight. Brawn gallops down the hill, dirt and stones flying from his hooves. His focus comforts Alexis, the reins lying slack in her hands. Nearing the houses she tugs gently on them, but Brawn has already begun to slow.

'Quiet as you can,' she whispers in his ear. She breathes in deeply, enjoying the familiar smell of straw, something she's going to miss. Sticking to the main streets, they trot along. Her grip tightens as they approach the village. The markets cover the streets, fresh smells of bread, fruit and vegetables float past, but the cobbled paths are empty.

'They've gone,' she murmurs. She recalls the whisperings of people, the flitters of conversation she heard as she left the village only yesterday. *I heard they're close*, someone had said. *We should leave. Let's not listen to them. If we stay, who knows what will happen.* Brawn's hoof clips a cobblestone, sending a judder through her, waking her from her thoughts.

The streets narrow as they pass out of the hustle and bustle and the houses get farther apart. Staring down at the end of the lane, Alexis can make out the stone wall that surrounds her home. As they approach the solid wooden gates she loosens her grip. Bringing Brawn to a standstill she slips off of him, making sure Samuel stays slouched on his back. The large, heavy gates groan as she heaves them open. She leads Brawn through the courtyard, towards the dark house, then drapes his reins loosely through the iron loop attached to the wall.

'Wait here, boy,' she says to Brawn. The horse snorts then nuzzles her shoulder. She turns to Samuel who's slumped forward.

'Samuel.' She tugs on his arm. 'Samuel. I can't carry you, you need to wake up.' He groans but doesn't make any attempt to move. Alexis looks to the house. It's silent and still.

'Brawn, watch him,' she says, as she tests the door handle. It's unlocked and as she enters the kitchen a sweet, earthy aroma hits her.

'Mother! Father!' she calls out, just in case. No reply comes. 'They can't have been gone long,' she mumbles to herself, noticing the pot on the stove as she rushes through the kitchen. Once out in the hall she heads up the stairs, taking two steps at a time. She makes straight for her brother's room, glancing into her bedroom as she passes. It's just as she left it; the patterned quilt turned back, still looks inviting. A sudden urge to clamber into the bed and ignore everything that's happening grips her. She sighs, then turns and continues to her brother's room. His is just as tidy as hers. Heading straight to his wooden chest, she heaves the lid open. She rummages through his clothes, grabbing a pair of beige trousers and a white linen shirt, then tosses them into a worn satchel. Lastly, she picks up a pair of boots, hoping it will all fit Samuel.

Back downstairs, she takes a quick look in her father's study. The hundreds of books that line the walls, years of work and academia, all left behind. Just as she's wondering whether to leave a note, in case they return, the floor creaks behind her. She whirls round, grabbing the crossbow from her back in one swift movement.

'Alexis,' the man says, holding his hands up.

'Mantel,' she exclaims, quickly lowering her weapon. She feels a swell of relief in her chest as she sees the Davadore. Mantel moves into the room and Alexis notices the female Davadore standing in the doorway behind him. She nods at her. 'Nidel.'

Nidel nods back.

'What are you doing here, Alexis?' Mantel asks, softly.

Alexis looks towards the window, she can't see Brawn from here. She hopes the Davadores didn't see Samuel.

'I had to come back for something,' she says. 'And

I wanted to check my family were okay before we travelled north.'

'You should be miles from here by now,' Nidel retorts, her thin lips pursed. Alexis looks from one Davadore to the other, their pale faces seem starker in the dim room. They edge forward, lifting the hoods of their brown cloaks back.

'You really shouldn't be here, Alexis. Pemba could be close,' Mantel says.

'I know. I'm sorry, Mantel. I'll be back with Anka and the other Seekers shortly.' She keeps eye contact with the Davadore. 'Do you know where my family have fled to?'

Nidel sighs, gliding over to the desk. Her long dark hair is tied up so tight it pulls her already crease-free forehead even farther back.

'They're safe. They're with the other villagers,' Mantel replies, his eyes boring into hers. From all her training with them she's used to the Davadores' ways, their soulless glares and paper-thin skin. To her, their manner and appearance is customary, but she's aware that to others they may seem cold.

'Why are you here?' Alexis asks, immediately regretting her tone.

Nidel whirls, her thick cloak flowing around her, as if caught in a sudden sweeping current.

'We're here to make sure everyone has cleared out and is safe,' she says.

'Alexis,' Mantel cuts in. 'Do you still have it?' He glances to the pouch on her belt.

Alexis slowly turns her gaze from Nidel.

'Yes, of course, Mantel. It's safe.' She instinctively runs a finger over the leather that bears the weight of the artefact. 'Anka and I will continue the journey.'

Mantel nods slowly.

'Why don't you come with us?' Alexis asks.

'You know we can't. We must continue helping in the search to find and stop Pemba and his army. We trust you Alexis, and Anka.'

Alexis drops her eyes to the floor.

'We must go now,' Mantel says. 'And so must you.' His long pale fingers reach out and brush against her cheek. She lowers her head.

'We'll see you soon child.'

By the time she looks up they've gone and the room is empty once again. She raises a hand to her cheek, the imprint of his cold touch still there. Moments later, she rushes back into the hall, hoping the Davadores haven't seen Samuel. As she steps out into the courtyard she turns to the wall where she left Brawn. She stares, the iron ring bare, the courtyard now empty.

Chapter Seven

HIS EYES FLY OPEN AND he gasps, almost choking, his mouth as dry as sawdust. He looks about him, the strong smell of straw invading his nostrils. The bed of hay beneath him is rough. *Where the hell am I?* he thinks, feeling the sweat cling to his body. A grunt comes from above him and hay drops on his head. He looks up to find Brawn munching, quite happily it seems. Samuel touches his forehead gently, the throbbing still constant. The blood feels congealed beneath his fingertips.

'Samuel!' Alexis exclaims, standing in the stable doorway. 'How did you get in here?'

Samuel stares at her red cheeks. Her voice seems a little shaky. He doesn't answer, but looks up at Brawn again.

'Well done boy,' Alexis says, now next to the horse, patting his side.

Samuel stands, his legs wobbly, his clothes now drenched in sweat.

'You don't look so good,' Alexis says.
'Thanks.'

'Let's get you into the house for a minute. Then we've *got* to get going.'

Samuel nods, not having the energy to say anything, but hoping she means back to the forest. She puts her arm around his waist and he lets his arm hang on her shoulder. With the top of her head so close he can smell the sweet scent of her hair. He feels lightheaded and leans into her a little more as they make their way out of the stables and across the empty yard.

Samuel slumps forward onto the kitchen table. The thudding in his ears is loud again, like someone's stomping about inside his head. His whole body feels heavy. Through half closed eyes he watches Alexis at the stove as she pours steaming liquid into a slightly misshapen mug.

'Here,' she says, holding the cup out to him. 'Drink this. It will make you feel better.'

'What's wrong with me? Why do I feel so weird?' He takes the mug from her, his hand shaking as he stares at the murky green liquid. 'What is it?'

'It's tea. Drink it, it will help.'

He slowly lifts the cup to his lips and takes a small sip. It hits the back of his throat instantly, causing a fiery heat. Then, after a few seconds, it settles into a sweet subtle taste.

'It's got a kick,' he says, his voice strained from the heat.

'Wait here. I'll be right back.'

He nods, the movement not hurting quite so much.

'Strong stuff,' he says, then realises she's already left. He turns his gaze to the room he's in. There are pots and pans everywhere and cupboard doors open, as though someone's been looking for something. On the wall he notices an object which resembles a clock. At the centre it has three bronze coloured prongs, all different lengths. At the end of each spike is a circle and in between each of them are other shapes. A sudden movement outside the window catches his eye. He turns to find the small bird from before, looking at him through the glass. It hovers, its tiny wings beating so fast all he can see is colour.

'How are you feeling now?' Alexis asks, suddenly behind him.

'Will you stop creeping up on me like that!' He turns back to the window but the bird has gone. He blinks, wondering if it had been there at all.

'Bit better actually. Thanks.'

'Good. Then we should get going.'

Samuel watches her at the stove again, this time pouring the liquid into small glass bottles.

'What are you doing?'

'We should take some of this with us,' she replies, not turning round. 'Never know when we might need it.'

'What are you talking about?' Samuel scrapes the chair back as he stands. He feels the strength return to his legs, his muscles now able to hold him.

Alexis turns round to face him. Her forehead has the thinnest of wrinkles as she scrunches her brow and parts her lips to speak.

'Alexis!' a voice yells, before she can say anything.

The bottle drops from her hands, but her reactions are so quick she catches it just before it hits the floor. She glances at him before rushing to the kitchen window.

'Anka,' she mutters. 'Quick. Samuel, come with me. Quickly.' She grabs his arm and hauls him out of the kitchen and into a narrow corridor.

'What the hell–'

'Shhh. *Please*,' she urges, pushing him in front of her through a door, into another room. 'Wait here. Please be quiet. It's for your own good. Trust me.'

He opens his mouth to say something, but noticing her widened pupils, decides against it. He allows her to shut the door, not saying another word.

Chapter Eight

SAMUEL LEANS HIS EAR AGAINST THE DOOR. The smell of wood oil enters his nostrils as mumblings come from down the hall. From what he can make out it's Alexis and one other person. He steps back, unable to hear what they're saying.

'What am I doing?' he says to himself, as he looks about the small room. His legs feel stronger than a few minutes ago and he makes his way over to the far side, towards a bookshelf. As his eyes flit over the book spines he wonders if George and Ed are missing him yet, or if they're still trying to chat up the two girls they'd met the first day of the trip. His eyes stare at the book titles: *Black Beauty... Worlds and Their People... Travelling to Other Worlds... Plain Seeking... A Guide to The Milky Way and Universes... Earth... Retoru... Salverva... Minula...* He traces his finger along the edging of the books, then stops.

'Worlds and Their People. Travelling to Other Worlds.' The words sound loud in the small space and he pauses, wondering if Alexis and whoever is out there heard. No one comes and the mutterings continue. He wanders over to the desk. No computer, no phone, just a lot of papers and a dark metal box. Its surface is scratched and the lid has an intricate line of bronze cogs. It reminds him of the clock in the kitchen. He picks it up and tests the lid, but it's stuck fast.

'Anka, *please.*' Alexis' words filter through the wall, leading Samuel to take up position on his side of the door again.

'What would your father say?' He hears a male voice, but can only hear a muffled reply from Alexis. 'What are the Davadores going to say about this?' the guy speaks again.

'I've seen them, but they don't know. And you mustn't tell them.'

Samuel waits, catching only the odd word.

'Then you have to leave him here,' the voice booms through the door. '*We've* got to go.'

'*Anka.* You know I can't do that.' Alexis' voice rises. 'I can't leave him here,' she continues. 'He's my responsibility now. *I've* got to get him back, when I can. If he's with me I can at least *try* and keep him safe. If I leave him here how will he get home?'

No reply comes, but Samuel can hear boots clipping the floorboards every now and then. Moments later, Anka's voice comes, clear as anything.

'Let me see him. Where is he?'

'I don't think that's a good idea. He's weak and I don't want to scare him.'

Samuel wets his lips and swallows hard as he hears a grunt, a clipped sneer.

'Okay, he can come with us. I'll tell the others to go, they can warn the squads and continue tracking Pemba's army, give us a chance to get to Irith. It's probably best if I keep hold of it until we get there.'

'No, Anka, you have to go with them. You're the leader. They look up to you. You'll know what to do if things go wrong. I'll take Samuel with me to Irith's and we'll meet you there. You've got to make sure our people are safe.'

Samuel listens, his ear starting to hurt, pushed against the frame. He feels as though his heart is thumping against his ribcage.

'I don't know if I can do that, Alexis. We were meant to take the egg to Irith together. And you know I can't do it without you.'

'Egg?' Samuel murmurs, the floorboards groaning as he shifts his weight from one side to the other. With the sound of movement the voices stop and Samuel stiffens as footsteps approach.

Chapter Nine

'*ANKA*.' SAMUEL CAN HEAR the urgency in Alexis' voice. 'The army are closer than we realised and I have a better chance of getting the egg to Irith safely if someone's looking out for me. You can throw off the scent, detract their attention away from us.'

Samuel imagines her slender arms gripping hold of Anka, trying to deter him from coming down the hall.

'Please, Anka,' she continues.

Silence follows and Samuel wonders if they've gone outside. He slips his fingers into the gap between the door and its frame, wondering whether to take a look.

'Alright. But you must leave soon,' Anka finally replies.

'We'll be gone by tonight. You should go now, make a clear path for us.'

'Remember, stick to where you know, stop if you have to and be careful of everyone.' Anka's voice has softened a little.

'I know. We trained together, remember?'

Samuel moves back from the door.

'I'll see you soon,' Anka says.

Shortly after, Samuel hears a door swing shut and he hurries over to the window, being sure to keep out of sight. The guy he presumes is Anka strides across the paved garden. With his back to Samuel it's hard to tell, but he looks of similar age to Alexis and himself. His hair is dark and if it wasn't slicked back, would probably be quite long. He looks strong, his muscles defined, even through the long white shirt he's wearing. Samuel notices the straps, similar to Alexis', around his arms and legs. He wears a belt over one shoulder which runs down his chest. Attached to it is a knife and what looks like a tiny dagger, joined to a catapult-like contraption. A long sword, sits neatly in a sheath on his hip. Samuel's eyes settle on his neck, where he notices a group of circular tattoos that stand out against the guy's tanned skin. He moves a little closer to the window to get a better look, but his view is blocked by another, younger boy, hovering at the large gate. The boy holds two sets of reins, which are attached to two large brown horses. The boy is skinny and not that tall. His mousy coloured curls bound about his head as he hops back and forth on his feet, as if unable to stand still. His eyes are wide, his forehead creased, but when he sees Anka he breaks into a relieved smile. Anka doesn't seem to acknowledge him. Grabbing a set of reins from the boy he leaps up onto a horse, his sword bashing his side as he does so. The boy clambers up onto the other horse. Samuel watches Anka clip the heels of his knee-high boots into the horse's side. He takes a last glance at the house and Samuel senses an annoyance in his grey eyes. The steed obeys its rider and trots out of the gate with the boy in tow.

'Come on,' Alexis says, bursting back into the room. 'We've got to get going.'

Samuel steps back from her as she reaches out.

'Who was that? What were you talking about?' He feels his legs start to give way and his breathing strain again. For a second he wonders if it's her, having this effect on him.

Alexis dashes behind him, grabbing a chair and placing it beneath him before he has time to fall.

'Drink some more of this,' she says, flicking the lid of a small vial and placing it to Samuel's lips before he can stop her. The warm liquid coats his throat, keenly working its way down. He can feel it running through his body, striving to get to every part of him.

'Are you in some sort of trouble?' he asks her, finally feeling able to take a full breath. 'With the police or something?'

Alexis leans away from him, her lips set in a pout.

'Police?'

'Yeah. I overheard you and, and Anka, is that his name?'

Alexis nods.

'What was all that stuff you were saying about going somewhere, taking something? Where are your mum and dad?'

Alexis turns away from him.

'They're gone.'

'Gone?'

'Yes. Look, that doesn't matter right now.' She spins round to face him. 'We *have* to get going. None of this will make any sense to you, but if you can just be stronger.'

'I feel better. Maybe give me more of that drink.'

'No. We must save it. I don't know when we'll need it again.'

Samuel doesn't reply and they remain in silence for a minute or so.

'Samuel, I have to tell you something. And you have to just listen.'

'Is it about your family?' His eyes glance back to the books and he wonders if he's stumbled upon a group of UFO believers.

'In a way it is.'

Samuel sighs, a little heavier than he intended. His thoughts drift to Ed and George. He wonders if the girls they met are this unusual.

'There's a reason you feel so weak, Samuel, and it isn't because you hit your head. At least, that's only part of it.'

Samuel waits, wondering if he wants to hear what she's got to say. He's finding her an interesting distraction from his relentless thoughts of his brother.

'Did you see anything before, in the forest?' Alexis asks.

'Like what?'

'Something that might have looked a little strange to you.'

Samuel thinks back to the light. He hadn't thought too much about it since waking up. It almost feels like it was a dream now.

'There was a light,' he says, then smiles, thinking how dumb he sounds.

Alexis stares at him intently.

'Samuel, that light, what you saw, was what we call a gateway. It was a portal that led you to another world. It led you here, to White Plains.'

Chapter Ten

SAMUEL FEELS AS THOUGH HE'S UNDER WATER, or at least his head is, his ears full of liquid. He remembers the light in the forest and the opening more clearly now. The force he felt from it and the pain as he got sucked in had been almost unbearable. But then he'd woken in the forest. He hadn't seen Ed or George, but they could have been anywhere. The gurgling in his ears only begins to subside when he feels Alexis' hand on his arm.

'Samuel?' He watches her mouth form the word but he can't hear her. 'Samuel?' she repeats. This time her voice is clear. Her hand still rests on his arm and he feels a tingle on his skin as her fingers lightly press. He looks over at the books again and she follows his gaze.

'They're my father's. He's spent many years studying worlds. He's a Plain Seeker, like me. Or at least he was,' Alexis says.

Samuel swallows hard, then clears his throat, trying to waken his vocal chords.

'A Plain Seeker?' he croaks.

'Yes. There's not time to fully explain, but I seek out new plains, new worlds. There are lots of us here, an elite who have the gift. We're born with it, but our abilities don't form fully until around the age of thirteen.'

He stares at her, realising he probably looks vacant.

'Being a Seeker means I can travel to other worlds by opening gateways,' she continues.

'Hang on. Let me get this right. You're trying to tell me that I'm on another world? This isn't Earth? And you're someone who has special powers?' He gets up, forcing her to step back. 'It doesn't look that different,' he says, striding over to the window.

'Your world and mine are similar in many ways.'

Samuel studies the world outside, realising that, although it doesn't look very different, it definitely feels different.

'How is this is even possible?'

'There are hundreds of universes, Samuel. Your world isn't the only one to have life on it.'

He feels his skin prickle and he turns to face her.

'That's not what I meant. I meant how did I get here? How did I come through the gateway?'

Alexis looks behind her, to the door.

'I don't know who opened it but it was left open by accident. Non-Seekers shouldn't travel through portals, not without a guide. That's why you feel so weak. That's why I brought you back; I had hoped my family would still be here. I wanted to speak with my father.'

'So no one has ever travelled through a gateway before?'

'It *has* happened, I just wasn't sure how it would affect you.' Alexis drops her gaze to the floor.

'This is crazy.' Samuel sits down, then stands up again almost straight away. He has a sudden urge to run, but he doesn't think his legs will co-operate.

'I wanted to send you back. But then *they* came. And now it's too late. You've got to come with me.'

He feels the blood rush to his face. He tries to stop it by taking a deep breath, something he's learnt to do when he feels the anger build. After a few seconds the rush subsides, but the niggling feeling in his gut won't go.

'I know something happened. Something pretty weird. But if this is real, if I *am* in another world, then why can't you take me back now?'

'It's complicated.'

A short, sharp exhale of air escapes him. He thinks of all the times girls have said that to him. Between him and Ethan it was always Ethan that had found it easy to talk to girls, to make them laugh and like him. When it came to himself, girls would be kind, but they'd always find an excuse to turn him down. He used to find it funny, knowing that it couldn't have been his looks, since he and Ethan were twins. His trouble had been that he was quieter, he held back a little more than his brother, knowing that Ethan would comfortably take the lead.

'Samuel, Samuel are you listening to me?' Alexis says.

He shakes his head a little, trying to focus on the present.

'You've got to take me back.'

Alexis exhales, louder than necessary.

'What about my mum and dad. They'll be going mad. You *have* to take me home.'

'Let me show you something,' she says, grabbing a book off the shelf. Looking at the contents, she runs her index finger down the flecked paper, before flicking through the pages.

'Look.'

Samuel studies the page. The pictures are like ones he used to see in text books at school: white dots cover the paper. The centre is a dusty pink, whilst the edges seem to shimmer grey and blue.

'What am I meant to be looking at?' he asks.

'This here' – she points to an edge on the sphere – 'is Earth. And right around here' – her finger traces a line around the page – 'is White Plains.'

He takes the book from her, holding it up closer to his face.

'That far?'

'Yes. But not if you can open gateways.'

'You just can't right now,' he replies, closing the book and placing it back on the shelf.

'If I could explain it all now I would, but we've got to get going.' She moves over to the door.

Samuel notices the bag on the floor, then turns back to the window.

'Samue–'

'Hey what's that?' he says, noticing smoke outside, drifting over the high wall.

Alexis rushes to the window.

'They're already here,' she says. 'Come on.'

She grabs his arm, yanking him towards the door, then throws him against the wall.

'Wait there,' she says, reaching for the bag. She pulls out a dagger and stuffs it into a sheath on her belt, then swings the bag up over her shoulder, the crossbow still on her back.

'You've got to come with me. You're going to have trust me.'

'But–'

'Samuel.'

She grabs his arms, and he feels again how strong she is. 'Warlord Pemba, and his army will destroy everything if we don't stop them. We're in the middle of a war here.' She moves closer and he can see the pulse in her neck throb beneath her skin. 'If we don't stop them, it won't just be my world at risk, Samuel. Earth will be too.'

Chapter Eleven

A SCREECH COMES FROM OUTSIDE and Samuel throws his hands to his ears, the piercing noise almost unbearable. Seconds later it stops. He looks back at Alexis and nods. She holds his stare for a few moments, then takes his hand and pulls him behind her.

'Stay close to me and do what I say,' she whispers.

Samuel barely has time to look around as they creep through the house. They make their way back down the narrow hall to the kitchen and out the door. Alexis places a hand on his chest.

'Wait here.'

She holds the crossbow out in front of her as she runs across the courtyard, her feet barely seeming to touch the ground. She reaches the stables a few seconds later and disappears inside. Samuel watches as the fog drifts through the trees, working its way over the wall, as if searching for something. The crackling sound of fire, the smoke's origin, is distant but clear.

'*Samuel,*' Alexis calls. 'Come here, quickly.'

He takes a last look round before dashing over to

her. His muscles twinge, still a little shaky.

'You get on Brawn, I'll ride Paladin,' Alexis says, guiding a dark brown horse out of the stalls. She hands Brawn's reins over to him. 'You won't need to do much, as horses go, Brawn's pretty astute.'

Samuel watches Alexis mount her horse in one swift motion.

'Come on, get on.'

He moves the satchel aside that's attached to the horse, then clumsily puts his foot in the stirrup. His knee buckles as he pushes off from the ground and he falls back.

'Still a little weak,' he mumbles, avoiding Alexis' gaze. He tries again, this time pushing a few times before leaving the ground. The saddle creaks under him as he settles into it.

'Brawn, you stay behind me,' Alexis says to the horse. Brawn snorts and lifts one hoof from the floor.

They trot out of the stables, towards the wooden gates. Alexis jumps down to open them. Once back on her horse she turns to him.

'We're going to head out of here and straight for the trees. The forest is about half a mile away, so we'll be out in the open. Keep low, don't look up and stay on your horse.'

'Don't look up?'

Alexis doesn't respond, instead she looks back to the house. Samuel can't read her expression and before he has time to say anything she kicks her heels into her horse's side and clicks her tongue. Just as he wonders whether he should do the same, Brawn moves off. Samuel falls forward, finding his face full of horse hair as Brawn's mane lifts up and down in the wind. He grips the reins, leaning back a little, trying to find his balance. Brawn follows Alexis and Paladin down the cobbled street at a steady pace. With trees one side of them and the wall that surrounds the house on the other, Samuel feels as though they're fairly enclosed. Moments later however both the wall and the trees end and all he can see is a winding path, leading out into vast open fields.

'Is this a good idea?' he calls, forgetting to stay quiet. Alexis turns her head slightly but doesn't reply. She's leant forward a little and looks more than comfortable with the horse's stride. She kicks her heels into the horse's side once more and their pace quickens. Samuel hasn't ridden much before, but he's sure horses normally gain speed over time. Brawn, however seems to go from a trot to a canter in an instant. He squeezes his calves, feeling the horse's powerful muscles ripple beneath him.

As they hurtle forward, the air that had begun to feel stifling from the smoke, begins to clear and the sound of the blazing fire quietens as they leave it behind them. After a few minutes Samuel relaxes his grip on the leather and loosens his shoulders. He can see the forest up ahead, just like Alexis had said. He focuses on her back, her long hair bouncing against it.

Her legs look strong as they hold her up, off the saddle every so often.

They race up the hill, towards the edge of the trees. Just before they reach them a shriek sounds above Samuel's head. He brings his hands to his ears once again. Seconds later an arrow, alight with flames, spears the ground in front of Alexis. Paladin whines, rearing up. Brawn swerves round the horse and the arrow. The whooshing sound of more arrows comes from behind him as he and Brawn enter the forest. Samuel turns to see Alexis trying to calm her horse. He pulls on Brawn's reins and the horse veers round, kicking up dirt from the dry ground.

'Alexis!' he yells, raising his voice above the barrage of arrows that continue to rain down. 'Keep going!' she replies, still trying to calm Paladin. It's too late for her to follow them into the safety of the trees; a line of fire has formed between them. Above, in the sky, is a rolling black cloud. Samuel can't see what's shooting the arrows, but every so often he catches a glimpse of dark blue feathers, then a wing, then lots of wings.

'Go, Brawn!' Alexis shouts. The horse whinnies, then turns, before Samuel even has a chance to say anything. They enter deeper into the forest, dodging around trees and fallen branches. Within seconds Paladin's whines, and the crackling of fire quietens and all Samuel can do is grip tightly to Brawn's reins.

Chapter Twelve

Brawn continues to canter through the forest, his stamina not wavering. His ears twitch round as if constantly alert.

'Brawn, we can't just leave her,' Samuel says to the horse. 'We've got to go back.' Brawn flicks his mane, but keeps going. The deeper they go, the dimmer the light, as the trees blanket the sky. The only sound he can hear is his rapid breathing and the occasional grunt from the horse. With sunlight unable to break through the dense trees he feels his stomach twist and his palms sweat, leaving a slight residue on the leather reins. Shadows dance about around him, as forest life continues and a steady flutter of wings, flitting through the trees beside them, catches his eye. The small colourful bird darts about, as if trying to keep up. Brawn's hooves clop against stones, as the earth beneath them becomes rockier. Minutes later they enter a clearing and the horse slows, before coming to a standstill. Samuel looks around for the bird, but it's gone. He jumps down from Brawn.

'What the hell happened here?' he says, staring at

the broken rubble. It takes him a moment to realise he's standing within the remains of a house. There are barely any walls left and no ceiling, just broken bricks. He wanders through the wreckage, where the burnt remains of the home and what was once in them, are scattered across the ground. He frowns, as the smell of ash prickles at his nose as he bends to pick up a small round object. It's unrecognisable and still warm from the flames and his fingers leave an imprint, its material now soft. Turning it over in his hands, he wonders what it was. His foot kicks against something solid and he looks down. Bile rises to the back of his throat as he realises what he's looking at. Underneath all the debris is a lot of soot, but through this he can make out flesh, human flesh. As his eyes flick over the ground he realises there is more, there are bodies everywhere.

'Samuel!' a familiar voice calls out.

He spins round, searching for Alexis. Paladin bursts through the trees on the opposite side of the glade. Alexis is atop the horse, her hair splayed out behind her, her pale cheeks flush.

'Alexis!' he yells, running towards her.

She brings the horse to an abrupt stop.

'We've got to get out of here,' he says, a little breathless. 'They're dead. They're all dead.'

Alexis jumps down from her horse and loops the reins over a nearby branch. She runs over to the

dissected houses and bodies. Samuel follows, hesitant-
ly.

'I'd hoped they'd all cleared out,' she murmurs.

'What's going on? What the hell was that back
there?'

'Harpies,' she says, staring at the massacre.
'They're part of Pemba's army.'

'Harpies?' Samuel repeats the word, running his
hand down the back of his neck, his muscles tight.
He's relieved he's not alone anymore, but more than
that, he's glad she's safe.

'Did they follow you?' he asks.

Alexis looks back to the trees.

'No, I think I lost them. Harpies don't particularly
like the forest, they prefer to fly out in the open. I
couldn't see the rest of Pemba's army.'

'The rest?' Samuel scans the forest trees.

Alexis sweeps her hair back in one swift movement, tucking it up away from her face.

'Pemba leads an army of all sorts: harpies, orcs,
orglins and men and women, just like you and me.'
She carefully moves around the bodies and bricks as
she speaks. 'He's gathered his army from all different
worlds.'

Samuel watches her bend near a pile of ash. His
thoughts stumble over one another as he tries to take
in what she's saying, but not look at what's right in
front of him.

'What do they want?' he asks. 'Why are they fighting you?'

'It's a lot to try and explain.' She looks away from him, to the ruins. 'Come on. We can't stay here,' she says, making her way back to her horse.

Samuel looks at Brawn who's been standing patiently next to Paladin.

'Where are we going? Can't you open a gateway and send me home now?'

Alexis grips the horse's reins but falters. She's facing away from him, but he can see her shoulders tense as he asks the question.

'I can't take you back, Samuel. I tried–'

'I know you tried and then the army came, but no one's here now. I can't stay here. This is our chance.'

She turns round to face him.

'Samuel, gateways are forbidden. The Davadores–'

'Davadores…I heard that word before, back at the house.'

Alexis nods. 'The Davadores are a council of men and women,' she continues. 'They've been on this world for hundreds of years, training Plain Seekers at their sanctuary, the Lyceum. I studied there, along with Anka and many others.'

'So they're teachers?'

'In a way. They encourage us to watch over and travel to other worlds. By doing this we gain a greater understanding and knowledge of the universe and we bring that knowledge back here. But when Pemba arrived the Davadores stopped the use of gateways.'

'Why?'

'The Davadores found out they were using our gateways to plain jump. They've been able to destroy countless worlds.' She looks past Samuel, her eyes glazed. 'Thousands of people died before we realised.'

Samuel clenches his jaw. He can see the self blame etched in the creases on her face.

'If I were to open a gateway now, with them so close–'

'But maybe they wouldn't follow?' Samuel says, not taking his eyes from her.

'Maybe not.' She pauses, the lines on her brow softening. 'But I still can't risk it, not just because of what's happening, but because your body needs time to rest, to heal, before it can be put through such stress again. When anyone travels through a gateway there is a delay. It's more apparent when travelling between worlds than if you were to travel within the same, but this delay will have weakened your cells; your body needs time to adjust.'

'But the portal I travelled through, tha–'

'I told you before. That shouldn't have been open. I don't know who opened it. All I know is that Sith, a fellow Plain Seeker, found it and alerted me of its presence.'

'But you *were* going to try and send me back. Even

though you knew I was weak.'

Alexis looks as though she's about to speak, then drops her head. Samuel thinks about the portal in the forest. He recalls what she said about Earth and the danger it could be in. His mum and dad's faces come into his head. They've aged since the accident; Samuel couldn't see it before, but here, in his mind, he can see it clearly.

'Samuel,' Alexis says.

He squeezes his eyes together for a second, letting the image of them wash away, then he looks back at the human remains.

'I don't want my mum and dad in *any* danger. I can't lose them too.'

Alexis leaps onto Paladin.

'Then you've got to come with me,' she says. 'But first, you'll need to put these on.' She reaches into the satchel attached to the horse's side and pulls out some clothes.

Samuel feels his heart beat harder. He knows what Ethan would do if he were here. He glances round the clearing, then grabs the clothes from her.

'Okay, let's go,' he says, trying to ignore the sick feeling in his stomach.

Chapter Thirteen

As they leave the glade Samuel watches Alexis splash drops of clear liquid from a vial, onto the ground. It smells of something strong, like stained sheets. He scrunches up his nose as Alexis explains:

'It's a mixture of plant extracts and boar urine. It will mask our scent.'

Samuel allows Brawn to trot along calmly beside Paladin, the path just wide enough for them both. He feels uncomfortable in his new clothes, even though they fit him. As Alexis tucks the vial back in her bag her hair falls down in front of her face and she sharply flicks it back. As she does so he catches sight of a mark on the nape of her neck.

'Your tattoo,' he mutters. 'I saw the same one on Anka.'

Alexis whirls round, touching the back of her neck.

'It's our mark,' she replies, her lips barely moving.

'Your mark?'

'Yes. Plain Seekers all have it. We're born with it. It's faint, but it darkens over time.'

Samuel stares at her, but she's focused her gaze ahead.

'Is that what gives you your abilities?'

'No, not exactly.' She gently kicks her heels into Paladin's side, urging the horse on. 'It's there to show who we are. To tell people that we are a part of something. Sometimes I can feel it getting warmer, or it might hurt, if there's danger or I can sense something.'

'Can I see it?'

She turns to him, then without saying a word, gathers her hair, sweeping it round in front of her, to reveal the imprint on the back of her neck. Samuel clears his throat and leans closer. The tattoo is no more than a couple of inches long. Three solid circles run diagonally. Two ellipses encompass them, opposing each other, whilst smaller circles sit on the ellipses, creating what looks like a tiny universe. He reaches out, placing his index finger on her skin and traces one of the circles. She stiffens. His eyes are now distracted by the light hairs on her neck.

'So every Plain Seeker has one of these?' he asks.

'Yes. Unfortunately it's not unique,' she replies, letting go of her hair and allowing it to fall neatly back into place.

'I think it looks good on you.'

Alexis doesn't reply and Samuel fidgets back into the hard saddle.

A little later and he finds the courage to ask her where they're going. Alexis barely turns to him before giving a clipped response, 'North, to Irith. He's an enchanter. I have something for him.'

'An enchanter.' The word floats from Samuel's mouth, conjuring up images in his mind. He allows the silence to grow between them again, letting the rhythmic pace of the horse lull him. After a while the trees merge into one as he becomes sleepy and gives in to the weariness that feels a lot like jet-lag.

Chapter Fourteen

SAMUEL STIRS ON HIS HORSE, his body shivering a little at the chill that's lurked its way under his skin and into his bones. The forest is quiet and he can tell that they're on the darker side of the day. He swallows a few times, trying to get rid of the stale taste in his mouth.

'This enchanter, Irith. He can help us?' he asks Alexis, who is riding just in front.

'Yes.'

'Maybe when we reach him, you can take me home?'

Alexis adjusts the reins in her hands.

'As soon as it's safe, and you're strong enough, I'll take you back.'

Samuel fidgets in the saddle.

'Have you ever been to Earth?'

'Yes.'

Samuel wonders if she's always this abrupt. Then, as if having read his thoughts she adds, 'I like it, but it's loud and tense. It makes me nervous and excited at the same time. It's a strange place.'

Her words jar with Samuel as he realises he feels exactly the same a lot of the time.

'All worlds feel different to me,' she continues.

He turns to her, noticing the slight sheen of perspiration on her skin from the warm, but clear air.

'You don't seem to have as much stuff here,' he says.

'Why do you think we're travelling on horses?' Alexis' cheekbones stand out, as her mouth turns upwards; the first time he's really seen any hint of a smile. 'Other than walking or travelling on water, this is our quickest way of getting places. If I'm not Seeking.'

Samuel feels his skin tingle a little at the word.

'What do you need to take to Irith?' he asks her.

Alexis glances at the pouch that's gently tapping her side as they ride along.

'It's something that can help end the war.'

Samuel looks at her blankly. He wonders again if she's usually this blunt. As if reading his mind, Alexis expands.

'It's an ancient artefact. It once had a bearer, but he was murdered and the object was damaged.'

'Can I see it?' He leans towards her a little, but she pulls Paladin away.

'It's too dangerous to show you. We must keep going.'

Samuel moves back, looking to the path ahead.

'How long will it take us?'

'A day, maybe two.'

Paladin shifts back in line with Brawn, guided by Alexis' subtle movements.

'We can rest for a bit later,' Alexis says. 'Once we're deep enough into the forest.'

Samuel falls quiet again, as he feels a sudden tiredness seep into his muscles.

HE STARES AT THE HORSE'S SWISHING TAIL in front of him. The forest is dark, only the moonlight shines down when it finds gaps between the dense trees. Alexis has been quiet for a while, but he can tell she's alert. With the steadiness of Brawn's pace his eyelids grow heavy. He jerks, a sudden movement from the horse waking him. Moments later and darkness comes again, as he closes his eyes, unable to keep them open.

'Samuel.' Alexis' voice drifts by. 'Samuel,' she says again, sharply. Nausea sweeps over him as the tiredness leaves.

'What is it?' he asks, scanning the trees.

'There's something out there,' she replies, her crossbow held out steadily.

'Are you sure?' Samuel can't see much in the dim light, just the silver bark of the trees glistening a little.

'Yes. Even if my eyes deceive me, my mark

doesn't.'

He looks at the back of her, but her hair is covering her neck.

'Whoa, Paladin,' she says, her voice low but soft. The horse obediently stops and Brawn does the same. Samuel starts to take his foot out of the stirrup and swing his leg round, but Alexis grabs his arm. Her touch is warm and he feels the surface of his arms twitch. She doesn't speak, but holds her hand up.

Without the continuous clopping of the horse's hooves the forest is still, then crumbling dirt bounces around them. They both spin, searching for where the noise came from. A shape darts between two trees, metres away.

'There,' Samuel says, pointing towards it.

'I see it.' Alexis slips off her horse. 'Wait here.' She sprints to the nearest tree, her actions so nimble she barely makes a sound. The silhouette moves again. It's so quick it's hard to keep track of. Samuel slides down off Brawn, his descent almost silent. Alexis moves from tree to tree but the predator seems to be quicker, covering the area around them in seconds. Samuel creeps round Brawn, trying to keep track, but as whatever it is gets closer his head starts to spin. He stands still, focusing on the nearest tree. With his eyes adjusting to the light, he follows the contours of the tree's bark as it staggers its way up the trunk. The wood begins to ripple.

'Alexis,' he whispers, unable to see where she is. Seconds later a tall figure emerges in front of the tree. The creature's forehead is huge, hanging over its eyes, clearly blocking part of its vision. Its long, pointy nose sniffs at the air, its nostrils widening. Without warning It flings its arms forward, releasing a handful of small knives. They thunk into the tree next to him, each one miraculously going awry. The creature disappears, reappearing almost instantly, inches from him.

'Alex–' Samuel chokes on the word as the monster thrusts its hand forward, wrapping its long fingers around his throat.

Chapter Fifteen

THE MONSTER DIGS ITS FINGERS DEEPER into his neck. Samuel twists, trying to break free. A putrid smell enters his nostrils. The stench makes its way up to his eyes and he feels them burn as he blinks, tears forming. He stretches his toes, trying to find the earth, as the creature lifts him. A hiss then a thwack and the grip loosens. A heavy grunt leaves the monster's mouth and they both slump to the ground.

Samuel lies still in the darkness. He tries to move his arms but it's hopeless, the body of the creature presses him down. His breathing shallows, for fear of breathing too deeply and his ribs cracking. Being so close he can almost taste the oozing rancidness from the beast's skin. He hears a quiet groan. The monster's head drags down over his chest, then it rolls away and he inhales deeply, his lungs filling with air again.

'Samuel,' Alexis says, dropping to her knees beside him, then grabbing his arm and pulling him up.

'I'm okay.' He takes a few more breaths. 'What was that?'

'An orglin.'

Samuel stares down at it. Its face is buried in the grass. Its dirty, fleshless legs poke out from the rags it's wearing and sticking out of its back is a bolt from Alexis' crossbow.

'Is it dead?'

Alexis nudges the beast with her foot, but the creature doesn't respond.

'It came out of nowhere,' he says.

'Orglins can teleport.'

Samuel looks to her. The sweat that had formed on his forehead is now clammy.

'Are there more of them out there?'

'They normally travel in packs, but it looks like this one was alone. It might have got separated from the others, or took off by itself.'

'Why would it do that?'

'Caught our scent, most likely. They're pretty devious creatures; rather than alerting its pack it could have decided to go off on its own search. If I hadn't killed it when I did, it would have killed you then made its call to the others.'

Samuel shivers.

'We shouldn't stay here any longer,' Alexis says. 'Help me get him to that tree. I'll cover him over with some branches and try to hide his stench.'

Samuel takes one of the orglin's arms. Its dark skin feels as rough as it looks, and when Samuel peers closer he notices patches of tiny pimples covering its body.

'I've never seen anything like it,' he murmurs.

Alexis pulls the bolt from the creature and wipes it on the grass before putting it back in her sheath. She hurriedly covers the body with bracken, until he disappears from sight.

SAMUEL RUBS HIS ARMS, as the early morning dampness clings to him.

'Let's stop here for a rest,' Alexis says. 'Looks like there's a den over there.' She jumps down from Paladin before the horse has come to a stand still.

'Here, give me a hand,' she says, as she undoes the buckle on a rolled up tarpaulin attached to the horse's saddle. Together they drape the sheet over the horses.

'Won't that come off when they lie down?' Samuel asks.

'Horses don't always lie down to sleep.' She runs her hand down Brawn's leg to his knee. 'The joints in his knees lock, which means he can sleep standing up, but he's relaxed. The sheet should stay on, giving them some form of camouflage.'

Samuel takes a last glance at the horses before he squeezes through the overgrown forest. Branches snag on his clothes and the deep smell of leaves mixed with dirt attacks his nostrils. In front of him Alexis takes out a knife and slices through some of the nettles that have wound their way around the trees. Moments later they're standing in an empty lair that's no bigger than two metres wide.

'It's small but well covered, and the nettles will give good defence. We can't stop for long though.' She picks up some ferns that are scattered on the floor and sits them amongst the trees, creating even more of a shield.

'It's pretty good,' Samuel says. 'Have you got any food in there?' He motions to her bag.

'Plenty of anasi beans.'

'Anasi beans?'

'My mother grows them.'

'I'll go for anything right now,' he says, feeling his stomach grumble at just the mention of food.

'YOU SLEEP. I'LL KEEP WATCH,' Alexis says, as she swallows her last mouthful.

Samuel wonders whether to protest but his head is starting to ache again, and even though he no longer feels comfortable in small spaces, all he wants to do is close his eyes. Nettles scratch his arms and twigs dig into his back as he tries to get comfortable. He places his hands on his stomach, not wanting to take up too much room. Through half closed eyes he watches

Alexis quietly pull out a heavy-looking jacket from her bag. She wrestles with it in the small space, then, finally getting it on, she ties her hair up away from her face. She grabs hold of a small satchel that she's brought into the den and places it underneath her head, as she wriggles down next to him. She's so close he can feel the heat from her body. He closes his eyes completely and breathes in, expanding his chest. A heavy scent of leather comes with the intake of breath, and he realises her coat is make from animal-skin. Feeling the pulse in his stomach he begins to tap his finger to the beat of his heart, and after a while the mindless action becomes slower as sleep drags him.

Chapter Sixteen

'ETHAN!' SAMUEL YELLS. 'Ethan where are you?' He sits up, banging his head on a branch.

'Shhh, Samuel. Be quiet. You were dreaming.' Alexis places her hand gently on top of his. He clenches hold of it, trying to remember where he is.

'Alexis?'

'Yes.'

He looks at her pale face, then down at their hands, realising his fingers are still wrapped around hers. He lets go.

'Sorry.'

Alexis shrugs.

Samuel rubs the back of his neck, the sweat now cold on his skin.

'Bad dream,' he says. 'How long was I asleep for?'

'Not long, maybe an hour.' She continues to stare at him, then adds, 'You called out to someone.'

'Huh?'

'Just before you woke up. You said the name, Ethan.'

'Really? I don't remember. Is there anything I can

have to drink? My mouth's really dry.'

Alexis hesitates, then rummages in her bag.

'There's water or some tea. It will be cold, but is still good.'

Samuel opts for the small bottle of tea, and gulps the liquid down.

'Has it been quiet?' he asks, wiping his mouth.

Alexis nods. 'Another hour and then we'll be on our way.' She lies back down.

Samuel leans his elbows on his knees. His dream of Ethan trapped in the car is still clouding his mind. The silence of the forest seems so loud.

'I lied just now,' he says, after a few minutes.

Alexis is quiet, and he wonders if she's fallen asleep. He clears his throat.

'What do you mean?' she replies, her voice soft.

'I was calling out to my brother.' His voice cracks and he pauses.

Alexis fidgets, but he doesn't turn to look at her.

'Ethan is – was – my brother. He died in a car crash, almost a year ago.' He stares at his hands, concentrating on the lines in his skin as he speaks. 'I've had the dreams, nightmares, pretty much every night since, always the same sort of thing.' He rubs the back of his neck vigorously.

She doesn't say anything, but edges in a little closer and places a hand gently on his arm. He stiffens, but doesn't move away, glad for the human contact. It isn't long before his eyes feel heavy, and he closes them again, listening to her steady breaths as they lull him back to sleep.

HE WAKES ABRUPTLY AND looks down to find Alexis' head buried in his chest, and his arms wrapped around her back. His relaxed muscles instantly stiffen and he carefully slides away from her. She stirs, then turns to face the other way. The pouch attached to her belt drapes down onto her back, and he wonders if it holds more vials of the tea that made him feel better. He gently loosens the straps, gives a small tug, and the bag falls into his palm. He crawls out of the cramped space, quietly picking up another bag along the way.

Out in the forest, streams of sunlight find their way through the trees, waking the birds and other forest life. He breathes in as he stretches. His body feels stronger, even from the small amount of sleep.

'Morning, you two. You sleep okay?' he says to Brawn and Paladin, who seem to be happily munching on some grass. Paladin ignores him but Brawn lifts his head, his ears twitching round. He snorts, digging his front hoof into the soil.

'You pleased to see me, boy?' He runs his hand up Brawn's nose. A white patch has appeared on one of his ears. 'I'm sure *that* wasn't there before, was it?' He studies the horse's coat for a few moments more, then his stomach growls and he realises how hungry he is. He bends and searches through Alexis' bag, hoping there's more food. He pulls out a leather hip flask. Prising the cork out he smells a slight mustiness from the leather casing. He pauses, then places the flask to his lips. The liquid fills his mouth, then the familiar tang hits his tonsils. He swallows the mouthful of tea before taking a few more swigs, then lays the flask on the grass and looks at the small bag he'd removed from her belt.

'What does she keep in here then?' he murmurs, unclipping the popper. He tips it upside down and a small wooden cube, no bigger than his palm, falls out. The box is solid, all except for a hairline crack running all the way round it. After a few moments a faint glow begins to creep out from the fracture. Samuel almost drops it, but catches it just before it hits the ground.

Brawn snorts and shakes his head from side to side, but Samuel barely glances at him. He tightens his grip on the box, and stuffs the pouch into his pocket. On closer inspection, he notices that the crack is about half an inch from the top, making it appear as though there is a lid. Gripping the cube in one hand, he tugs on the top with the other. Nothing happens, but the light fades a little. He fiddles with the box but it's stuck solid. A small part of the wood on one side is far lighter in colour than the rest. He presses his finger against it. Nothing. He pushes harder and the thin line of light glows again. This time it spreads out, lighting up around the whole cube. He looks up, checking to make sure no one is about. The forest is clear and quiet. He runs his finger over the smooth wood, noticing another light patch. His brow creases with concentration. Once again he pushes it, then breathes in sharply when another strip of light appears. Each time a ribbon of light materialises, he spots another square of lighter wood. He continues to push each piece until nearly every inch of the cube is covered in thin strips of light, all crossing over one another. He tries to pull the lid again but it's still stuck. Locking his hand down, he twists, and a satisfying click signals that it's opened. Light leaks out fast, causing him to wince and hold it back. Brawn starts rearing up, whining.

'Shhh. It's okay,' Samuel says. 'I just want to look.' His hands shake a little, but he forces the lid off. The light dims and he peers inside. An oval object sits clasped inside a metal claw. The object has a black tint but at the same time looks translucent. A crack runs through it, a break which doesn't look like it should be there. Three long prongs hold the egg-like object delicately. They run up the sides and thin out to a point.

'Is this it? Is this the artefact she's carrying?' he

murmurs, unable to take his eyes off it. He slowly lifts his hand until it's hovering just above the egg.

'No! Don't touch it!' Alexis yells.

Samuel jumps and his finger slips. He touches the tip of the egg and feels a jolt. He sees Alexis' face, frozen, her mouth open, and her eyes wide. A second later and everything turns white.

Chapter Seventeen

ALEXIS STARES AT THE EMPTY SPACE. Her mouth is open, but she can't speak. She drops the flask that she'd been holding and the water drips out, getting sucked into the arid earth, as she runs over to where he was just standing.

'Samuel? Samuel!' She looks about her, but he and the egg are gone. Brawn whinnies, scraping his front hoof in the dirt.

'It's alright boy.' She raises her arm, trying to calm the horse. 'We'll find him.' She runs around grabbing their things and bundling them back into the bags.

'The Davadores will know what to do.'

Brawn rears up beside her.

'What's wrong?' she says to the horse. 'You don't think I should tell them?' A low rumbling comes from Brawn's nostrils. 'What do I do then? Tell Anka? I can't arrive at Irith's without the egg.' The horse's eyes are wider and brighter than normal. She holds his reins and hushes soothing tones.

'Where are you, Samuel?' she murmurs, looking around at the soundless forest.

His lungs feel like they're about to explode as he struggles to find air. He tries moving, but his limbs won't work. A surge of energy rushes through him, causing him to gasp. His chest expands, as he finally feels the oxygen circulate. Dropping to the ground, the box he was holding, lands neatly in the red earth. His face almost touches the soil as he gulps in air. After a few moments he draws longer breaths, slowing his heart rate and letting the dizziness subside. He clenches his fists, scrunching the dirt up in them.

'Alexis?' he says, lifting his head. The forest has gone and has been replaced with earthy cliffs. 'Alexis!' The word reverberates around the ravine. No answer comes. He clambers to his feet, brushing the remnants of dirt from his hands. The red rocky face of the cliffs stretch up so high he can't see beyond them. He scoops up the box at his feet. The object is still clasped in the claw, but the blackness of the egg now swirls on the surface.

'Hey, get off me!' a voice says.

Samuel looks up but can't see anyone. Laughter bounces off the rocks and he instinctively dives behind a boulder.

'You're no fun anymore,' the voice says again.

Samuel peers around the rock into the ravine. Two men are walking towards him, and as they get closer,

Samuel can see they're older than him. They look almost identical, with one just slightly bigger, his muscles more defined. Their brown wavy hair is almost shoulder length and they're both wearing long shorts that are frayed at the bottom. Neither has a top on, the sweat from the scorching red sun clinging to their skin. One shoves the other, almost pushing him to the ground. Samuel notices their bare feet; they're filthy, as though they've never worn shoes.

'I said stop it.' The guy growls, ramming back. It looks hard, but they're both laughing.

'You've got stronger, Faro.'

Samuel holds his breath as they approach. For the few seconds it takes for them to pass he gets a better look at their faces. They really do look the same, even their eye colour, each having one green and one blue. Samuel hears a quiet hiss and looks down to find an orange beetle, scurrying near his foot. He carefully steps to the side, but then a scratching sound comes from behind him, and more hissing. Once the men are at a safe distance he turns around. Covering the cliff wall, a few feet away, are hundreds of beetles, all scuttling across the stone. He shudders, quickly stepping backwards and patting his clothes to check none are on him. Wiping his clammy hands on his trousers he turns to look back to the men. They're making their way down through a crevice in the rocks. He looks back to the cliffs and round the ravine, but there are no other signs of human life. Making a decision he follows them, being sure to keep his distance.

He treads carefully down the rock face, trying not to let any stones fall. The men's deep voices carry back to him on the breeze. As he descends he loses sight of them for a few moments. Picking his pace up, he's glad for the sturdy boots Alexis gave him. He turns the corner and stops still. One of the men is less than a few metres away. Samuel watches as the man peers into a cave.

'Hey, Pemba, look at this!' he calls.

'Come on, Faro, we don't have time.'

'Wait a minute. There's something in here. Look,' Faro says.

The other guy makes his way back, and Samuel watches them enter the cave.

'What is that?'

Samuel strains to listen, but all he can hear are muffled voices. He edges farther down the rocks. Just as he's about to reach the cave entrance, a flash of light radiates from the opening, causing him to lose his footing and slide on the dry dirt. He grapples for the rock but the stone crumbles beneath his fingers and he tumbles, falling faster and faster, unable to right himself. The ground becomes softer, almost wet. The clouds move as if on fast forward. Finally, the earth evens out and he stops, flat on his back. He breathes heavily, squinting up at the bright sky. After a few deep breaths he picks himself up again. The landscape around him has changed. The cliffs have been replaced with open marshy land and a few hundred yards away is a windmill. With nothing else in sight, Samuel begins to make his way over to the building. He drags his feet through the marshy bog, his legs feeling sluggish. As he approaches the windmill standing above the marshland, he can see it's sitting atop wooden stilts. He studies the structure. It's timber frame is a rich, deep colour. Its sails are gigantic and turn ever so slightly in the breeze.

'No!' a deep voice bellows.

Samuel drops to his knees and crawls behind a swamp plant. The cold water seeps into his trousers as he crouches, waiting.

'You don't understand,' a voice urges.

Samuel watches as a man emerges from the windmill. He's wearing a black robe, and his hair is darker, but it's definitely one of the men from the ravine.

'I do, brother. But you must understand that we are responsible now. We must ensure it is safe.'

Moments later and Samuel sees the owner of the second voice. He's wearing a grey robe and holding a box almost identical to the one in Samuel's hand.

'I'm tired of being responsible. You have no idea. It's okay for you, you don't mind the solitude. But I can't bear it anymore.' The dark-robed man has turned to face his brother. He has deeper strokes on his face than before. He reaches out to the box but his brother steps back.

'Think of everything we could do with it, Faro. Everything we could have. Think of what it's given us already.' His voice is strained.

Faro doesn't reply. He's clutching hold of the box.

He sighs, a loud weary sigh. 'Pemba, brother, we–'

'Forget it. You'll never understand.' Pemba turns from his brother and sails down the wooden steps, as though he's gliding on air. Samuel slowly lies flat on his stomach, hoping the reeds cover him and the ripples don't give him away. As the man gets to the swamp he turns in Samuel's direction. Samuel doesn't move. He holds his breath, the plant tickling his nose. The man scowls, then a few moments later hurries off through the swamp. Samuel looks back to Faro, who is watching after his brother, now clasping the box in both hands.

Samuel starts to stand but the reeds have wrapped around him, clinging to his body. He wriggles but they tighten their grip and he feels a surge in his chest. He looks down and sees his reflection in the water. With his matted hair, wide eyes and taut skin, he might as well be looking at his brother.

'Help!' he yells, as he gets dragged down. He struggles, pulling at the plant. 'Help!' His ears and nose fill with water, as the cold stabs at his skin. The pressure in his chest is almost unbearable, but he clings on to the wooden box, gasping, no longer able to keep his mouth shut. Darkness comes and he closes his eyes, as the reeds wrap around his face and hands.

Chapter Eighteen

SAMUEL OPENS HIS EYES. He grunts, grabbing his face, but there's nothing there. It takes him a moment to realise he's no longer under water. His clothes are dry, like nothing even happened. He's no longer in the swamp, but inside, surrounded by circular walls. Light fills the room through a large window; he hurries over to it. Outside is the vast bog.

'The windmill,' he mutters, spinning round and finding himself faced with a wall, lined with hundreds of books. He turns his attention back to the window. Next to it is a door, and to the side of that is a set of stairs that wind up the edge of the building. Above him he hears muffled whispering. He starts to make his way up the staircase and as he nears the top he finds Faro with his back to him, bent over. Samuel edges a little farther up, hoping the stairs don't creak. Faro turns slightly and Samuel sees the box from the cave, now sitting on the table. It's open and an egg is on show. It isn't the same as the egg that Samuel has in his box. This one is translucent, with a yellow centre, like the sun. He takes another step, then ducks as Faro whips round. Samuel peeks out from behind the banister and sees Faro's arms stretched out, his brow creased with more lines.

'I hope I won't need you,' Faro says, staring at a second wooden box in his hands. Samuel strains, reaching up on his toes. His eyes widen as he sees what's in the box: the same egg that he found in Alexis' bag. He looks down at the cube in his own hands, then quietly pulls the lid off. The dark egg is still there.

'There are two eggs,' he murmurs, glancing back to Faro, then at the egg on the table. Just as he closes the lid on his own box a low rumble sounds from outside.

'Pemba?' Faro says, now at the top of the stairs. Samuel steps back, startled. His foot slips and he loses his balance. As he tumbles back he draws the box in close to his chest. Faro is now directly in his line of sight, but the man doesn't seem to see him. Everything around him begins to change. The stairs disappear, the walls disintegrate and the sky that's now above him turns black. He shuts his eyes, waiting for the impact. His shoulder blades tense as his back hits hard ground and the jolt reverberates through his entire body. He clambers to his feet once more, rubbing his shoulder, the cobbled street having jabbed into it. On one side of him is a building, with lots of windows, its bricks crumbling. On the other, is an imposing partition with built in arches that run all the way down. Seeing that one end of the road is closed off by a high brick wall, he starts to make his way towards the other end, where he can hear voices. As he turns the corner he enters a large open courtyard. It's busy with people milling about chatting, some sitting at tables, eating and drinking. He runs over to a small group of men and women.

'Hey, can you help me? Where am I?' They carry on speaking, not taking any notice. 'Hey, can you hear me?'

He waves his hand in front of them, but they don't flinch. He moves past them to another group of women, where he lingers, trying to work out what language they're speaking. They talk fast, unfamiliar words rolling off their tongue with ease. Sighing, he wanders across the square, weaving in and out of people and tables before ducking into an alley. The passageway has a stale smell and lots of twists and turns, narrowing in some places, then widening out in others. Footsteps pound behind him, clipping the stones. He quickens his pace and tightens his grip on the box, wanting to get out of the backstreet. As the footsteps get louder, Samuel starts to jog, ignoring the ache in his back. Finally he reaches the end, stumbling out into a busy city street. He darts to the side of the alley, and pauses to catch his breath. Seconds later, a grey-haired figure emerges and hurries past, down the street, his robe spread out behind him.

'Faro,' Samuel mutters, recognising the man, even from his bent frame. He follows, side-stepping people as they come towards him. He's so focused on the man he almost bumps into a statue. The faded, grey stone is covered in moss and has a small plaque on the base, which is inscribed with symbols. Moving round it he searches for Faro, but he's disappeared.

'Damn it,' he mutters. The man is the only constant thing he's seen here, and he has a feeling he must stick with him. The street in front of him separates off into a crossroads. Having no idea of which way to go, he opts for his usual choice, left. As he hurries on, the air begins to cool and a wind starts to whip around at his clothes. The sky darkens and the clouds swirl. Behind the building to his right is a large structure, reaching up to the sky. He takes a side road through some houses and exits out onto another main road. Here, a circular building towers above him, with open arches almost all the way round.

'Pemba!' a voice yells.

Samuel turns and spies Faro a few hundred yards away. He follows the man's gaze upwards to find Pemba hovering above the building. His skin looks pale and tough. A set of wings spring up behind him, spreading out as if about to take flight. Samuel steps back. A second later and a woman with wings reveals herself.

'Pemba, you cannot do this,' Faro yells.

Pemba stares down at his brother, his face set, his eyes vacant of emotion. Samuel starts to make his way towards Faro, still staring up at the concrete oval. As he moves past the arches, shadows form on the walls and he sees creatures in the alcoves, standing to attention, like guards, each with a spear by their side.

'Orglins,' he murmurs.

'Pemba, please,' Faro says, now standing at the base of the building, metres from Samuel.

'Give me the Orbis, Faro,' Pemba replies.

'This isn't what you want. I know it isn't.' Faro stares up at his brother, but Pemba doesn't respond. Even from far below, Samuel can see Pemba's eyes darken more. He raises his arm and the bird woman behind him snaps her head to where he points.

'Go,' he says. Samuel barely hears the word, but sees the command form on Pemba's lips. The woman screeches, drawing back her wings and plunging towards the ground, heading straight for Samuel.

Chapter Nineteen

SHE SWOOPS OVER HIS HEAD, so close he can almost feel the wind from the feathers ruffle his hair. She doesn't land, instead hovering just above the ground behind him. An arrow is drawn in her bow, but she doesn't shoot. She opens her mouth wide and flames escape her. The fire rushes out, swirling in every direction as if unsure of what it must latch onto first. It licks at the brick walls, then getting no joy makes its way to one of the few trees that line the concrete landscape. It travels so fast, swallowing the tree whole.

'A harpy?' Samuel murmurs.

Screams come from passers by. The harpy turns to them, her mouth still wide. The fire runs along the ground, hissing and spitting as it itches to reach them.

'No!' Samuel yells. He dives for the harpy, flailing through the air, but doesn't make contact. Instead he soars straight through her and lands with a heavy thud. He flips over, the harpy just above him. Her wings are so large they block his view of anything else. He waits for the screams to get louder as the flames find their targets. But moments later a flash of white lightning fills the sky behind the harpy and the screams deaden. The bird woman drops to the ground, the tip of her wing landing inches from Samuel's foot. He turns to the passers by, but the road is empty. Faro hovers above him, a cane in his hand, aimed at the harpy, daring her to move.

'Brother, do not make me do this,' Faro says, turning to Pemba who is now surrounded by an army of harpies.

'Give me the Orbis,' Pemba demands. He raises his hands and Samuel watches as a dark orb of electricity grows between them.

'Don't you see? We were chosen to look after it. To look after everything that is held within it. Why do you want to destroy that?' Faro says.

'I don't want to destroy it. We've been given a chance to use the strength and powers that the Orbis has given us, for greater things. We can do anything we want, *be* anyone we want. Any world can be ours.' Pemba doesn't take his eyes from his brother as he speaks. 'Don't you want more?'

'I want what is best for everyone, Pemba.'

'Then you're a fool. We had nothing, and we'll have nothing, if we don't act. I won't ask you again. Give it to me.' Pemba's voice deepens. He doesn't wait any longer. Throwing his shoulders forward, he expels a ball of light from his hands. Faro swings his cane away from the harpy, blocking Pemba's attack, and dispersing the dark current before it hits him. His cane holds steady as Pemba continues to launch bolts of lightning at him.

Samuel can't move, enraptured by Faro and the shield of white light he's built to protect himself. He feels the heat of the power from the force of Pemba's assault.

'Come on,' he murmurs, as Faro is forced to the ground, not far from Samuel. He's knelt down, his head bent forward, but his cane remaining strong and upright.

'Stop,' Faro whispers, but the strikes continue. 'Stop,' he says again, this time a little louder.

Pemba shows no sign of giving up.

'Stop!' Faro yells. 'Stop!'

Pemba slowly drops his hands, a deep laugh emanating from him.

'What did you say?'

'I said stop. You're, you're stronger than me.'

'No!' Samuel yells, but no one turns to him.

Pemba drifts down, towards his brother.

'Can I have it?' he says, holding his hand out.

Faro looks up at him, sweat is pouring from his face. His hand shakes as he reaches into his tunic.

'No, Faro, you can't!' Samuel yells, scrabbling to his feet.

Faro pulls out the box.

'Let me show you something first,' he says, moving the box in his hands, twisting and turning it, until finally he unlocks the lid. Pemba, now almost on top of him, reaches out.

'I'm sorry, brother. I'm sorry, but I cannot let you do this.' Faro holds the open box towards Pemba, turning his head away. Pemba's smile disappears as he stares into it. A white light emerges, spreading across everything. Faro looks down, his face creased with sadness. Pemba appears frozen, his mouth open, his hand still. The light gets so bright Samuel can't look anymore. He closes his eyes, just for a second, but when he opens them the light has gone and Pemba has disappeared. Samuel watches Faro hang his head, the box still in his grasp as he fiddles with the lid. Samuel looks down at the box in his own hands. He undoes the top and stares at the dark egg. His hand shakes a little as he reaches out to feel the smooth, cold object beneath his fingertips. He feels the familiar rush and watches as the buildings crumble and the world spins once again.

Chapter Twenty

Alexis swings up onto Paladin, both horses loaded with their bags.

'Stay close to me Brawn,' she says to the horse, looking at his empty saddle. She inhales deeply, then signals for Paladin to move. The horse trots forward and Brawn falls back behind them. They've travelled no more than fifty yards when she feels her skin tingle.

'Samuel?' she says, turning round to find him lying face down in the dirt. 'Samuel!' She pulls on the reins, leaping off the horse before Paladin's even come to a standstill. She drops to her knees and lifts his hair that's flopped down, away from his face, then hauls him onto his back. The box is clasped in his hands. His eyes are closed, his skin covered in dirt. Close up she can see a little fine stubble on his face, beginning to poke its way through. She bends and puts her ear to his mouth. He smells like her brother when he's been working in the stables, only a little sweeter. Air from his nose tickles her ear and she can feel his pulse beating against her fingers. She leans back, releasing the breath that she'd been holding. A snort comes from behind her and a breeze ripples through her hair. She looks round to find Brawn staring down at Samuel.

'Something to drink, that will help.' She grabs the flask from Brawn's side and yanks the stopper out, before carefully lifting Samuel's head onto her lap. She places a few drops of tea into Samuel's mouth, biting her lip in anticipation. Then she dabs some water on his forehead, temples and neck.

'Please wake up,' she says, not knowing what else to do.

After a minute or two his eyelids twitch and she watches his fingers tighten around the box.

'Alexis?' he croaks, his eyes finally opening.

She leans back, her heart pounding. He sits up suddenly, scrambling away from her.

'Pemba. Faro. They–'

'What? What did you see?'

Samuel turns to her. His face is contorted, his eyes glazed.

'*This* is what's so important? This is what you're taking to Irith?' he asks, holding the box up.

Alexis moves back, patting the dirt from her clothes.

'Yes, and you shouldn't have taken it from me.' She reaches out for the box but Samuel draws it in close. 'It's a basilarium,' she explains.

'A what?'

'A basilarium. It holds something of great importance.' She nods towards it. 'The object in it is called the Egg of Darkness.'

The slight colour that had returned to Samuel's face disappears.

'Have some more of this,' she says, handing him the flask. He takes it from her, his hand shaking as he sips the liquid.

'What did you see?'

Samuel swallows and she watches the skin on his neck roll over his adams apple.

'I saw Pemba, and Faro. I saw what they found, what made them strong. Then I saw Faro trap his brother.' He stares down at the basilarium.

Alexis feels her chest tighten.

'So you know about the Orbis?'

Samuel looks up at her, his mouth closed, twisted, as if he's biting the inside of his cheek.

'I saw another basilarium, another egg. It looked so different to this one.' He falls silent as he traces his finger over the contours of the box.

Alexis watches his hand, mesmerised by his gentleness.

'What you describe is the Orbis. It's an egg which holds all life in it. All worlds,' she says.

'And that's what Pemba has been searching for?'

Alexis nods.

'But how did he escape the Egg of Darkness?'

She sighs, knowing Samuel won't stop asking questions until she tells him everything.

'The Darkness is a barren place, with no light, or life in it. Faro knew it would keep Pemba weak. After Faro trapped him he assigned a bearer to the egg and sent it to another world, far away from himself and the Orbis. A few months before you came here, the bearer was killed. The egg's seal got damaged, allowing light to get in and Pemba used that light to grow stronger, until he was able to break free.'

Alexis watches Samuel's reaction. His chest flattens as he breathes out heavily.

'Where is Faro now?' he asks.

'No one knows. Some say he travels from plain to plain with the Orbis, keeping it safe.'

'Have you touched the Egg of Darkness? Have you seen?' he asks.

'I was entrusted the egg by the Davadores. I was given the responsibility of taking it to Irith. But I was ordered not to touch it. After seeing what happened to you, I guess that's why.'

Samuel nods slowly.

'But what *did* happen to me? Where was I?'

'I think you were in Nekton.'

'Nekton? What's that?'

'It's a space in between worlds. It links worlds together. Rather than you being inside the egg, the

Darkness, I think you got caught between plains. Nekton doesn't have any sense of time, which is why you were able to see things that have already happened. The egg showed you its history.'

'That's why no one could see me,' he murmurs, rubbing his face as if trying to take it all in. 'But there's something I don't get.'

'What's that?'

'Why did they give it to *you*? I overheard you and Anka talking before. I heard him say he couldn't do it without you.'

Alexis clenches her jaw, unable to stop herself. She takes a moment, wondering how best to explain.

'He meant finding Irith.'

'*Finding* Irith? I thought that's where we were going?'

'We are.'

'I don't understand.'

She fiddles with one of the straps on her wrist, running her fingers over the taut leather.

'I didn't tell you everything before,' she says. 'My abilities, they allow me to do a little more than others.'

'What do you mean?'

'As well as opening gateways to other worlds, I can also locate people. If I have something of theirs, or something that is connected to them, I can use it to find their location.'

Samuel doesn't reply. He stands up, now looking

much stronger.

'You mean, no one knows where Irith is except you?' he says, standing above her.

She looks up at him and slowly shakes her head.

Chapter Twenty One

ALEXIS TAKES A WHILE TO REPLY, wishing she didn't have to explain it all to him, but knowing he might be in more danger if she doesn't.

'The Davadores said the object, the Egg of Darkness, would be the connection and show me where Irith is. And it did.'

'Why would the egg be connected to Irith?'

'I don't know,' she replies. 'I just know I need to get it to him fast, and hopefully he can mend it.'

Samuel strides over to Brawn.

'I *thought* it was damaged. It has a crack running across it.'

Alexis nods.

'I can see why the Davadores need you,' he says, stroking the horse's side.

'You should have some food and then we must get going,' she replies, springing to her feet. 'Let me take that.' She reaches out again for the basilarium, but Samuel jerks back.

'Samuel. Give it to me. It's too dangerous for you to have. And you must eat, regain your strength.'

'It's weird,' he says, his eyes focused on the box, his voice robotic. 'When I got back to you, I felt like I'd travelled through another gateway. But that didn't last long. And now I feel stronger than before.'

Alexis steps forward. She places a hand on his arm and feels his muscle tense. The touch seems to waken him from his trance.

'Eat something,' she says again, slowly taking the basilarium from his grip.

He nods, rubbing the back of his neck, then producing the pouch from his pocket he hands it to her. She puts the cube back in it, then swiftly ties the bag to her belt, before pulling out some food that she'd packed from home.

'There's something else I'm still not sure about,' he says, taking the parcel of food she's holding out to him.

'What?'

'If Pemba wants the Orbis. Why is he here?'

Alexis brushes the crumbs from her hands.

'Because, he wants the Egg of Darkness too,' she says. 'If it's fixed, then he can be trapped in it again. He'll do anything to stop that from happening.'

Samuel stops chewing.

'But that means he's after you. You're the least safe person to be around.' He swallows forcefully and Alexis can almost feel the food getting stuck in his throat. She feels her face redden.

'It all happened so fast. I'd wanted to leave you with my family. Somewhere safe, until I could get you home. But I was too late, they'd gone.'

Samuel takes a swig of water. She listens to the gulp as it travels down his throat.

'I can't let Pemba get the egg. I had no choice,' she says. 'And now, neither do you.'

Samuel falters, the drinks flask halfway to his mouth.

'What do you mean?'

Alexis adjusts the crossbow on her back.

'Before you came here, I wasn't being tracked. The gateway you came through from Earth changed that.'

Samuel stares at her quizzically.

'For a short amount of time after a gateway is closed, a trace of the other world is left behind,' Alexis explains. 'For a portal to have been opened now, when it's forbidden under Davadore law ... Pemba might think it's to do with the egg.'

'You think they'll have seen traces of Earth?'

'No. I believe that the gateway was closed long enough for any particles to have disappeared, but Pemba has been trapped for so long, he's been able to study worlds, to watch them.' She feels a breeze tickle her arms. 'He might know where you're from. He might have your scent now as well, especially as you've touched the egg.' She lowers her eyes for a second. 'I don't think they're just tracking me. I think they're tracking you too.'

Chapter Twenty Two

Samuel looks at the piece of food in his hand. His stomach rumbles but he doesn't feel hungry anymore.

'I think Pemba knows you touched the egg,' Alexis says. She's barely taken her eyes from him. He has so many thoughts he can't seem to latch onto one.

'What are we gonna do?'

Alexis tightens the straps on Paladin's side, then does the same to Brawn.

'Keep going. We're going to do what I've been trying all along; get the egg to Irith.'

'But what if he can't help?'

'He *will*,' Alexis replies. 'He will.'

Samuel doesn't like to push her any further. Having been so curt until now, her repetition is clear to him that the thought has crossed her mind.

Samuel stares at the fine hairs on Brawn's mane as the horse follows behind Alexis.

'I'm sure Brawn's coat is changing colour,' he says,

inspecting the white flecks that seem to be spreading throughout his coat.

Alexis looks back at him.

'Hopefully.'

'What do you mean?'

'If it's turning white, that's a good sign.' She slows Paladin so she's trotting alongside him. 'Brawn isn't from here. I rescued him from a world called Fortis.' She reaches out and pats Brawn's side. The horse responds, throwing his head towards her.

'It's a world close to this one. It's one of the worlds Pemba and his army have already destroyed, looking for the Orbis and the Egg of Darkness. If I hadn't brought Brawn back here, he would have been killed. I wish I could have saved others, but there wasn't time.'

'You saved him, though.' Samuel runs his fingers through Brawn's hair. 'So, why is he black?'

'All horses on Fortis are white, but I think the shock and the stress from Pemba's army, caused him to turn this colour. He must feel comfortable with you, now his hair's turning white again. I hope it returns completely. He's one of a kind now; he'll be sought after, especially with the intelligence that Fortisian horses have.'

Samuel sits up in the saddle and turns to her.

'What do you mean?'

'His speed and intelligence are far greater than

horses here, or on Earth.'

'I thought he was fast, when he led me into the forest,' Samuel replies.

'That was fast, but he can do better. Wait until he's returned to his usual self. I'm sure he'll get his full speed and strength back then.'

Samuel feels a rush of excitement in his belly. He'd known there was something different about Brawn and now he realises it's because the horse understands him. He feels comforted by this and eagerly pats Brawn's side.

Alexis taps her heels into Paladin and the horse speeds up.

'Hey, where are you going?' Samuel calls.

'There's a lake up ahead, I can hear it.'

Samuel listens and watches Brawn's ears twitch.

'I can't hear anything!'

Alexis doesn't reply but veers off into the thick of the forest. Brawn canters behind them, at a reasonable pace, one which Samuel now realises is no exertion for the horse at all. Samuel bends every now and then, avoiding low branches. A few moments later he sees rippling water through a gap in the trees. Brawn's pace changes as the solid dirt turns to white sand, and he feels his hooves sink a little into the softer ground. He tries to remain steady on the steed, but his heart beats a little faster as the horse's legs seem to descend further.

Chapter Twenty Three

BRAWN IS PERSISTENT, struggling with the perilous ground, and ploughing on through the trees. It takes a few minutes, but they finally reach the other side and Samuel is able to take a deep breath, allowing his uneasiness to recede. The sand seems to have hardened a little, and Brawn moves effortlessly again.

'This is a lake?' Samuel says, once they've caught up with her.

The water's edge starts a few metres in front of them, but the other side of the lake is nowhere in sight.

'Are you sure? Looks more like an ocean.'

Alexis laughs, the first time since he's met her.

'It's called Lake Avania.'

She dismounts Paladin and walks to the edge of the water. He watches her as she bends down, cupping the water in her hands and then taking a sip. Her hair slowly falls away from her neck as she bends over, revealing the mark on her pale skin. He slips off Brawn and walks forward a little.

'You said before, that your dad was a Plain Seeker.

Does he have the same powers as you?'

Alexis drops her hands, the water splashing back into the lake. She stands up straight, her back to him.

'He's not a Plain Seeker anymore. Not an active one. He's forbidden to use his powers.'

'Why? What happened?' he asks, moving closer to her.

Alexis briefly runs her fingers over her mark, then gathers her hair to cover it.

'It's a long story and we don't have time.' She bends again, filling her flask up. 'You'll want to fill a couple of these. This is good, pure water.'

He does as she says and takes the canteen out of the holder attached to Brawn's side, then dips it into the lake.

'You don't have to tell me. But if it's to do with what's happening here, then maybe I should know,' he says.

'It has nothing to do with it.'

Samuel looks away. He makes sure his flask is filled to the top before sticking the cork back in.

'It's difficult for me,' she mutters.

Samuel pretends to be way more interested in the flask than he is.

'To be a Plain Seeker at least one of your parents has to be. But that doesn't mean every child will be; my brother isn't. We all treasure the gift and to be told you can't use it, is a disgrace.'

Samuel remains quiet, letting her speak. Every time she pauses her lips push forward, as if she's forcing words back.

'My father used to travel to worlds all the time and sometimes with his friend, Orlo. But over time, Orlo became obsessed with finding new worlds and entering into them to explore. He was always bringing things back.' Alexis turns to face him. 'As a general rule we're only allowed to bring one thing back from each world, and we have to acquire it in the correct way. Earth, for instance; I would need to buy something, or make sure the object I wanted had been discarded, before bringing it back here.'

'Do you mean like a book?'

'Yes, it could be. Why?'

'I saw *Black Beauty* when we were at your house.'

'That's my fathers. He's always called me Beauty and he brought that back when he travelled to Earth years ago.' She smiles, and he can see in her mind she's replaying a memory.

'What about Orlo?'

'He went against the Davadores' rules. It was clear he was out of control. He got greedy, with everything new worlds have to offer. The Davadores had to put a stop to it. They thought my father was involved and forbade him to open any more gateways.'

Samuel holds her gaze.

'I'm sorry they didn't believe your dad.'

Alexis raises her eyebrows, her eyes widening.

'They were just doing what's right. Trying to keep our world safe. We're seekers, not destroyers. We must enter in and out of worlds carefully, something Orlo had neglected by the end.'

'Do you always agree with the Davadore's rules?'

Alexis turns away from him again, scraping her foot over her tracks in the light sand.

'The Davadores have aided us. They've helped our world grow,' she says. 'We mustn't interfere with other worlds. It could change things.'

Samuel looks out across the lake. The water darkens and wind ripples across its surface. Paladin whines and sinks her hooves into the soft sand.

'It's alright girl,' Alexis says, grabbing hold of the horse's reins.

'What's wrong with her?' Samuel asks, being careful not to get in the way of the powerful beast.

'I don't know.' Alexis casts her gaze to the edge of the forest. At the same time the horse throws her head up and down, as she rears back. Her hooves land with a heavy thud and she charges forward.

'Paladin, no!' Alexis yells, running after the horse. 'Wait here!' she calls back to him. Her speed increases, her stride fluid and within seconds she's disappeared.

Samuel jogs after them, but Brawn blocks his path. He moves to look around the horse, but there's no sign of Paladin or Alexis. Brawn snorts, pushing his head into Samuel's shoulder, gently but firmly.

'Okay, okay,' he says, placing a hand on the horse's muzzle. He continues to stroke the horse, as his eyes avert back to the forest.

'Alexis?' Movement amongst the trees catches his attention. He runs his hand along Brawn's side as he edges round him.

'Good boy.'

He concentrates on the line of trees, dropping his hand as he moves slowly towards them. Brawn turns, but doesn't try to stop him. A branch cracks loudly.

'Hey! Who's there?'

His eyes are a little fuzzy in the dim light as he enters back into the forest. He feels the coolness on his arms once again as the trees create an umbrella above him. The bark creaks on the large trunks, but he can't hear anything else.

'Must have been an animal or something,' he says, turning back to Brawn.

He relaxes, his stomach muscles having tensed. A sudden pain shoots through his shoulder and a force pushes him to the ground. It happens so quickly he doesn't have time to call out. Twigs scratch against his face and soil finds its way into his mouth. He flips himself over but is pinned down. His eyes sting from the dirt that flies into them, and he grapples with the muscle that's holding him. Through blurry vision he sees a muddy face, partly covered by a mop of hair.

He stops thrashing for a second. The pause surprises his attacker and Samuel lunges up, wrapping his arms around the boy and overturning him, so he's on top. He presses hard into the boy's shoulders and the boy gives a small yelp. The face below him changes, taking on the look of a wild animal. His blonde eyes focus behind Samuel and Samuel turns his head. A large brown horse looms tall next to them. From this angle he can't see its rider, but a glance at the legs tells him it's a guy. The boy beneath him takes his chance, twisting his body and shoving Samuel hard. The close impact winds him and he flops to the ground, spluttering for air. The spasm in his stomach subsides after a few seconds as he manages to get a breath. He looks up and sees the boy a short distance away.

'Wait,' Samuel croaks.

The boy falters, turning to glance at him, then peers deeper into the forest. He looks back and forth a few times as Samuel tries to stand, his stomach still cramping. The boy begins to back away, and after a few steps he turns completely and runs off through the trees. Samuel looks round for the mysterious rider, but the forest is now empty of human life.

Chapter Twenty Four

'SAMUEL!' ALEXIS CALLS, RUNNING TOWARDS HIM. He hasn't moved from when the boy fled, moments before.

'I'm okay. Did you catch up with Paladin?'

'Yes. I've tied her up back there.'

'I think I know what scared her,' Samuel says, telling Alexis about the boy.

'Which way did he go?'

Samuel points in the general direction, now not entirely sure, all the trees looking the same.

'I'll go look for him.'

'I don't think he was here to hurt us. To be honest, I think he was scared. Some other guy was here, on a horse, I think that scared him off too.'

Alexis looks toward the trees where Samuel pointed.

'Maybe villagers?' she says.

Samuel finally gets up, brushing the dirt from his clothes.

'Is there a village nearby?'

'Kirkela. It's not far. We can stop there for supplies.'

Samuel nods. 'The boy can't have been older than fifteen or sixteen, but I get the feeling the rider was older, though all I saw were his legs.' Samuel rubs his chest where the boy had pushed down on him. 'The boy was pretty strong.'

Alexis smiles and Samuel coughs, feeling the blood rise to the surface of his cheeks.

'Come on. We can probably make it to Kirkela before nightfall,' she says.

SINCE THE RUN IN WITH THE BOY, they'd mainly ridden in silence. Samuel hadn't felt a need to speak. He'd been staring at Alexis in front, letting his eyes glaze over. With no distractions, his mind is usually focused on his brother. It had become normal for him to think about him, replaying memories, good and bad. The quietness in his mind was suddenly unnerving.

'How much farther is it to the village?' he asks.

Alexis doesn't reply. She looks as though she's buried in her own worries.

'Alexis?'

'It shouldn't be long now. We should let Anka know of our progress. He and the others must meet us at Irith's.'

'How are you gonna do that?'

Alexis reaches into the satchel attached to Paladin's side.

'We have ways of communicating here,' she says, pulling out a bit of crumpled paper. 'Do you remember the bird you saw, back in the forest, just after you came through the gateway?'

Samuel recalls the colourful little bird that had danced at his feet.

'I've seen the bird since then,' he says.

Alexis looks up sharply. Her small nose twitches.

'You didn't tell me.'

Samuel shrugs.

'This might be a little easier than I thought then. That bird you saw is called an altaira. They're birds that come to you if you're ever in need, most of the time in immediate danger.'

Samuel looks up at the cover of the trees, seeing glimpses of the sky.

'But I saw the bird when we were at yours,' he says.

'That is rare, but I have heard it happen before.'

'Really?'

Alexis pulls something out of the bag. She holds it up to her face, then licks the end of what looks like a small piece of lead.

'Yes. Sometimes an altaira can attach itself to someone. It came to you when you needed it, back in the forest, then for whatever reason it feels it must keep returning to you.'

The thought comforts Samuel.

'How do I get it to come to me when I want it to?' he asks.

'You can try calling for it.' Alexis brings Paladin to a halt. 'Focus all your energy on imagining the bird in front of you. Don't think about anything else. Remember how it looks, its colours. Hear the tiny beating of wings as it soars towards you, then comes to land at your feet.'

Samuel balances himself as Brawn comes to a stand still. He stares at the closest branch, trying to picture the bird perched on it, then he holds his breath and waits.

'Nothing's happening,' he says, after a minute or two.

Alexis swings round, so she's sitting with both legs on one side of her horse, nearest to him.

'Close your eyes.'

He does as she says, feeling a little stupid. He concentrates on the insides of his eyelids, the red darkness. As he shuts his sight off, his other senses heighten. His smell is the first, as a slight wind blows, sending a mixed scent of grass and dirt his way. Sound is next, the trees groaning, as if tired from their constant standing. After a few seconds the bird's tiny head pecking at the grass comes to mind. Its feathers blow from the flurry of air and he thinks about its wings and how they look like they've been dipped in paint, all the colours running into one. He tries to remember if the bird made any noise, but all he can hear are fluttering wings.

'Look,' Alexis whispers.

He opens his eyes and realises what he heard wasn't in his head. The bird dives, landing neatly on a branch. It tucks its wings to its sides, hopping nearer the end of the bough.

'I did it!' Samuel leans forward. 'Come on, come here, it's alright.' He holds his hand out to the bird. 'What do I do now? How will she understand me?'

'They can understand us. We just need to give her a message to take to Anka and the others.' She scribbles something on the piece of paper, then gently rolls it up, before handing it to him.

He takes it, then holds the paper between his thumb and forefinger, his arm outstretched. The bird flits down from the branch and lands on top of Brawn's head. Samuel moves back a little, wondering what Brawn will do, but the horse remains still as the bird looks up at him, her small eyes shining. She tilts her head one way, then the other. He slowly stretches his fingers nearer, trying so hard to stay still, not knowing if sudden movements will scare the bird. After a moment she leans her head forward and clamps her beak down on the paper.

'She definitely likes you,' Alexis says.

'Go on then, little bird, off you go.'

She spreads her wings and floats up into the air, hovering for a moment. Then, her wings beat faster and she flies off, dipping up and down, avoiding the branches of any trees that enter her path. Samuel smiles as he turns to Alexis.

'Now what?' he asks.

'We let her do her job. It shouldn't take long for her to get the message to the others.'

'What if the message gets intercepted?'

Alexis picks up Paladin's reins.

'Altaira are fast and very clever. They rarely get caught,' she says. 'And if they do, they destroy the message.'

Samuel looks through the trees, at the invisible path the altaira flew off on.

'How do they destroy it?'

'They swallow it. Just like they would a bug.'

Samuel glances at her, but she's already ahead of him. He hopes she's right, and the little bird is fast enough.

Chapter Twenty Five

SAMUEL WATCHES ALEXIS RUB THE BACK of her neck, then reach round for the crossbow on her back.

'Are you okay?' he asks, seeing her mark glowing.

'Something's wrong,' she replies, drawing on Paladin's reins to slow the horse. 'Look.' She sits forward, pointing the crossbow at the top of the trees. Samuel follows her gaze. The trees are less dense, allowing the early evening sun to throw some light on them. He watches wisps of smoke float above the forest in the distance.

'Kirkela?' he asks.

'Yes.'

'What's wrong?'

'I don't know. Either the smoke is from the villagers or–'

'Or it's Pemba's army?' he says.

Alexis clicks her tongue, ordering Paladin to pick up the pace.

Until now Samuel has tried not to ask too many questions, afraid of the answers. But he's intrigued by the sparsity of human existence in White Plains. Since being here, he's only seen the forest and Alexis' small village.

'Do you have any cities here?' He finally plucks up the courage to ask her.

Alexis turns her head a little towards him, and he waits for a clipped response.

'There are some areas of larger population. But we mainly live in small groups, villages. And each village is different.'

'What do you mean?'

Alexis turns her concentration back to the path in front of them.

'White Plains is built up from ideas that other worlds have to offer. A lot of what you've seen may seem similar to Earth. Your world has some interesting concepts, especially for habitation.'

'Habitation?'

'Yes. The way you structure your buildings. A lot of us here base our homes on this. If you went somewhere like Fortis, Brawn's world, it would be very different. Their houses are built half below and half above the ground. This works for them; the atmosphere there is hot and humid and they need to take shelter, to stay cool. But I don't really like the idea of being below the surface for too long.'

'Are you claustrophobic?'

Alexis raises her eyebrows and tilts her head slightly.

'I don't like small spaces.'

Samuel nods, familiar with that dread. Every time he's in a car now the feeling creeps in.

'I guess that's my nature. Being a Plain Seeker, I thrive on the open air,' Alexis adds.

Samuel wants to ask more about Plain Seekers, but he doesn't want to push her. Her crispness appears to have softened a little, but if she's like other girls he has a feeling that could change at any moment.

An arrow twangs into the trunk of a tree near him, making both horses rear up.

'Get down!' Alexis calls, jumping from her horse.

Samuel stares at the arrow.

'Get down!' she yells again, as she moves backwards, her crossbow aimed at the sky.

Samuel leans forward, swinging his leg over Brawn and dropping with a thud.

'Move. There.' Alexis points to a cluster of trees that will give more cover.

Samuel does as she says, while Brawn remains beside him, acting as a shield. A large shadow skims across the ground. He hears a low thunk as the bolt leaves Alexis' crossbow.

'Do you see them?' he asks, feeling the adrenaline pump through him.

Alexis doesn't reply but continues to scan the night sky. Another shadow dances across the forest. She turns and fires again, then quickly reloads the weapon.

'*Come on.* Where are you?' she mutters.

A screech sounds above them and the harpy swoops low to the ground. It hovers, its large wings beating, creating a current that Samuel can feel on his skin even metres away. The harpy opens her mouth and Samuel tenses, waiting for the fire.

Chapter Twenty Six

THE HEAT DOESN'T COME. Instead, a shriek escapes from the harpy's stretched mouth. The sound is so loud and high pitched that Alexis drops her weapon and they both cover their ears.

'She's calling to the others,' Alexis says.

Moments later and the screeching stops. Alexis jabs her foot under the crossbow and flicks it up into the air, catching it neatly in her hand, before spinning round to face him.

'I've got to go after them, try and lead them away. You stay here.' She takes a dagger from her boot and slices the straps on the satchel attached to Paladin's side, then thrusts the bag into his arms.

'There's food and water in here. If anything happens to me you must get to Kirkela. They'll help you there.'

'We should stay together,' Samuel says.

A nearby tree crackles and hisses as it's suddenly engulfed in flames.

'Stay with Brawn and try and keep out of sight.' Alexis hesitates, taking one last look at him, then running off in the direction of the harpies.

'Alexis,' Samuel says. His attempt to follow her is intercepted by a burnt branch which falls in front of him. 'Brawn, we can't just let her go out there.'

The horse lifts his hoof off the ground then puts it down, before repeating the action with his other leg, steadily moving backwards. Paladin remains quite still, as if too scared to move. Samuel ties the two ends of the bag strap together and slings it over his shoulder. He roots around in the other bags attached to Paladin, being careful not to be too rough, in case she bolts.

'There must be some sort of weapon in here,' he mutters. Right at the bottom of one of the bags, his fingers close around something cold. He pulls the hard object out of the bag. The dagger is small, but the blade looks sharp. The steady clapping of wings above him comes again, only this time he can tell there's more than one harpy. In the distance he hears the storm of arrows and imagines them raining down on Alexis.

'I can't wait here,' he says, tracing Alexis' footsteps. He moves with haste but keeps low to the ground. He doesn't turn to see if Brawn and Paladin have followed. With one hand hovered over the bag on his side, his other grips the dagger, holding it out in front of him. He's never used a knife on anything other than dead meat. An image of raw chicken and a knife slicing through it with ease, materialises in his mind. Just as the thought has fully formed, an arrow slices past his left ear, grazing it ever so slightly. The pain is sharp and sudden and he clamps his fingers around his ear, feeling the warm blood. When he looks up he sees where the arrow came from. A harpy is now standing a few metres away. He darts behind the nearest tree, waiting for more arrows to come. Resting his face against the cool bark he carefully edges round the other side of the large trunk. With daylight decreasing, all sorts of shapes begin to skip about. The harpy stands in the same spot. Slowly she raises one wing. Samuel watches as the other harpies move from behind the trees, into view. Each of them lifts one navy coloured wing in response. With a quick glance he counts about ten. He moves back behind the tree and slides to the ground, trying to control his breathing and ignore his thumping heart. The heat from the burning trees warms the cool dusk air. His neck aches, the way it always does now when he feels stressed. Just as he's wondering what to do, twigs and leaves scatter at his feet, causing him to look up. Flying across the tops of the trees is a harpy, and dangling in its claws is Alexis.

He jumps to his feet, leaving the safety of the large tree and runs, his feet pounding into the ground.

'Alexis!' he yells, keeping an eye on the harpy above him, whilst dodging bracken and fallen branches. A horse whines to his left. He turns, expecting to see either Brawn or Paladin, but instead he sees the brown horse again, galloping parallel through the trees. He doesn't stop running, but strains to get a look at the rider this time. With the speed of the horse and the denseness of the forest, he still struggles to see who it is, but the slicked back hair reminds him of Alexis' friend, Anka. He trips on a tree root, almost toppling over but righting himself at the last moment. Once steady, he searches the sky again for Alexis. She's just ahead and looking down at him, struggling hard in the harpy's talons. He watches as she reaches to her boot and withdraws a knife. She slashes the weapon above her head, but the harpy jostles her so she can't attack. Her eyes widen as she stares at him, then takes the dagger to her waist and slices. The pouch holding the basilarium drops, plummeting with a sense of purpose. Samuel sprints, pushing his aching muscles harder. The bag falls through the trees just ahead of him, barely making a sound. He dives forward into a thicket, discovering the basilarium nestled in some twigs. Not wasting any time he bursts from the copse, sprinting forward, searching the sky again for Alexis, but the trees are too dense and he can no longer see her. After a while his legs feel as though they're on fire and he trips again, but this time lands heavily on his knees. He doesn't attempt to get up, the sky is empty, and the horseman is nowhere in sight. He lowers his head, not knowing what to do.

A few minutes later and a quiet squawk rouses him. Lifting his head he sees the harpies have surrounded him once again. He stays still, but his eyes drop to the small bag. *The egg,* he thinks, slipping his hand inside and pulling the basilarium out. Quickly unlocking it he pulls the lid off. The egg sits there, as it did before, the desire to touch it still strong. He looks up at the harpies. Each one of them is staring at him, their heads slightly tilted to the side. Their faces are human, but their noses are long and sharp. Behind one of the harpies he spots Paladin, then Brawn, his dark eyes shining through the dingy light. He pauses for just a second, before deciding.

'Brawn, Paladin, run!' he yells. The horses hesitate, then Brawn obeys and Paladin follows. Samuel takes a last look at the harpies, who are now advancing in. He grips the dagger and with just one finger touches the tip of the egg. The last thing he hears is a piercing scream that echoes round each of his assailants, as he disappears from sight.

Chapter Twenty Seven

HE CLOSES HIS EYES BRIEFLY, and embraces the wind tugging at his clothes. When he opens them again, he finds himself tucked into an alcove, with stone walls looming tall around him. Peering out of the recess he spots a large grassy courtyard. High walls surround it, with wooden doors built into them, all the way along each side. Behind the wall at the far end stands a large tower with red clay tiles. A loud crack reverberates around the inner walls. Seconds later, the noise comes again.

Whack.

Whack.

He steps forward a little, to see where the noise is coming from. Standing on the grass are Anka and Alexis. They look slightly younger than they are now. Both seem focused, their brows creased, their movements quick and sharp as they battle against each other. The wooden poles they're holding are about a metre long and they jab them back and forth, blocking each other's attack.

Samuel watches Alexis, her actions almost effortless. Her hair is tied back in a plait and it whips about her as she swings round, crouching to the floor to avoid Anka's assault. Still bent she swipes her pole, thrusting it against Anka's calves. He grunts as his legs buckle, then he falls back. She jumps on top of him placing the pole across his chest.

'You're down,' she says, smiling.

Samuel waits for Anka's response, expecting hostility, but instead his face changes from discomfort to a smile. He propels Alexis backwards, then rolls on top of her, pinning her down. They both laugh and Samuel looks away, gripping the stone wall next to him. Just as he's wondering whether to leave the alcove he notices a man in the shadows. His long brown cloak blends into the darkness, making him harder to see, but his pale face is a stark contrast against the orange stone walls. He's also watching Anka and Alexis, his lip curled in a smile. A loud bell rings on top of the tower and the two Plain Seekers immediately scramble up off the ground and hurry away, the cloaked man watching after them. Samuel steps forward, but the world begins to spin: the outer walls diminish, the grass square disappears and interior walls begin to build up around him. Within seconds he's standing in the corner of a small room, waiting for the dizziness to subside. The room looks like a study, with shelves full of books and a desk covered in papers. More books pile up on the floor and on one side of the room is a wooden door. Before Samuel can move, the door flies open and a man crashes in. He scrabbles over to the desk, sweat trickling down his receding hairline. His brown tunic clings to his belly as he fumbles with a set of keys attached to his belt.

'Come on, *come on,*' the man mutters. He unlocks the desk drawer and shoves his hands inside. Samuel moves around the room, trying to see what it is he's looking for. Moments later and the man triumphantly stands back, pulling out an object.

'A basilarium,' Samuel says, seeing the familiar artefact.

The man looks up, his small eyes glancing around the room. He shakes his head and a drop of sweat falls to the floor. Sniffing loudly he tucks the basilarium into his robe, before hurrying to the other side of the room, where a large tapestry hangs on the wall. A bang on the door reverberates around the small space and Samuel feels his heart rate quicken. Instinctively he drops to the floor behind the desk.

The man stumbles backwards as the banging gets louder. His large fingers grab onto the wall hanging, pulling it down around him to reveal a small secret door. He grapples with the keys once again. The thudding on the other side of the room continues as the man tries to slide the key into the lock. A second later and the wood on the far door splinters and the shouts on the other side increase.

'*No*. No, please,' the man says, as the door is forced open. Feet pound into the room and Samuel strains to look round the table. All he can see are two sets of legs.

'Please, you don't understand, you can't do this,' the man cries, his attempts at escape now hopeless.

'Be quiet,' comes an unrecognisable voice. 'Give us the basilarium.'

The man shakes his head, his mouth open.

'He must be the bearer,' Samuel mumbles to himself, still unable to see the attackers. The only visible part of them now is their weather-beaten boots. A slit about two inches long across one shoe is the only distinctive blemish. He inches further behind the table, knowing this has already happened, that there's nothing he can do. He knows no one can see him, but something keeps him from standing. The room has fallen silent. He peers out once again, just as he hears a gasp. The bearer clutches his chest as blood oozes from the wound and through his fingers. Samuel feels the sick gurgle in his belly as the blood drips onto the stone floor. The basilarium smacks to the ground a few feet from him. He imagines the man's grip having slowly released as the life seeped out of him. He tucks himself under the desk, unable to look. A shadow passes across the small hole in the wooden table. He lightly presses his face up against it and stares at the defect on the boot. He can't see much else, other than the back of a guy, who's bending to pick the basilarium up. Something passes across the hole, momentarily blocking the light. Then Samuel sees it; the mark on the neck. The same mark that Alexis has.

'A Plain Seeker,' he mutters, pressing his face further against the wood. But it's no good, he can't see anything else. He edges backwards on his hands, away from the table, wanting to see who killed the bearer. His hand touches something cold and he looks round to find his basilarium, which has dropped from his grasp. The egg is now exposed and his fingers are touching its cool surface. He clambers to his feet but the colours of the world begin to drain away, and the two men standing over the dead bearer, are now just a blur.

Chapter Twenty Eight

GRASS SEEDS IRRITATE HIS NOSE as his face touches the forest floor. He can't keep the sick down any longer, and he clutches his stomach as his muscles contract. After a few moments he wipes his mouth and stands. The forest is quiet, but the drifting smoke tells him he must be near Kirkela. There are now no signs of the harpies; the burnt out trees are the only clue that they were ever there.

'Brawn. Brawn,' he says, in hushed tones. Daylight has almost disappeared and he hopes he can reach Kirkela before it's gone altogether. He retrieves the basilarium from the ground. Just as he's about to twist the lid back on, he notices markings on the egg that weren't there before. The wavy lines look like some sort of map. A pain shoots through his ear, causing him to falter. He brings his hand up and feels the crust of dried blood from where the arrow skimmed it. A branch snaps to his left and he ducks, but not quickly enough. The arrow spears into his shoulder, bringing an instant heat to his body. The basilarium falls from his grasp as he drops down, rolling onto his side. His right hand clutches around the arrow head that's almost completely embedded in his skin. The harpy swoops to him, her face just within reach of his. Her small beady eyes bore down at him, and a small shriek comes from her beak-like mouth.

'Get away from me!' he says, throwing his arm up at her.

She flings her head backwards, screaming like a banshee, before whipping her wings round. Samuel sees an arrow sticking out from her back, then he hears a whack as another hits her, piercing her feathers. She raises her wings as if to fly off, but the arrow has left her lame.

Samuel feels an icy sensation seeping through his shoulder, where the arrow is lodged. At the same time he feels his clothes sticking to his back. He tries to move his arm but it's paralysed.

'Gideon, get her!' a woman yells.

He strains to look past the harpy who's now in a heap on the ground, her wings draped over her. His focus blurs as the world seems to be moving, either that or his brain is rolling about in his skull. He widens his eyes, trying to stop the dizziness. Another harpy is hovering over the wounded one. After a moment or two he realises it isn't a harpy, but a bird, one who's just as large, but whose wings are shades of brown and white. He blinks hard as the bird begins to change shape. Its claws shrink and become rounder.

Its legs become smooth and its puffed out chest gets smaller, as its wings dissolve. Within moments the bird has transformed into a woman. Samuel blinks again, feeling drowsy and wondering if he's imagining things. With one arm now useless, he uses his other clumsily, to grab the basilarium and shove it back into the pouch.

'Quick, Gideon,' the woman says.

Just as she speaks Samuel sees a pair of amber, glass-like eyes moving out of the shadows. He holds his breath, unable to talk. A large black panther stalks forward, then pounces on the harpy. The harpy retaliates, attempting to throw her wings up, but the panther's shoulder blades roll forward and its large paws scratch at her face, forcing her down. The silent struggle doesn't last long as the harpy is overpowered.

'We must take her back to Kirkela,' the woman says. 'You bring her, I'll get the boy.'

Samuel wonders if she means him. He opens his mouth but all that comes out is a groan.

'Don't speak,' the woman says, now bending over him.

Looking up into her dark eyes he feels instantly calmer. She places a hand gently on the base of the arrow that's still sticking out of him. Her dark, smooth skin stands out against the wooden arrow.

'The bearer…I saw…Plain Seekers. What, who,

who are you?' he stutters.

'I'm Senta. That's Gideon.' She points to the panther. 'What's *your* name?'

'Samuel,' he replies, then averts his eyes from her for a moment. The large cat begins to change. Its back legs grow and its front legs leave the ground. The hair on the beast falls to the floor and tan skin takes its place. Samuel wheezes, as the panther is now a man. His face is strong, his body solid.

'We're going to help you,' Senta says. 'Try not to speak. These arrows, they're poisonous. We need to get you back to our village.'

Samuel wants to stand. He wants to run, but the paralysis feels as though it's spreading.

'Help me,' he says.

'Come on, Senta. Let's get going,' Gideon demands, now having scooped the harpy up and draped her over his back.

Samuel feels a breeze on his head. He looks up and sees Brawn's face.

'Brawn,' he murmurs.

'Drink this,' Senta says, placing a vial on his lips, not giving him a chance to protest. Samuel gags a little, then swallows the liquid, barely tasting it. He concentrates on his breathing, the only thing he feels he can control. His eyelids close as he feels Senta hauling him up. He knows the light of consciousness is fading, and for once, he welcomes it.

Chapter Twenty Nine

ALEXIS' HEAD IS POUNDING, her eyes are hazy and she can't work out where she is or what's happened. The last thing she remembers is seeing Samuel's face staring up at her from beneath the trees as the harpy held her in her grasp. She recalls the panic in his rich brown eyes and she shudders. She hopes he retrieved the basilarium and made it to Kirkela. She had no other choice, she couldn't have let them take her *and* the egg. The familiar smell of hay drifts up. It rustles as she struggles to sit. It's dark but she knows she's inside, the air is too still.

'Hello?' Her voice is raspy and dry from lack of water.

No reply comes, but a small dot of light flickers. Black lines cross in front of her eyes as she searches, looking to see where she is. Her heartbeat rises as she realises there are bars surrounding her. She scrabbles round on the floor, her legs heavy. Looking up, she can see the extent of the domed cage encompassing her.

'Help!'

Her voice bounces off the jagged walls that she now sees bordering the cage. She looks down at her legs, they're covered in blood and bruises. Thick shackles wrap around each ankle and attach to chains, which run across the base of the cage and hook up to rings. Her eyes adjust to the light and she slowly moves around the edge of the cage, the rattling chains following her. It takes less than nine steps to cross the enclosure, and she studies each bar, each slim gap as she goes. There's no way out. She drops a pebble through the cage and waits for the impact; it's a few seconds before she hears it.

'I just need to focus.'

She closes her eyes, forcing her body to relax. It takes a little longer than usual, with the constant dripping of water running down the cave walls and off to whatever lies beneath. Eventually the familiar feeling of serenity washes over her. The trickling sound of water pours into her ears, as she imagines the particles colliding together. The well known spirit builds inside her. She opens her eyes and a small light begins to take shape in the cage. A leap of hope forms in her stomach as the portal grows, but then a searing pain courses through her body. She falls to the ground, as shocks of electricity shoot through her. The gateway shimmers, before disappearing altogether.

'No!' She reaches out but the electricity fires through her once again. She looks once more to the chains around her ankles. The sliver of light running up and down the shackles identifies them as necarsus chains; impenetrable without some form of special weapon.

'Please altaira, please, I need you.' Her plea is met with silence, and she slumps down against the frame of the cage.

'What have I done? I've failed everyone.' She closes her eyes and grips hold of the cold metal bars.

'Be strong,' she murmurs to herself. 'You've got to be strong.'

HER MUSCLES FEEL LIKE THEY'RE RIPPING as she strains her arm further through the thin gap between the bars. The trickling water is inches away from her outstretched fingers.

'Just a little more. *Come on.*' The burning ache begins to work its way from her shoulder down her arm. Finally, a single drop falls onto her index finger. She greedily brings her arm back into the cage and rubs it onto her lips. The liquid feels like silk and her dry mouth is grateful for it. With barely any light she has no real idea of time. She knows she must be somewhere well hidden, as no altairas have come to her aid. She's never felt so trapped.

SHE WAKES UP, HAVING DRIFTED OFF. A burning sensation comes from her mark, and she slowly moves away from the edge of the cage. A stench of death invades her nostrils.

'Where is it?' A strong voice seemingly full of loathing escapes from the darkness. 'Where is he?' The voice comes again. She turns her head, trying to work out where it's coming from, the sound seeming to bounce off every rock.

'Who's there?'

'Answer me. Tell me where they are?' A hand grips the side of the cage. She flinches but doesn't make any other movement. The pale fingers are long and bony, the fingernails yellow and rotting.

'Where's what?' she replies, her voice calmer than her churning insides.

'You know what. Tell me!'

'I don't know what you're talking about. Who *are* you? Show your face.'

'Stop playing with me, child. Tell me where the egg is. Tell me where Faro is.'

Alexis feels her stomach tense. *Pemba? He doesn't have the egg. He doesn't have Samuel. He still needs me.* She remains still.

'I don't know what you're talking about.'

Another hand curls its fingers around the bars.

'Harpies are strong creatures, but they're not very bright,' Pemba hisses. 'They were meant to bring the egg when they grabbed you. What more can you expect I guess, from a species whose world is ruled only by them?'

Alexis focuses past the cage bars, trying to get a glimpse of him. All she can see is a thin pair of grey lips. The saliva on them reflects every now and then, in what little light there is.

'Where am I?' she asks.

'You stupid girl, you won't win.' Pemba rattles the cage. 'You have no idea what you're a part of. They're just using you.'

The snarled words jar her like a jagged knife through her chest. A light flickers but Pemba stays well hidden in the shadows. She dives forward, slipping her hands through the bars and wrapping them around the angular wrists. She digs her nails in, pressing as hard as she can, with what little strength she has left. A howl pierces the darkness and she feels the skin beneath her fingernails give way, but she continues to press down. The wrists writhe, twisting to be free. Finally they pull back, leaving the torn skin behind. Alexis looks down at her hands, the pallid skin mixed with crimson blood under her nails.

'You're still weak,' she says. 'You're pathetic.' She claws her arms through the bars, reaching out into the shadows, but her hands touch nothing. He's gone.

Chapter Thirty

'SAMUEL,' A VOICE WHISPERS. 'Samuel.'

'Who's there?' Samuel replies, forcing his eyes open. The room is dark and empty, except for the bed he's lying on, and a chair over the other side of the room. He touches his face, his cheeks are cold. His skin feels rough from a few days' stubble.

'Samuel,' the voice comes again. The word floats across the room, just a whisper. His heart thumps an irregular rhythm as he scrabbles out from the blanket. He searches the room but the night sky is too cloudy and all he can make out are shadows, cast by the trees outside.

'Over here, boy.' The curtains flutter. Samuel dives towards the window, but the material is limp in his hands, the space empty. He stares out at the ground below.

'Who's there?'

Fingers curl around his shoulder, digging their way into him. He whirls round, the fingernails ripping at his skin as he tries to pull free.

'Pemba?' He almost chokes as the hand slides around his neck. Everything about the man looks weaker than when he saw him in Nekton. Even his eyes are now just two small black pools. Pemba tightens his grip, his mouth curling upwards. His skin is tight, a little translucent, the veins showing through under his eyes and cheeks.

'The Darkness. It, it's ruined you,' Samuel says, as the long fingernails dig deeper into his skin.

'I'm getting stronger,' Pemba hisses. 'Now where is he? And where's the egg?'

'I, I.' Samuel can't speak, the pressure on his throat is too much. The giddiness fills his head. He shuts his eyes, afraid they'll burst from their sockets if he keeps them open.

'Welcome it.' Pemba murmurs in his ear. 'It will make everything easier.'

Samuel winces as Pemba catches a muscle in his neck. *No. No, it's not going to end like this.* He forces his eyes open, bringing his hand up to Pemba's shoulder. He grabs his robe, then clutches at his long, coarse hair, curling it round his fingers, tighter and tighter. Not waiting any longer, he yanks hard. The slight release on his skin is enough for him to drop down and out of Pemba's grasp. As he comes back up the hand hits him, right across the temple. White dots fill the dark room and he falls to the ground.

THE AIR FILLS HIS LUNGS FORCEFULLY as his eyes fly

open. He sits up, expecting to be in the middle of the room, but instead he's back in bed under the blankets. The room is lit only by the stars shining through a gap in the curtain. There's no disruption and no sign of Pemba. He touches his neck and feels the slight bruising. Up against the far wall is the chair with a satchel on it. *The egg,* he thinks, leaping out of bed, but falling straight over, his balance unsteady. He looks down to find his left arm bandaged. He remembers the harpy, the arrow, and then the creatures transforming into humans. Tentatively he tries to check the wound, but his shoulder has been bandaged up tight. There's a slight brown stain, from where the blood has seeped through. He clenches his hand a few times, checking the movement. Apart from a little stiffness in his fingers and an ache in his shoulder, it feels fine. As he gets up, his hand brushes against a metal bowl on the floor. Remnants of a dark liquid line the bottom of it. He staggers over to the chair, still feeling a little woozy. His heart thumps a harder beat as he flips open the bag and finds the pouch, empty. He searches the rest of the small room for the basilarium, his movements rapid, if a little shaky, but it's no good, it's gone. Alexis' pained face, as she was taken away, appears in his mind.

After a few minutes he sinks down against the door. He runs his hands vigorously over his face, the pouch still clenched between his fingers.

'I can't believe I lost the egg,' he murmurs.

Chapter Thirty One

SECONDS PASS AND AS HIS THOUGHTS quieten he hears low murmurings of chatter. He slides up the door frame, being careful not to make a sound. Opening the door just a crack allows him to hear the words more clearly.

'He'll be fine,' a woman says.

'But what about the egg?' a man replies.

'He kept muttering something about a map. I thought it was just the poison, making him delirious.'

'The map,' Samuel murmurs, remembering what the egg had showed him. He recognises the voice as Senta, the woman from the forest.

'I suppose you'll be taking it now.' The man's voice is deep and Samuel recalls the face of the panther, then the man, who Senta called Gideon. He clenches his fist, before flinging the door open and almost tumbling out. The door opposite is ajar and he can see shapes moving about in the room beyond. He barges in, not thinking about anything other than the egg.

'Where is it?' he says, ignoring the pain in his

shoulder. Glaring around the room full of people, he recognises Senta and Gideon straight away. They're standing on the far side of the room, quite close together. Between him and them, a fire blazes in the centre of the snug room. The smoke floats upwards, towards a funnel, which appears to be filtering the fumes out. He moves around the low-ceilinged space, steering clear of the fire, seeing Senta and Gideon properly for the first time. Senta's leather clothes leave much of her flawless skin exposed. His sudden interruption has clearly surprised her, as she stands poised, in one hand holding forward a long wooden spear. As he looks her up and down he notices she's fitted with weapons: attached to her waist is a large sabre, the blade covered in blood. Sticking out at the top of her back is a large bow and he can just make out the tips of the arrows. His eyes flick over her wrists and ankles, noticing metal plates.

'Samuel,' Gideon says, stepping forward. His wide forehead creases and his large eyes narrow. A long metal rod with an orb on each end, sits in his hand. It retracts suddenly and he stuffs it into a casing on his belt. Samuel looks at the man. At a guess he'd say he was in his thirties.

'Where's the egg,' Samuel repeats, now turning to the rest of the room. Next to Gideon is a man and woman, who, judging by their slightly greying hair and wrinkles, are a little older than his own parents.

They're both small, ordinary looking. The woman has an apron on and her dishevelled blonde hair has flecks of white in it. Her hazel eyes look warm and he feels the panic in his chest ease a little.

'Samuel, you're awake,' Senta says, seeming to find her voice and moving towards him. 'How are you feeling?'

'Yes dear, do you feel better? Come, come sit down.' The woman with the hazel eyes scuttles over to him and ushers him to a nearby seat. As soon as he's sat, the woman checks his bandage. He winces but sinks into the high-back chair, glad to feel something soft beneath him.

'Still a little tender?' she asks.

'Stop fussing over him,' the small man says. Samuel can barely see his mouth, his face is hidden under a wild growing beard, one which covers the lower part of his face, then grows up and round to join the hair on his head. The wrinkles under his eyes seem to deepen the more he stares at him.

'Calder. He's been hurt,' she replies, smoothing the front of her apron.

'Samuel, this is Calder and his wife, Faedean. They helped remove the poison from the harpy's arrow. It had buried itself quite deep.'

Samuel looks up at the man who spoke. He's much taller than Calder and Faedean and even with his weathered face, has a sense of gentle authority about him. His dark grey hair, that looks like it was once brown, falls wispily in curls every which way on top of his head. His protruding eyes are dark and striking, but seem to reflect a sadness. Samuel's observations take no more than a couple of seconds of each of them.

'Where am I?' he asks, ignoring what the man said.

'You're in Kirkela,' Senta replies. 'Samuel, this is Toko.' She glances at the curly-haired man.

'Why won't you tell me where it is?' He knows he's being abrupt but all he can think about is Alexis, and the basilarium.

'It's safe, Samuel.' A voice floats from a corner of the room, and he strains to look behind Faedean, who's still fussing over his shoulder. A man steps out of the shadows, his cloak sweeping behind him. The man's dark, slicked back hair and cold glaring eyes are familiar. It takes Samuel a few seconds before he realises it's the same man he saw when he was in Nekton.

Chapter Thirty Two

'THIS IS MANTEL,' TOKO SAYS. Samuel doesn't respond, having almost instantly recognised the Davadore who had been watching Alexis and Anka training. The air in the room suddenly feels cooler, the flames straying away from Mantel, as if trying to flee. He senses everyone is waiting for Mantel to speak.

'You're a Davadore,' Samuel says. Mantel nods, lifting back his hood. 'Do you have the egg?' Samuel asks, standing from the soft chair.

'We have it safe,' Toko answers him.

'You were fortunate Senta and Gideon came along,' Mantel says. 'What happened to Alexis?'

'The harpies. They took her,' Samuel replies. 'She told me to bring the egg here if anything happened to her.'

He continues to hold Mantel's stare, wondering whether to tell him about the bearer, and that it was Plain Seekers who murdered him. *Maybe he already knows.* He questions if what he saw was actually real. 'We have to help her,' he says. 'We have to help Alexis.'

Mantel places a hand underneath his cloak, to expose a cream tunic. Attached to his roped belt is a long thin sword. His thread-like eyebrows crease inwards.

'I'm afraid we can't,' he says. 'We have no way of knowing where she is.'

'There must be some way of finding out? What about an altaira?'

Mantel's face changes, the softness of concern fades and slight surprise settles in its place. Samuel wonders if he knows he's not from White Plains.

'It's too risky. The best way to help Alexis now is to find Pemba and stop him, before he destroys this world.'

'How do you plan on getting the egg to Irith now?' Toko asks Mantel.

'I think Samuel should continue with it,' the davadore replies, without hesitation. 'Alexis trusted him and I'm needed elsewhere to try and stop this war. If a map presented itself to Samuel then that's a good sign. It will lead to Irith, and if you're willing, Toko, I think you and the others should go with him.'

'I don't think that's such a good idea,' Calder says, stepping forward. 'Surely it's too dangerous?'

'You don't have to go, Calder,' Mantel replies.

Calder stiffens at his words. He twists some of his beard hair between his thumb and forefinger, whilst clearing his throat a couple of times.

'He's right, my friend,' Toko says, placing a hand on the man's shoulder. 'You've got Faedean, and–' he puts his back to Samuel, '–Phoenix, to look after.' Samuel just catches the name.

'We'll help,' Senta says, speaking for both her and Gideon.

Mantel nods, slowly. He taps the handle of his sword and Samuel notices his slim feminine fingers; they are nothing like that of a fighter.

'How do you know the map will lead us to Irith?' Samuel asks.

The soft babbling stops and Samuel feels all eyes turn to Mantel. The Davadore seems a little taken aback, but he recovers quickly with a thin smile.

'The egg was created by a powerful man, Faro, and that power meant the egg's sole purpose was to keep Pemba trapped. Now the egg is damaged it will want to be repaired. It will lead you to the person who can do that.'

Samuel hopes he's right, for his sake as much as Alexis' and everyone else's. He's desperate to find Alexis, but his need to get to Irith is also a selfish one. He hopes Irith, this so called enchanter, can help get him home, if only to warn his family of the danger.

'Here,' Toko says, now in front of him. Samuel hadn't seen him move. He looks down at Toko's outstretched arms. In his hands is the basilarium. The recognised tug emanates from it once again. He glances round at the others to see if they can feel it too. If they do, they seem to be good at hiding it. Slowly he takes the wooden cube from Toko.

'Thank you,' he says.

'Don't you want to see the map on it?' Gideon asks Mantel.

'No,' the Davadore replies, holding his hand up. 'No, it's okay.' He softens his voice and drops his arm. 'The less people that see it, the better.'

'We should get going as soon as possible then,' Toko says.

Mantel nods, a sharp flick of his head. 'I'll be on my way. I'll let Anka and the other Plain Seekers know. When you arrive at Iriths you must send an altaira. Anka and the others will then be able to find you.' He glides towards the door, but stops before leaving. 'The other Davadores and I *are* trying to stop Pemba and his army.'

Samuel can feel the tension in the room, everyone's posture a little rigid. Finally Faedean breaks the silence.

'We know, Mantel. We know you are.'

The Davadore drops his head, then turns and leaves the room without saying another word.

SAMUEL COUNTS THE SECONDS that nobody speaks

after Mantel has gone. Toko is the first to break the silence.

'We must gather just a few things and be on our way. Senta, Gideon, you go sort out our, guest.'

Samuel looks up sharply. *Guest?*

'Wait a sec. What was that I saw in the forest?' he asks, directing his question at Senta. 'You looked like a harpy, and you–' he turns to Gideon '–you were a big black cat.'

Senta brings a hand up to her mouth instantly, trying to hide her snigger.

'I think you mean a panther,' Gideon replies, adjusting the leather straps around his lower arm.

'Samuel, they're shapeshifters,' Toko says, a hint of confusion in his voice, as if Samuel should know.

Samuel grips the basilarium tighter. His eyes are tired from the dimness. Aside from the fire, there's only one other light in the room. The strange lamp has a round base, with a single piece of metal piping for the stand. Fitted half way up is an old fashioned tap, with a large droplet of glass hanging from it. The globule is the source of light and above it is a bent piece of piping, with another tap sitting on top.

'Who are *you*?' Calder asks, his stocky legs taking a step towards him and interrupting Samuel from his observations.

'Samuel. Mantel told us Alexis was travelling from Rythe. Is that where you're from?' Toko's voice is rich, his words rippling off his tongue. Samuel doesn't hear a strand of threat in them, but his presence is commanding.

'Yes. No. I'm not from Rythe.' He looks down at his feet.

'Does it matter where he's from?' Faedean says. 'What matters is that we must get him and the egg to Irith, safely.'

'*You* are not doing anything of the sort,' Calder replies. 'You must go with the other villagers, somewhere safe.'

'But, Calder. I don't think *they'll* want me with them.'

Samuel notices the slight tone that forms Faedean's words.

'Does this mean you'll be coming with us then?' Gideon asks Calder.

Calder stares at the shapeshifter from beneath his bushy eyebrows.

'Samuel, why don't you come and show me the map, whilst the others get things ready,' Toko says.

Samuel slides a glance at Senta and realises she's watching him quite closely. Her mouth twitches upwards as he takes a last look at her, then the others, before following Toko out of the room.

Chapter Thirty Three

'WHY DID MANTEL SAY THAT, before he left?' Samuel asks Toko, as the man shuts the door behind them. He takes a quick glance around the room they're now in. Toko doesn't reply, instead he walks over to a glassless window, then lifts up a large paving slab and slots it into a groove that surrounds the opening. The light immediately disappears from the small room. Samuel edges back to the door, barely able to see anything.

'We don't want anyone looking in,' Toko says.

A moment later and Samuel hears tapping, followed by a yellow, greenish glow, which emerges from across the room. Toko continues to tap his finger against a lantern, until the light gets brighter and begins to move about inside the glass.

'What is that?' he asks, mesmerised by the light.

'These are hotaru,' Toko replies. 'They're little creatures that sleep in the day. But you can fool them into thinking it's night-time.' He smiles and stops his gentle knocking on the glass, once all the insects are awake. Samuel moves closer, counting at least twenty.

'They look like fireflies,' he says.

'Where are you from, Samuel?'

Samuel breaks his gaze from the creatures. A lump finds its way into his throat.

'I know you're not from here. I think Mantel knows it too. I don't know why he's letting you carry on with the egg, but he must have good reason.'

Samuel doesn't respond; he'd wondered the same thing. It had been odd that Mantel wouldn't even look at the egg. He watches Toko slide a latch on the top of the lantern and open the lid just a crack. One of the hotaru is lucky enough to feel the air and darts upwards, squeezing through and out into the room. Once it's found its freedom it doesn't hang about. It dashes through the air, leaving a streak of light in its path. After it's explored the area and realised it can't escape, it flies up to him. The creature is half the size of his pinky finger and has tiny wings that move so fast, Samuel can barely see them. The hotaru is hovering inches from his face. Samuel reaches out with his index finger, but before he can get close the insect darts to the side, out of reach. It makes its way back to the lantern and Toko opens the cap wide so it can soar back in.

'Now, about this map,' Toko says, slipping the catch back in place.

Samuel knows he has no choice but to show him. He doesn't know White Plains, he can't read the map, but maybe Toko can. His fingers work around the box, without him even thinking about it. He pulls the lid off. The dark shiny exterior of the egg is now covered in further markings.

'Here, let me take a look,' Toko says, holding his hand out.

'No! Don't touch it. I mean, I don't think we should touch it.'

Toko's eyes narrow, but he doesn't press any further. Samuel holds the basilarium nearer to the man, allowing him to study it.

'It's pretty impressive. It looks so delicate,' Toko says, after a minute.

'Does it make sense to you?'

'Well, it's difficult to see … Wait there a minute.' His forehead creases as he starts to search the room. 'I'm sure Calder has some,' he murmurs, whilst rooting through drawers. 'Ah, here they are.' He pulls out a pair of unusual glasses and places them on his face.

'What are they?' Samuel asks, staring at the bronze goggles that protrude from Toko's head.

'I should be able to see a little clearer with these,' he replies, flipping a small lens down in front of his eyes. 'Let me take another look.' He places his fingers carefully on the basilarium, whilst Samuel still has hold.

'Nope, not quite,' he says, moving his face closer

and fiddling with another, even smaller lens, that's sitting on top of the glasses. It slides down into place, in front of the others. 'There we go, that's better.' He studies the egg, murmuring every now and then.

'Look, here,' he says, lifting the lenses up. 'These tiny marks, they're names of towns and forests.'

'So, where's Irith?'

Toko studies the egg again. 'The map ends here.' He points north. Samuel moves the egg away from his finger. 'Sorry. This area has a faint circle around it. It must be in this vicinity.'

'Well, how big is that area?'

'It's hard to say. Fairly large.'

Samuel leans heavily against the wall, his hope waning.

'I don't think it's that far from here, maybe just a day.'

'This egg. This is why they took Alexis.' Samuel inhales deeply. 'What do you think they'll do when they find out she doesn't have it?'

Toko treads the small space in front of him.

'I don't know,' he replies, taking the glasses off and tapping his finger on the silver handle of his sword. 'But if we get the egg to Irith, he will help. And the Davadores are doing all they can.'

Samuel doesn't like the uncertainty, but he knows there's nothing else he can do. He watches Toko, his stride strong.

'You're right. I'm not from White Plains,' he says. 'I'm from another world.'

Toko stops pacing.

'Earth.'

The room becomes quiet. The hotaru even seem to stop jittering about.

'Earth.' Toko says the word slowly, as if seeing what it feels like on his tongue. 'Can't say I've heard of that. How did you get to be here?'

'Well ... It's complicated. It was an accident.' Samuel avoids eye contact.

Toko doesn't speak for a few moments.

'Are you going to tell the others?'

Toko doesn't respond, but places the glasses on the desk. Samuel wonders whether he heard him.

'They're good people. And they will help you. They don't need to know any more than they already do.' Toko turns to look at the lantern of light. 'You've been honest with me, Samuel, now I'll be honest with you. You asked me why Mantel said what he did. The Davadores have been a part of this world since, I can't even remember. They've helped all of us, especially our main asset, Plain Seekers. But some people, some of us, are wary of them. We don't agree with all of the things they've done. They ordered people to stay in their homes, saying we would be safe from Pemba's army. Then it became clear that village after village was being destroyed.' He rubs his lower lip. 'We must protect what little families we have.'

'*Little* families?' Samuel asks, intrigued by Toko's choice of words.

Toko glances to the door.

'There are other things, other *ways* the Davadores have, that people are opposed to.'

Samuel waits for Toko to continue, for him to turn his attention from the door.

'Some of their rules, if you want to use such a word, are restrictive.'

'I know, gateways are forbidden. Alexis said–'

'No, it's not to do with that. You see, Samuel, to keep our world running as best as possible, the Davadores believe that it shouldn't be overcrowded. Population is handled in a certain way.'

Samuel feels his stomach tighten.

'How do you mean?'

'There is a per-household rule.'

'You can't tell people whether they can or can't have a baby,' Samuel says, feeling a tingle of heat run through his chest.

'Everyone is allowed a child. They just can't have more than two,' Toko replies, stopping abruptly. Samuel can see by the man's sunken shoulders that he despises his own words.

'What happens if they disobey this ruling?'

Toko sighs. 'In the small instances where people don't comply, the third child is named a tertia, and great dishonour is brought upon the family.'

Chapter Thirty Four

'TOKO!' THE DOOR FLIES OPEN, interrupting Samuel's wild thoughts. Gideon barely enters the room. His eyebrows slant down, setting his face in a frown.

'Toko, we can't find Phoenix.' His words resonate in the confined space. The heaviness that had settled in the air from their conversation, now disperses and is replaced with an eerie hysteria.

'When did Calder and Faedean last see him? He can't be far. Have you checked the stables?'

'Yes. First place we looked.'

'You and Senta go check the surrounding area. And the village. We'll look again here.'

Gideon barely waits for Toko to stop speaking before he turns on his heels and marches out of the room.

'Toko, what you said–'

'Not now, Samuel. We must find Phoenix.'

'Who?'

'Calder and Faedean's son. He's fifteen, but he has a tendency to run off.' Toko makes towards the door. 'He always comes back. But what with the army and everything … I should make sure he's okay. He, he's a little different than others.'

'Different?'

'Yes.' Toko turns to face him. 'There's something else, about the rule of two children.' He lowers his voice and barely moves his lips. 'If your first child is divergent, in certain respects, then you're not allowed to have another.'

Samuel feels a shiver creep into his bones and the skin on his neck ripple.

'Is that why Calder's not very friendly?' he asks.

Toko doesn't respond, but his mouth twitches, as if wanting to say something.

'Stay here. I'll go help the others.' He leaves, swinging the door shut behind him. Samuel feels the draught as the air sucks towards the door then back into the room. He turns round. His eyes have grown used to the faint light of the hotaru, who are still humming about inside the glass. As he stares at them he recalls Toko's words, *the stables. Brawn*, he thinks, picking up the basilarium from the desk and slipping out of the room. The short hallway has a few doors leading off it. Most of them are closed. He turns right, noticing the yellow stone-washed ceilings getting even lower as he turns another corner. The house is higgledy piggledy, with twists and turns and crooked walls. Finally the hallway ends with a small door. He looks outside, through a barred opening, then pushes out into the fresh air.

Staying close to the property wall, he sees no sign of the others, or of any other houses; the building looks settled amid acres of land. He jogs over to the stables, which can't be more than fifty yards away. The stifling atmosphere hits him as he enters. The strongest smell is the leather, coming from all the horse tack neatly hanging near the door. Next, as he passes the feeders, is a sweet aroma. He lets his eyes adjust to the dimly lit stalls as he edges along the wall, peering into each one as he goes.

'Brawn?' he whispers.

A strong scent of manure permeates throughout. Most of the stalls have horses, but none holds Brawn or Paladin. As he's nearing the end he hears a familiar whine.

'Brawn?' He peers into the stall to his left and comes face to face with the dark-haired beast. He chuckles, as the horse nudges his nose into his hair. 'Am I pleased to see you, boy.' He rubs the horse's muzzle and as he does he notices the streak of white hair, now running down the horse's side. 'Where's Paladin?' Brawn clops his hoof on the hard ground then moves aside. Samuel sees Paladin at the back of the stall, happily munching on some hay. 'Well done, boy. Alexis will be glad I didn't lose her horses.' The words seem empty in the airless stables. 'I will find her,' he says, patting the horse.

The rough sound of metal on concrete fills his hears, and he whips round. The noise is coming from the farthest stall. He runs his hand along the pleasing cold stone wall as he makes his way towards it. The noise gets louder, the scratching frantic, then slow, then frantic again. Treading as quietly as he can, he approaches the last enclosure. He counts to three, before finally rounding the corner and peering inside.

Chapter Thirty Five

AS HIS EYES ADJUST HE FINDS himself staring down at a boy lying on the concrete floor, something shiny in his hand. The boy suddenly looks up, aware of Samuel standing there. His eyes are wild with panic, his face and hands splashed with mud.

'*You*. You're the one who attacked me in the forest,' Samuel says.

The boy's lower lip quivers as his eyes dart back and fourth between him and the stall door. In his hand, Samuel sees a knife.

'Whoa. It's alright,' he says, raising his hands. 'I'm not going to hurt you. It's Phoenix, right?' He steps aside, wanting the boy to know he's not trapped. 'Your mum and dad are looking for you.' A strand of the boy's dark hair has made it loose and tumbles down in front of his eyes, causing him to blow it out of the way every few seconds. Its darkness is such a contrast to his blonde eyes, something Samuel hadn't noticed before, in the struggle.

'They're always looking for me,' Phoenix replies, his eyes falling back to the floor, his fright seeming to have suddenly left him. 'I didn't attack you.' His voice is a little whiny and doesn't fit his strong build. 'I didn't mean to hurt you.' Sweat glistens on his brow.

'It's okay. You didn't. Not much.' Samuel smiles, lowering his hands a little as the boy digs the knife back into the ground. 'You're strong for fifteen,' he says, recalling Toko telling him the boy's age.

'I've always been strong. I've always been bigger than my ma and pa. I think that's why the others don't like me.'

'Others?'

'Yeah. The other people in the village. That's why we live out here, away from them. They think I'm stupid.'

Samuel realises why he hadn't seen other houses. They're outcasts. Living out here because their child is a little different, like Toko said.

'We should go and find your mum and dad. They're worried about you.'

Phoenix's strokes get faster. The scraping of the metal on concrete begins to vibrate through Samuel's head.

'What's in your hand?' Phoenix asks, without looking up.

Samuel had almost forgotten he was holding the basilarium, its form feeling like it's moulded to his hand.

'This? Just something of mine,' he replies. 'What

are you doing there?' He edges closer, distracting Phoenix from the egg. Phoenix barely stirs. But after a while he uncurls his fist, loosening the grip on the knife and exposing the floor beneath his hands.

'I don't think someone who's stupid could do something like that,' Samuel says, pointing to the intricate drawing he's done of Brawn. Phoenix shrugs.

'I've not watched him for long. It just stays in here.' He puts his finger to his temple.

Samuel nods, brushing some of the sand with his feet, to reveal more of the etching.

'That's a nice looking knife,' Samuel says, motioning to the wooden handled blade. 'I've always wanted one like that. It looks nice and new. My dad gave me his old one, one he had when he was growing up. I still have it, or at least I did…' He trails off.

'My pa gave me this one,' Phoenix says. 'Did you lose yours?'

'Not exactly. I hope it's safe. It's a little difficult to explain.'

'It has me and my pa's initials on it.' Phoenix thrusts his arm out towards Samuel, the knife still clasped in his hand.

'That's cool. I wish mine had that.' Samuel leans against the stable door, taking a quick glance out, checking for the others. There's no sign of them. 'What *were* you doing out there in the forest?' he asks.

'Please don't tell my ma and pa. I'm not meant to

be out there, not on my own. I'm not meant to go anywhere, really.' Phoenix's eyes widen and he starts to tremble.

'It's alright, I won't tell them.' His words seem to fall flat as Phoenix starts to groan. Samuel reaches out, placing a hand on the boy's shoulder, loosely, but tight enough to get his attention. Phoenix jerks back and Samuel releases his grip, but waits until he's calm and looking directly at him.

'I won't tell them. I promise.' He speaks steadily and calmly, hoping he listens, hoping he knows what a promise is. After a few minutes, Phoenix stops moaning.

'I'm never allowed to go anywhere. I just wanted to explore. I did it once, ages ago. I didn't go far, but then I got braver.' Phoenix lifts his chin. 'One day I went into the forest and I was gone for ages. It didn't matter though, it was night-time.' Samuel nods, letting Phoenix know he's listening. 'After that I kept going out. I see things at night that no one else sees, they're all in bed. All the animals come out. They don't mind me, they've got used to me, I think.'

'You like animals, hey?'

Phoenix stares at him. 'Yes, I like them. I like all animals.'

'It wasn't night-time when I saw you out there though.' Samuel kneels down at the edge of the stall door.

'I try and go whenever I can now. I was on my way back home when I saw you and that girl.'

'Phoenix I know you're strong and you're fast, but I don't think you should go out on your own for a while. There's a lot going on out there and your mum and dad will want you to be safe. I won't tell them, but just promise me that you won't go out on your own for a while.'

Phoenix stares down at the sand, at the image of Brawn.

'I don't know you,' he says.

'I know you don't. But I'm not going to hurt you. The girl, the one I was with, in the forest. She's been taken.'

Samuel doesn't know how much the boy knows and he doesn't want to scare him by telling him more than what's needed.

Phoenix swirls his finger through the sand, creating meaningless patterns.

'I'll stay here,' he says.

Samuel nods, relaxing his jaw, the ache from clenching only just entering his consciousness. Before he can say anything he hears footsteps on the hard stable floor. Phoenix glares at him, but before either of them can do anything a figure appears in the doorway.

Chapter Thirty Six

'PHOENIX, THERE YOU ARE,' CALDER SAYS. His tone now showing no sign of gruffness. 'Are you alright?' He bends over his son, but doesn't attempt to touch him.

'Sorry,' Samuel says, standing. 'I was going to come and find you, let you know he was here.'

Calder grunts, then mutters a thanks. His skin looks softer, now that his frown has dissolved.

'Phoenix!' Faedean exclaims, rushing in and throwing her arms around her son.

'Ma. Get off me.' Phoenix pulls away.

'Sorry, love.' She backs off, but not before running a hand through his hair and down his shoulder.

'Faedean, you take him back to the house. Let the others know we've found him and finish gathering your things. Samuel, come with me a moment.' Calder gets up and walks out, not giving Samuel a chance to reply.

CALDER LEADS HIM OUTSIDE AND OVER to a small building made of large stone slabs. As they enter, the strong smell of coal smoke stains the air, but underneath is a sweeter odour, like burnt honey. Samuel notices the tools hanging off every available wall and table space, even off the brick chimney on the far side.

'It's a forge,' Calder says. 'It's for the fire, to heat the metal.' He turns to a rusted chest and starts rummaging through it. 'Here. Take this.'

Samuel looks down at the dagger Calder is offering, slowly accepting the gift.

'For protection,' Calder clarifies. The blade catches the light as Samuel turns it over in his hand. It's bigger than the one he found in Alexis' bag and its thick inner edge curves in a wave. The handle feels steady in his hands and the leather strap wound tightly round it, allows him a better grip.

'Thanks.'

'You'll want to keep it on you, just in case,' Calder adds, holding up a sheath attached to a belt, to go around Samuel's waist. Samuel takes it from him, nodding his thanks again.

'And this is yours.' He passes Samuel his satchel. 'You'll need to keep that somewhere safe.' He gestures to the wooden cube. Samuel loops the bag over his shoulder, across his chest, then tucks the basilarium inside, stuffing Alexis' pouch in the bag as well. Calder watches him, rubbing his fingers through his beard.

'Thanks for being kind to Phoenix,' he says.

'You don't need to thank me.'

Calder doesn't reply, but wrinkles appear at the corner of his eyes as he settles into a smile. He picks a sledge hammer up from the workbench and tucks it neatly into his trousers. Screams break the comfortable silence, echoing out and bouncing off the instruments in the room, before rocketing their way into Samuel's ears.

'What the hell is that?' Samuel says, quickly tying the belt round his waist and following Calder outside.

'Calder!' Toko runs from the house, his sword drawn. 'Calder, the army are back. The harpies are attacking the village. We must leave, now.'

Gideon emerges from an outhouse, his mace fully extended in his hand.

'Gideon, is she still tied up?' Toko asks.

Samuel looks towards the outbuilding. He recollects when the harpy shot him in the forest. His grogginess from the poison had led him to forget, but now he remembers; Gideon had brought back a harpy. He makes a run for the entrance, where Gideon emerged, ignoring the shouts aimed at him. Once inside he takes a quick look round. Bales of hay are stacked high to the roof. A rusty bit of machinery stands over on the far side. Other than that, the barn appears empty. Then, in the darkest corner, he sees it.

Tied to the wall with some thick rope around her stomach and each ankle is the harpy. Her wings spread out across the floor, and he can see where the arrow sliced through, her feathers around the slash ruffled and wilted. She lifts her head, her long straggly hair half covering her face. Her beady eyes stare at him, then she jerks forward, the rope restraining her at the last minute. The screams of the villagers continue outside and Samuel's sure he can now hear the crackling of the harpies inferno.

'She won't say anything,' Gideon says, behind him. 'And we don't have time to waste on her.'

'Maybe she will if I threaten to pluck out more of her feathers.' Samuel steps forward, the knife Calder gave him still in his hand. He tries to keep it steady. 'Where is she?' he asks. 'Where have they taken Alexis?'

The harpy sneers at him, then screeches, 'I'll never tell!' Her voice sounds unnatural, as though she rarely speaks.

'What are they here for? Have they come back for you?' Gideon asks her.

The harpy turns to him, throwing her head forward. A gurgling sound comes from her throat, then a second later she hurtles spit at him.

Samuel stares at the creature in shock. He feels a heat through his bag, leaking from the egg. The rage manifests inside him and he steps forward, reaching out with his dagger. A hand grabs his wrist.

'Samuel, we've got to go,' Toko says.

Samuel grips the strap of his satchel, but loosens his hold on the knife. He takes a last look at the harpy. Her feathered chest rises and falls, as her head droops once again.

Back outside, Samuel can see the smoke ascending as the village burns, just beyond the line of trees that separates Faedean and Calder's house from the others. He can't see any harpies in the sky. A skin tingling scream breaks out. Faedean runs from the house.

'He's gone!' she yells. 'They've taken him.'

She falls into Calder's arms.

'Phoenix?' Calder asks, bending as Faedean drops to the ground, unable to stand.

'Our son. A harpy. She just came and took him. I couldn't stop her.'

Samuel feels the blood pump through him.

'Why? Why would they have taken him?' Faedean's words come out in gasps.

'Maybe it wasn't the harpy they came back for,' Gideon says, turning to Samuel.

Chapter Thirty Seven

'Gideon, find Senta. See if she can fly up and follow them. We need to get Faedean safe and get to Irith,' Toko says. 'But first, we need to get away from the village, without them seeing us.'

Faedean is still clinging to Calder.

'We'll find him. We'll find him, love, don't worry.'

Samuel can hear Calder hushing softly in her ear, as he helps her to her feet.

'Wait. I've got to get Brawn and Paladin,' Samuel says, running towards the stables.

'Samuel,' Toko calls, his heavy footsteps plodding behind, but Samuel ignores him, heading straight for Brawn's stall. The horses are still saddled up and Samuel grabs Brawn's reins whilst Toko takes care of Paladin.

'Come on, boy. We've got to go,' Samuel says, leading Brawn outside where Calder and Faedean are waiting.

'Round the side. This way,' Toko says, taking the lead as they edge along the outside wall of the stables. Samuel follows him, with Calder and Faedean behind.

'Toko,'–Calder says, holding Faedean up, almost dragging her along–'That way.' He throws his head towards a stretch of trees. Toko nods silently.

As they reach the corner of the building, Toko holds his hand up, signalling for them to wait. He takes a step forward, his sword poised in front. A second later and he makes the short sprint to the safety of the trees, with Paladin by his side. *Runs fast for an older guy,* Samuel thinks, tucking the knife into its sheath on his right hip and shifting the satchel on his left, getting ready to run. He looks up at Brawn, then lets go of his reins.

'Stick with me,' he says to the horse. He waits for Toko's signal, then steps out of the safety of the overhung roof. With a glance to his left he sees the fields rolling out, but no sign of the army. Brawn trots next to him, not leaving his side. Samuel exhales as he reaches Toko. Faedean and Calder are next, then they all follow Toko deeper into the forest. The noise of the fire dwindles as they get further away; a few minutes later and Samuel can't hear them at all. Toko stops abruptly as they reach the bottom of a steep incline. The trees growing upward slant at such an angle Samuel wonders how they don't topple over. At the brow of the high ground is a line of people, men and women, standing there, watching.

'Toko?' he says, the uncertainty clear in his voice.

'It's okay, Samuel. They're here for Faedean,' Toko

replies, before turning to Calder. A slight whimper comes from Faedean, then she stands straight, steady, brushing any tear stains from her face.

'Are you sure they want me to go with them?'

'They will keep you safe,' Toko replies.

'It feels strange, to be going with them, having been separate from the village for so long.' She says the words to no one in particular, as if just wanting to say them out loud.

'I'm sorry, Faedean,' Toko says. 'The divide has gone on for too long. But you'll be far safer with them, than us.'

Faedean nods before turning to her husband.

'You *will* find him, won't you?' she says.

Samuel looks away, not wanting to see the sadness in either of their eyes, or wanting to hear Calder's reply.

'Be safe.' He hears Faedean say. 'All of you, be safe.' She stands among them, small and harmless. He thinks of his own mum and feels a twinge in his chest. He glances at Calder who can barely take his eyes from the ground. With a last look at her husband, Faedean turns and makes her way up the hill to the villagers. A tall, thin haired man, steps forward as she approaches. He nods at Toko who replies with a similar tweak of his head. Some of the women smile a little, and Samuel hopes she'll be okay with them. Before they traipse off she turns one last time and looks to Calder. Samuel watches his beard twitch as his mouth turns upwards beneath it. The reassuring smile is enough for her, and she turns back round. As soon as they're out of sight, Calder's face drops. Toko places a hand on his friend's shoulder but Calder can't seem to bear the gesture. He hangs his head, his shoulders drooping.

'Let's go,' he says.

Chapter Thirty Eight

The further they get from the village, the more on edge Toko and Calder seem. Samuel is at the back with Brawn. No one has spoken a word since they left Faedean, what must be a couple of hours ago. Toko tramples ahead with purpose, while Calder keeps his head low, lifting it only when Toko hesitates for a moment. The further north they go, the hillier the forest gets, and Samuel is glad for the short rest he had at Calder's. He thinks about Alexis, and the look on her face as she was lifted away by the harpy. Then he recalls his brother's face. He can see it amongst the flames that engulfed the car. It always feels like he's watching himself die.

Without warning, Calder yanks his sledge hammer free from his clothes and swings his arm back, the weapon coming within inches of Samuel's chest. Samuel has no time to speak. Calder flings the weapon forward and Samuel watches in horror as it pummels into the figure that's emerged from the trees, just to their left. Calder lunges, jumping on top of the beast. He grunts heavily as both he and the creature thud to the ground. Toko turns, a little way ahead of them. He lets go of Paladin's reins and runs back, his sword at the ready.

Brawn's whining awakens Samuel from his stupor. He reaches for his dagger and runs to help Calder who's straddling the monster, the handle of his sledge hammer pressed against the marred throat. Calder is half the size of the beast, but his rage aids him, the struggle lasting only seconds.

'Calder,' Toko says, now by his friend's side. Calder continues to pummel the creature.

'It's dead.' Toko gently drags Calder away, who collapses on the ground, panting heavily.

'What *is* that?' Samuel exclaims. The large figure looks like a human, at first glance. It has two legs, two arms, a torso and head, but that's where the resemblance ends. Its large, pointy ears, stick out from beneath a copper helmet, with the armour curving around the monster's misshapen head. Its long straggly hair seems to hang down in clumps, half covering its scarred face. The nose on the creature snarls up, with a silver ring looped through it. Half its teeth are missing, with just two fangs poking out from the bottom of its jaw. Samuel looks at the oozing dent, printed in its chest from Calder's hammer.

'Toko!' Samuel shouts, as the creature opens its eyes. With one slice Toko cuts through the thick-skinned neck, spraying a dark liquid, some of which splatters down onto Samuel's shoes. The creature's eyes, dark and red, roll back in their sockets. Samuel stares at the beast, unable to speak, his hand still gripping the dagger.

'Now it's dead,' Toko says.

Samuel bends a little closer to the creature, then flies back, as a stench hits him. He flings his hand to his nose.

'What's that smell?' he says.

'It's just his odour.'

'It smells rotten.'

'Well, look at him, he looks pretty rotten.'

Samuel stares at Toko, unsure if he's making a joke.

'What is it?' Samuel asks again.

'It's an orc,' Calder replies, now standing. 'I'd heard some had left their own world to join Pemba's army.'

'An orc. I didn't think they were real,' Samuel says.

'Not real?' Calder frowns at him.

'Come on you two, we need to keep going,' Toko urges, wiping his sword through the grass. Samuel ignores Calder's continuing stare and takes one last glance at the orc. A shudder goes through him as he looks at its monstrous face. *I've got to get home,* he thinks.

Chapter Thirty Nine

'DO YOU THINK THERE ARE other orcs out here?' Samuel asks Toko, keeping his eyes to the ground as they move through the undergrowth. Toko slashes his sword through the bracken, creating a path.

'I don't know. There's another small village a little east of here. Perhaps Pemba's army are there.'

Samuel looks round at the scattered trees. Their bark looks a little different. The spongy texture moulds to his fingers as he places a hand on one as they pass by. He wipes the brown residue onto his trousers. The sun is warm on his head and for a moment he enjoys it working its way down his neck and shoulders and onto his back. The warmth doesn't last long as Toko and Calder stop abruptly. Calder turns and holds a finger up to his mouth. Samuel tucks himself behind a tree, Brawn behind him, obeying the man's gesture. Calder points forward, making eye contact with his friend. Toko nods but doesn't say a word as Samuel peers round the trunk. About a hundred feet away is a broken wall, but that isn't what Calder is pointing at. Samuel sees three figures crouching beside the barrier, with their backs to them. Under the shadow of the trees he can only really make out their shapes, but they don't look like any of the monsters he's seen.

'Maybe they need help?' he says.

'No,' Toko replies. 'Something isn't right.'

Samuel pinches the bark of the tree beneath his fingers. After a minute or two he watches as the trio slowly stand. Once stood, the light finds its way to them and Samuel sees the men in their military uniforms. One of them turns slightly, facing more towards them. Samuel gasps, unable to hide his surprise.

'What's wrong?' Toko asks.

'They're human,' Samuel replies.

'Yes. Not from this world, though.'

Samuel knows they're not from this world. Their khaki green clothes bear a military flag which he's seen hundreds of times, including at the army base near camp. He steps forward, away from the protection of the trees.

'They must be here to help,' he murmurs.

'Get back,' Calder orders, pulling him into the shadows just as orglins approach the men. 'Stay quiet.' Calder's hand is clenched around the hammer. The soldiers don't move. Their guns hang loosely by their sides. Samuel feels sick as he stands rigid, the blood rushing from his head. Slowly he pulls the dagger from its holder. Low murmurings come from the group. The human voices are a higher pitch, but Samuel can't make out anything that's being said.

After a few moments, one of the orglins turns to the side. It's hunched over, as though it can't stand upright. It lifts its head towards the sky and inhales, as if having caught a scent. Then it disappears, evaporating.

'Where did it go?' Samuel asks, but before Calder can answer, the creature appears metres from where it was. It lifts its head again, but Toko and Calder don't move.

'This way,' the orglin snarls. Samuel hears the words come from the beast's mouth, low like a rumble. If he hadn't been listening so intently, and the wind not carried in their direction, he might have missed it. The hideous creatures turn and slope off, the men following behind.

'That can't be right,' Samuel mutters, once they're alone again.

Calder lowers his sledge hammer. 'Nasty creatures those orglins.'

'Yeah, but the men, they – Look,' he says, pointing to one of the orglins who has held back. As he does so, air whooshes past his ear and a second later the orglin topples forward, an arrow stuck straight into its chest. Samuel spins round and pushes his arms out in front of him, ready.

Running through the forest towards them, bow in hand, is Senta.

'Did you find them? Did you find Phoenix?' Calder asks, rushing forward.

Senta looks over to her prey, the orglin, before dropping her head. Seconds later, Gideon reaches them, placing a hand on Calder's shoulder.

'I'm sorry, we lost them.'

Calder nods and Samuel can see his hand trembling as he pats Gideon's arm.

'Those men we saw, the humans,' Samuel says, still unable to process what he's just seen. 'Are they part of Pemba's army?'

Everyone turns to him.

'It looks that way,' Toko replies. 'Why?'

Samuel feels his legs weaken.

'It's just – they're from my world.'

Chapter Forty

Toko looks to Calder, whose eyebrows begin to crease inwards, causing his eyes to narrow.

'*Your* world. What do you mean *your* world?'

'It's alright, Calder,' Toko says, turning to him. The lines on his face are harsh but his eyes remain soft. 'Samuel isn't from this world, my friend.'

Samuel feels Calder's cold stare. He finds himself glaring at the ground, unable to look him in the eyes.

'Samuel?' Calder asks.

'I'm sorry. I'm sorry I didn't tell you. It's my fault the army came here. It's my fault Phoenix is gone.'

'No, Samuel,' Toko says. 'The army reaching Kirkela was inevitable. They're everywhere now. We *can* stop them, but I need your help, Calder.' Toko steps in between them both. Calder's face is pale, his eyes dark and round, peering out from beneath his unruly hair. He nods solemnly.

'Calder, I *am* sorry,' Samuel pleads, placing one foot nearer to him. Calder nods again, pushing his bottom lip out. He shifts his trousers up a little higher around his waist.

'Samuel, I think you should wait here, whilst we go and check out the village. We'll make sure it's clear,' Toko says. 'Senta, you stay here with him and the horses. Wait for our signal.'

Senta looks at Samuel from beneath her long eyelashes and he feels his skin prickle with heat.

'I don't need looking after,' he says. 'Shouldn't we stick together?'

'Maybe he's right.' Senta steps forward. The light in her dark eyes dancing back and forth.

Toko sighs. His face looks even more worn as creases grow round his mouth and eyes.

'We won't be long.'

Samuel watches as he, Calder and Gideon stalk off towards the village. Once they're out of sight he leans back against the closest tree trunk. The rough bark jabs into his top, and he flinches as pain keenly grips his shoulder.

'Is that still hurting?' Senta asks, pinching his shirt and lifting it. Her invasion takes him by surprise, but he stands still, letting her examine the wound. 'It's healing well,' she says, tucking the end of the bandage back in place. 'Faedean and Calder got the poison out just in time.' Her eyes skim briefly over his body before she drops his top. He looks at the dagger he's still holding, then turns to her.

'What happened back there, with the harpies?'

'We couldn't get close to them,' she replies, running a hand along the blade of her spear. 'Here, you should have this.' She reaches behind her and pulls a crossbow out of a holder. 'I discovered it just before we found you, in the forest.'

'This is Alexis',' Samuel says, taking the weapon from her.

'There was this too.' Senta opens his hand, placing something in his palm. He looks down to find Alexis' necklace with the feather still attached. He wraps the leather round his fingers as Brawn nudges his muzzle against him, sniffing the pendant. Samuel runs his hand up the horse's nose. *Alexis, where are you?* He thrusts the necklace into his trousers, pushing it deep into his pocket, so it doesn't fall out.

'Thanks.'

Senta doesn't reply but holds Paladin's reins in her hand, tilting her head slightly upwards, as if listening.

Minutes pass and he begins to kick his heel into the tree, bark crumbling beneath his shoe. He turns the knife over in his hand before placing it back in the sheath on his belt.

'We better stay quiet,' Senta says.

He looks up, dropping his foot instantly. 'I can't just stand around here doing nothing. There must be something we can do to help?'

'We should wait here, like Toko asked.'

'But what if they're in danger? What if they need our help?'

'They'll let us know if they do.'

'But what if they can't?' Samuel glares at her, but she looks away, towards the village. After a few moments of hesitation she turns back to him.

'Stay behind me, and don't make a sound.'

'Okay,' Samuel says, pulling the dagger out from his belt once again, his grip firm on the smooth handle. 'Brawn, you stay here with Paladin.' The horse whips his head up and down in response. Samuel pats his side, then follows Senta through the trees.

He stays close behind her, like she asked, as they dart between the trees. They stop and start, with her signalling each time for him to follow her. The air thickens and his clothes cling to his skin. Every now and then he catches her scent, a sweet and earthy mixture, causing him to lose his focus a little.

'Where are they?' he whispers, as the village comes into sight. The hairs prickle on his neck as they leave the trees and make their way through the rubble. A dark figure swoops down from a pillar of bricks, making a loud thud on impact.

'Senta, look out!' he yells. The words echo around the wreckage. Senta falls to the ground in front of him, the monster on top of her. A wheeze escapes her mouth as dust flies up around her body. Samuel stands frozen as the orc rips the spear from her hands, throwing it out of reach. Something tickles his cheek and he jerks his head. The altaira flicks her wings against his face again, as if trying to wake him from his daze.

'Find Alexis. *Please,*' he urges the little bird. The altaira's head darts from side to side, then she flits off and is out of sight in seconds. A rage manifests inside Samuel as he sees the orc on top of Senta, its large hands gripping her wrists. He lunges forward, his arm stretched out, the dagger jabbing in front. He feels the point of the dagger meet the creature, breaking through its tough skin, before sliding in. A loud roar comes from its mouth, as it flings its arm back, away from the object that's hurt him. The dagger slices through as Samuel keeps his grip. In one swift movement the orc spins round, thrusting its arm at him, hitting his chest and throwing him backwards through the air. The dagger flies from his hands and he recoils as his back smacks against a rock. His eyes roll uncontrollably in their sockets, and a sharp pain shoots through his stomach. The air is knocked out of him, catching in his lungs before finally rushing upward and into his throat. Gasping, he turns onto his side, fumbling for the dagger. Warm liquid drops on to the back of his neck. He looks up to find the orc towering over him, saliva dripping from his mouth, his nostrils flared. He flinches as the creature draws back his arm, then closes his eyes and waits.

Chapter Forty One

THE BLOW DOESN'T COME. Samuel opens his eyes and finds the orc gawking down at him. His pained expression is unmoving, and when Samuel looks down he realises why; the tip of Senta's spear is poking through its chest. He looks behind the orc to Senta. Her breathing is heavy and tiny veins mark the white of her eyes, as she grips the handle of her spear.

'Senta,' Toko says, running over, with Calder and Gideon not far behind. 'Are you alright?'

Senta becomes mobile again, loosening her grip and stance. Her eyes clear and the richness in them returns as she nods her head in response. She twists the handle of her weapon and the spear tears through the orc's body, before she pulls it free. Blood drips onto the grass next to Samuel's feet. The monster falls slowly, his last noise a loud thud as he hits the ground. Samuel grabs his dagger with shaking hands from the grass beside him.

'Thanks,' he says to Senta.

She nods. 'Just returning the favour.'

Calder extends his hand out for Samuel to take

and Samuel accepts, scrambling to his feet.

'I think the rest of the army have moved on,' Toko says.

'What about the villagers?' Samuel asks, looking round at the red dust covering the ground from the ruins.

'Looks like they all cleared out,' Gideon says. 'Where are the horses?'

Samuel looks behind him. 'We left them just back there.'

'I'll go get them,' Gideon asserts, as he begins running back to the trees. 'I'll catch up. You keep going!'

'Let's fill up our flasks and then carry on,' Toko says.

THE SUN HAS SET AND the night finally begins to creep in. Samuel knows they're not going to stop and rest, they haven't stopped since the village, hours before. As he walks safely beside Brawn, he empties the contents of his flask, letting the cool liquid coat his throat. Senta has hold of Paladin, who is trotting along behind. Gideon, Toko and Calder are up front. Samuel occasionally hears the odd mumble, a passing of words between them.

'How will we travel in the dark?' he asks, almost

stumbling on a tree root. No one answers, but they slow to a stop just ahead. Calder reaches down to his bag and rummages through it, before pulling out a glass jar. Samuel edges closer.

'The hotaru,' he murmurs, seeing the little insects stirring inside the container.

'They'll wake up in a minute,' Calder says, holding the glass up close to his face and squinting. 'Come on, it's time.'

'Won't they fly away?' Samuel asks, looking at Toko, but Toko shakes his head.

'They've been with me for many years,' Calder says. Samuel watches the hotaru fly out, surrounding him, like a glowing halo. With all of them flying together they shine a light that's bright enough for him to clearly see the path ahead, and they continue on their way.

After a few minutes he becomes enthralled by their soft glow and feels himself lulled into a sleepless coma.

'Maybe you should check the egg again. See if we're on the right track,' Toko says, walking next to him. Samuel shakes the sleepiness away and swings his satchel round in front of him, carefully taking the basilarium out. No one stops, but he can feel everyone tense, glancing at him every now and then, as if wanting to see the egg.

'It's clearer,' he says, once he's undone the lid.

'The map is darker.'

'Let me see,' Toko replies.

Samuel tilts the box.

'It must be as we're getting closer. We should be there tomorrow, hopefully.'

Samuel doesn't reply, intrigued by the lines as they curve around the egg, up to the tip. He studies the circle that Toko pointed out, hoping to see a symbol, anything that might show Irith's exact location, but some parts are still faded. He puts the basilarium back in his bag, praying Toko's right and they'll be there soon.

Chapter Forty Two

SAMUEL STARES AT THE BACK of Gideon as he marches on in front. He can't be more than ten years older than himself, but his strong silence seems self assured, and fitting for his panther form.

'What sort of things can you and Gideon shapeshift into?' he asks Senta, who's now walking beside him, holding Paladin's reins loosely in her hands.

'Most things,' she replies. 'Though we have our favourites. Like you saw, mine's a bird and Gideon's is a panther. There are different types of shapeshifters. Some can shift only into other human beings, others can shift into animals and some into objects.'

'What sort of objects?'

'Anything really. Like that.' She points to a large stumpy tree.

Samuel considers what she's said for a moment before answering.

'What sort of shifters are you two?'

'We're a hybrid, we can take on the form of other humans and animals.' She leans towards him and

Samuel finds himself unable to look away from her dark eyes. Out of nowhere a wild looking dog, similar to a jackal, runs out from the trees. He fumbles to draw his dagger but Senta lightly places a hand on his wrist. Her white teeth are a stark contrast against her dark skin as she smiles.

'What are you doing? Stop mucking about,' Calder says.

Samuel glares at the jackal, his dagger still clasped in his hand. He watches as the dog transforms in front of him. First, its snout shrinks back into its face, then its eyes become smaller, and its hair falls away. The animal begins to grow, its front legs becoming shorter and its back legs longer. Within seconds, Gideon stands in front of him.

'I forgot to mention, we've got very good hearing,' Senta says.

'Come on, we've got to keep the pace,' Toko calls back.

Gideon shakes his body, shedding the last few hairs, then he strides along next to Samuel.

'I saw you back there, when you helped Senta,' Gideon says, after a moment's silence. 'You may need to learn a few moves if you want to use that dagger well, and protect yourself.'

Samuel flicks his eyes over Gideon's mace.

'How do you mean?'

'Well, you need to get a feel for the weapon. Here,

give me the dagger.'

Samuel pulls the blade slowly from its sheath and hands it over.

'This is a small, light weapon. You can make minimal movements with your wrist to swipe or jab at your opponent. A bit different to that.' Gideon points to the large sabre attached to Senta's belt. Senta draws the sword and walks backward, facing them. 'Don't grip it too tight,' he continues. 'You need to be firm, but you don't want to lose feeling in your fingers.' He slices the blade through the air, then jabs it forward. 'There are just two moves I'll teach you. The parry, to deflect or block your enemy's attack.' Senta lunges forward but Gideon swipes the dagger downward, his body barely moving, all the energy focused in his arm. The sword meets the dagger and a clang rings out. As Senta swings the blade upwards, aiming for Gideon's head, he brings the dagger round and up, blocking her attack. They battle back and forth for a few seconds, each blow Gideon deflects, his wrist twisting this way and that. Samuel is impressed by the counter attacks, not expecting the small knife to withstand blows from such a large sword.

'If you manage to do that,' Gideon says, 'and launch an attack, then your best bet is a flunge.'

Samuel raises his eyebrows, glancing at Senta, and seeing her grin.

'A flunge is a flying lunge, like this.' He grabs the

sword from Senta and runs towards Samuel, pushing off from the ground and drawing the sabre back, forcing the sword out as he comes to land. The blade stops centimetres from him. He does his best not to duck to the ground.

'This attack should hopefully mean you reach your opponent before they have time to react,' Gideon explains.

'What if I don't have time to … to flunge?' Samuel says.

'You need to mix up parries with counter-attacks. You must focus. Try to sense your opponent's move before they've even thought it.'

Samuel nods, taking his dagger back from Gideon. He rolls his shoulders, then tosses the weapon back and forth between his hands, trying to get more of a feel for it.

'If all else fails, then hide,' Gideon says. For the first time he smiles at Samuel, and all the seriousness disappears from his face. A few seconds later however-er, the smile fades and he strides ahead again. Senta turns back round, but slows her pace to walk beside Samuel. A pang of guilt hits him from out of nowhere and he flinches.

'You alright?' Senta asks.

'Yeah, yeah I'm okay,' he replies, not looking at her. He wonders what's going on back home. He feels sick knowing his mum and dad have no idea where he is. If they knew what he was doing, that someone was teaching him how to fight, they'd never believe it, especially some of the creatures he's already come up against.

'I hope it's not much further,' he says, not wanting to think about home, or his mum and dad. Senta looks up to the early morning sky, as if it will reveal some clue as to where they need to go.

'It's getting colder,' he says.

'It will do, the further north we travel.'

Samuel nods. His legs ache a little, his mouth is dry, and a deep rumble in his belly is becoming frequent. But he ignores it all, especially as Brawn is trotting along steadfast, his pace never seeming to falter.

SAMUEL LOOKS AT THE FOREST AROUND THEM. The trees seem thinner and more sparse.

'What's out there? Past the forest?' he asks Senta.

'The plains.'

'Can I see?'

'Samuel.' Toko interrupts. 'How's the map looking?'

Samuel glances at Senta, but she doesn't answer him. He checks on the egg again.

'Clearer,' he says, showing Toko.

'We're not far now, I'm sure.'

'Shall we go out in the open?' Senta suggests.

Toko stares ahead, as if listening for something. 'We'll go and check. You wait here, Samuel.'

'But I want to go with you.'

'We don't know what's out there. I can't risk it.'

Samuel looks to Senta in desperation, then to Gideon and Calder, but neither return his gaze.

'We'll be with him, Toko. It might be safer if we stick together,' Senta says.

Toko's brow furrows. 'Alright. But stay close to us.'

Samuel nods eagerly, then smiles at Senta, grateful for her persuasion.

'Follow me everyone,' Toko says. 'Listen out for the slightest thing. If anything looks or sounds unusual, we make our way back to the cover of the trees, no hesitation.' He pauses for a second then veers off through the woodland. Samuel follows the others, and within moments they stumble out onto the edge of the forest.

Chapter Forty Three

THE AIR CATCHES IN SAMUEL'S THROAT as the landscape reveals itself. The brink of the trees succumbs to a steep decline of reddy, brown earth. Crumbs of soil trickle south of the precipice, having been disturbed by the horses' hooves. He glances to his left and then his right, spotting the edge of the forest both ways, flowing out far into the distance. He gazes out at the horizon, and a wave of heathland shimmers below him. The whiteness is quite beautiful and so bright he almost can't look at it.

'Keep moving, Samuel,' Toko says.

The horses advance cautiously along the edge of the cliff.

'Wait. What's that, over there?' Senta points into the distance. Samuel turns to look to where her outstretched finger indicates. On the peak of one of the waves is a twinkling white vision.

'What is it? I can't really make it out,' he says.

'Look closer.'

Samuel squints, covering his eyes with his hand, shading them from the bouncing light reflecting off the waves beneath them. The white light seems to be moving, fluttering almost.

'What is that?'

'I believe *that* is where we need to be,' Toko says.

'But there's nothing there.' Samuel struggles to see anything that might resemble a house, something that might suggest it's where Irith is.

'Try looking here,' Senta calls out, having moved a little further along the cliff. Samuel moves to stand next to her and Paladin. Brawn clops along, placing himself between Samuel and the ridge of the crag.

'Are they birds?' he asks, catching sight of a wing.

She smiles at him, then slowly nods.

'But–'

'They're doves,' Toko says. 'I've heard of this when people have spoken of Irith, and his home. The doves surround his house for protection. If you look in just the right light…' He trails off, moving along even further. 'See here,' he says. Samuel stands beside him, then stares again at the peak of the hill. As the light shines in a certain way he realises what it is he's looking at.

'I see it. A windmill,' he says.

'That's it. *That's* Irith's,' Toko replies.

Samuel stares at the familiar structure. He watches the birds hover, like a white wave, blanketing the monument. It's in the dips of the wave that he catches sight of the windmill a little more clearly. He recalls the last time he saw it, standing high on stilts above the marshland. *Can it be the same?*

'The air is so fresh out here. Can't we keep going?' He gestures to the plains beneath them.

'No. It's too exposed. We'd be easy targets.' Toko's words slash through the peacefulness. 'Come on, we should make our way back into the forest. It won't be long now.'

Samuel takes one last look at the rolling hills beneath him and then at the shimmering white doves.

'We're almost there,' he murmurs to Brawn.

'SAMUEL, STAY CLOSE TO ME,' Toko says, as they leave the forest. Irith's home is finally just metres ahead of them. The others surround him, but no one speaks. The air becomes a little hostile and he struggles to see out from behind their human shield.

'Gideon, Senta, you wait here with the horses. Guard the place. Let us know if you see or hear anything unusual,' Toko commands. They both nod, then Senta glances at Samuel before separating off and taking her station. Even though they're now just a few feet away the noise of the birds' wings is near silent, apart from the odd flutter. Samuel would have thought he'd feel unnerved by this many hundreds of birds close up, but instead he feels tranquil. Toko and

Calder are quiet, either side of him, and he wonders if they're feeling the same. Without warning, the birds fly apart, revealing a grand, dark wooden door. Samuel follows the grain of the wood upwards; it seems never-ending.

'What do I do?' he asks.

'You'd better knock,' Toko replies.

Samuel shifts his belt and sheath, then takes a few steps forward, away from Toko and Calder.

'You should send an altaira, to let Anka know where we are, like Mantel asked,' he says, glancing back at them. As he does, the bird's green and purple wings flutter in his mind, then as if it had been following them, it emerges from the clouds, swooping down and landing on Toko's shoulder. Toko seems unfazed and lifts a finger to rub the bird's chest.

'You should go in,' Toko says.

Samuel nods, as Calder smiles at him from underneath his beard, the same smile he gave Faedean when she left them. Inhaling silently, he keeps his chest pushed out, as he marches up to the entrance. He looks down to where the handle should be, but there isn't one. It has ancient, ornate hinges, but is completely solid. His hand hovers in front of it, before he curls it into a fist and raps sharply. The sound seems pitiful against the grand structure. He waits, but nothing happens.

'What if he's not here?' he says, turning round.

'What if something's already happened?'

Toko frowns. 'Try again.'

Samuel does as he says, but this time, as his fingers make contact with the wood, the door opens, silently. Cautiously, he places one foot over the threshold, his hand on his sheath. Once he's fully inside the door slams behind him. He spins round, but there's no handle on the inside either. His heart thuds, and he can almost feel it dangling behind his ribcage as his hands fumble against the rough wood. It's no use, there's no way out.

Chapter Forty Four

'COME IN,' A VOICE SAYS. Samuel whirls round but can't see who, or where the voice has come from.

'Irith?' He tries not to let his voice waver.

'Come in,' the man repeats, now sounding a little closer. Samuel looks up the winding stairs to find someone standing at the top. The figure begins to make its way down the staircase, treading carefully on each step, with one hand firmly gripping the railing. White, wavy hair with a yellow tinge, floats on top of the man's shoulders as he descends. He's much older than Samuel first thought, and it isn't until he's standing in front of him that Samuel realises how tall he is, his bent frame now straight. A white tunic hangs loosely around the man's shoulders and torso, flowing almost down to his knees. Grey trousers continue down to the man's worn feet, which sit snug in some tired-looking sandals. Samuel looks up at the man's face and finds himself staring into one bright green eye, the other an ocean blue.

'Faro?' he murmurs.

The name seems to take the man by surprise as he

flops into a chair with a grunt.

'I don't understand. Where's Irith?'

'Come, sit down,' Faro says. Samuel moves around the piles of books that are dotted all around the room; he's reminded of his college tutor's office. The ground floor of the windmill is open-plan; Samuel can see all the way around, except for the staircase which sits on one side.

'Please sit.'

Samuel does as he asks, sitting down a little clumsily into a large wooden chair opposite him. He glances to the silver-topped cane that Faro has leant against his chair, recalling the power that he'd seen come from it. Close up he can now see that a small white ceramic dove is perched on top. As Faro shifts in his chair the bird's wings flutter. Samuel blinks, wondering if he imagined it.

'My name's Samuel,' he says, dragging his eyes from the cane.

'Yes. I know who you are.'

Samuel fidgets, not knowing what to say or where to look. Faro doesn't say any more so Samuel casts his gaze around the room, looking at the set of globes, which are cradled in wooden stands. They all differ slightly in size and he begins to calculate in his head how many there are. It all gets too much as he realises there must be hundreds.

'They are all different worlds,' Faro says.

Samuel didn't realise he'd been watching him.

'*All* of them are different worlds? How many are there?' he asks, turning to face him.

'More than you can imagine. These are just some of the main ones. I have an extensive secret collection.'

His eyes twinkle.

'Did you know I was coming?' Samuel asks.

'Yes.'

'Have you come here for your brother?'

Faro looks away.

'He's coming for me.'

His skin, that Samuel had seen when in Nekton, was so young and full of colour, now looks pinched, tired and pale. But his eyes still shine as if he knows secrets no one else does. Samuel shakes his head a little at a question in his mind which voices itself over and over. Finally he gives in.

'You're him aren't you? You're Irith.'

Chapter Forty Five

'INDEED I AM,' FARO REPLIES, without blinking. 'I've tried many things to keep my identity secret. I've visited many different worlds over the years, and gone by many different names. Perhaps my downfall was staying here for too long.' His eyes flick around the room. 'Now it's too late.'

Samuel leans forward in his chair. 'And no one else knows that you're Faro?'

Faro's lips tighten. 'The Davadores know. They have been my trusted aides for many years here, on this world.'

'So that's the connection Alexis felt? That's why she knew where to find Irith,' Samuel shakes his head. 'I mean you. The link between you and the Egg of Darkness, is that you're its creator.' Samuel pauses. 'But why didn't the Davadores bring the egg to you themselves? If they knew it was you, that you could fix the egg, why give it to Alexis?'

He feels the burning desire for answers, working its way up through his chest and into his throat.

'The Davadores do not know where I reside. I've

always said if they did, it would make them vulnerable. Alexis has a great gift. They could trust her in bringing the egg to me safely.'

'But she didn't. She got taken.' Samuel can't shake the guilt.

'She didn't fail. Neither did you. The egg is here.' Faro's eyes flick to the satchel, and Samuel feels a heat rise through his hand as it hovers over the bag.

'But at what cost? What if she's–' Samuel jumps from the chair, his eyes stinging from tears. Faro doesn't respond, but stares at the empty seat.

'Do you know where she is? If she's still alive?' Samuel grits his teeth as soon as he speaks the words, not sure that he wants to hear the answer.

'I don't know. But she's strong.'

'We need to find her,' he urges, pacing the floor between them. Finally Faro looks up at him.

'There are other, more pressing matters, I'm afraid.'

'How can you say that?'

'Samuel, please, sit down. Alexis is strong, she can look after herself. I've watched her for some time. She's one of the best. We must concentrate on the other issue.'

He looks at the bag again. Samuel follows his eyes, wondering how he knows the egg is in there. He does as he asks, but sits rigid, hugging the satchel close.

'Can I?' Faro holds his arm out. Samuel stares at it,

slowly lifting back the material on the bag to expose the basilarium. A light is leaking from the lines, the heat becoming stronger.

'I want to ask you something first,' he says.

Faro's hand doesn't waver. 'You can't go home yet, Samuel.'

'How did you know what I was going to say?'

Faro slowly drops his arm.

'Come with me,' he says, using the cane to help push up from the chair. Samuel swings the bag over his neck, so the strap sits across his chest. He can still feel the heat from the egg but he ignores it, as he follows the old man up the stairs. The winding staircase takes him up to the first level and he sees Faro disappearing up another set. The windows are large and stretch up from the ground floor all the way to the top. Samuel pauses briefly to look out.

'Why aren't the birds covering the windmill anymore?' he calls out, as he sees the others standing loyally below.

'They are,' Faro replies.

'But I can see out…'

'Things aren't always what they seem, Samuel.' Faro leans over the railing, already having reached the top.

Samuel continues up, glancing to his left again, to look out the next panelled window. As he gets to the top step he looks about him, but Faro is nowhere to be seen. He wanders over to a globe that's tilted on its axis, on a tall stand. Bending slightly to get a closer look, he sees that the world is covered in blue, with only a handful of small islands dotted over it.

'That's Maris,' Faro says.

Samuel stumbles forward, almost knocking the stand, regaining his balance at the last second. Faro's sudden appearance is confusing, but then Samuel hears a click behind him, as though the bookshelf has moved and just slotted back into place.

'It's covered in water, hence the name,' Faro continues.

Samuel looks at him, trying to recall if he's ever heard the word before, at school, or college.

'Maris loosely means the sea.' Faro uses one finger to give the globe a soft spin. 'It's one of a few worlds where sea mammals rule.'

Samuel nods as his eyes drift around the space. The room is full of books, maps and objects he's never seen before.

'How many floors are there?' he asks, noticing there's another staircase over on the other side of the room.

'A few,' Faro replies. 'Here, I wanted to show you this.' He holds a book out and flicks through it. His crooked fingers fumble with the delicate pages, until he finds what he's looking for, then he hands the book to Samuel. Samuel stares at the drawing of a long, dark-haired figure, standing on the top of a hill, with his hands held high. Hundreds of orcs, harpies and other creatures stand tall behind him.

'Pemba,' he murmurs.

'Yes,' Faro replies. 'And this is what will happen if we don't mend the Egg of Darkness and stop him.' He turns the pages, until he finds one which shows an image of a world on fire. As he continues to turn the pages the images seem to come to life. The hissing fire and the screams of the people and animals whose lives it's taking, sail off the page and into Samuel's ears. The sounds make their way down his ear canals and into every part of him. They fill his head, until all he can hear is noise and all he can feel is pain.

Chapter Forty Six

NOT ABLE TO BEAR IT ANYMORE, Samuel grabs the book from Faro and slams it shut. The hell leaves him instantly. Faro calmly takes the book from him and places it on a table.

'I feel a responsibility, not just because he's my brother. But because *I* was the one that found the Orbis. I should have just left it, I should never have shown him.'

'Who are his army? Why do they follow him?' Samuel asks, feeling a little breathless after the cacophony that screamed through him.

'They're just like him, like my brother, in many ways.'

Faro pauses and Samuel can tell he finds it hard to use that word now.

'They are people, creatures, that have lived in the shadows. They think they've been overlooked, cheated by their own worlds. When I sent Pemba to the Darkness they retreated back into the shadows, but since he escaped he's reclaimed them. They want to be out in the light. Like him.'

Faro looks back down at the book. 'They help him grow stronger. The longer he's out of the darkness and the more death and destruction he and his army cause, the more power he gains.'

The heat from the egg still penetrates through the cloth bag, but Samuel also feels a cold reality as he thinks about the soldiers he saw.

'I think people from my world have joined him,' he says.

Faro nods despondently. 'People will do anything for power.'

Samuel knows Faro is right. People have started wars over countries, why not worlds; he just can't believe it was able to be kept secret.

'Do you have the Orbis here?' he asks.

A smile lifts Faro's cheeks a little.

'It is safe. But you know, Samuel, curiosity is not always a good thing.'

Samuel ignores him, wanting more answers. 'I saw what happened. Before you trapped Pemba in the Egg of Darkness.'

Faro doesn't reply, his face unreadable.

'When did you see that?'

Samuel turns back to the book, ignoring his question.

'Is the Orbis really as powerful as people say?'

'Yes.' Faro taps his finger on the cover of the book. 'It must always be kept safe. No one must ever touch it, except me. It's too dangerous. The same goes for the Egg of Darkness.'

Samuel feels the air catch in his throat. His heart thumps against his ribs as he tries to focus on the table in front of him.

'Why? What will happen if…' He looks at Faro, but the man's face is now blurry.

'Samuel?' He hears Faro's deep voice, but all he can do is stare at him and try to swallow; his throat is suddenly so dry he's unable to find the words.

'Samuel?'

Finally he forces the saliva down, and it eases into the cracks, allowing him to speak.

'I touched the Egg of Darkness,' he says.

Chapter Forty Seven

FARO PULLS A STOOL OUT from underneath the table, but Samuel doesn't sit.

'Is that when you saw me capture Pemba?' Faro asks.

'Yes. Why? Why must no one touch it?'

'I knew I felt it,' Faro murmurs. 'I felt something change, but I just thought–' He leans one hand against the table. 'I thought it was the egg getting closer to me. When you arrived here, I believed it was because Alexis had told you the way,' Faro pauses, glaring at the satchel hanging against Samuel's side. 'Let me see the egg. I must see it.'

His voice deepens as he reaches out for the bag, but Samuel steps back. A flash of darkness crosses Faro's face, but it's gone almost as quickly as it arrives.

'I'm sorry,' he says softly. 'Please. Please, let me see the egg.'

Samuel slowly pulls the basilarium out from the bag and hands it to him. He watches as Faro runs his fingers over it, muttering something. Then his hands work their way around the box, moving so fast they become a blur. In a few seconds, Samuel hears the familiar click and he watches Faro lift the lid off the box. A bright light fills the room and Samuel stumbles backwards, shielding his eyes. Faro holds the basilarium forward and Samuel waits for the light to be sucked back in before peering inside.

'This map.' Faro points to it. 'This is how you found me?'

Samuel stares at the lines on the egg that are now beginning to fade.

'Yeah, but it was clearer than that.'

'So it's true. You did touch it.' Faro's voice is soft once more.

'I told you I touched it. But the map, it was a lot clearer. Why is it disappearing?'

Without the dark lines of the map the hairline crack now seems much bigger.

'You *can* fix it, can't you?'

Faro holds the basilarium up close to his face, turning the cube until he's looked at the whole egg. His eyes seem to be far darker than before, but maybe that's just the light. He holds his hand up, raising the cane and pointing the dove inches from the egg. The cane darkens and the dove's wings beat, slowly at first, then faster. After a few seconds a bright light shoots forward from the dove and encompasses the egg. Sparks fly as Faro moves his cane around it. The dove works its way over the split and Samuel watches the broken egg begin to seal. Moments later Faro stumbles backwards, the light vanishing, the dove lifeless.

'What's wrong?' Samuel asks.

Faro slowly moves the cane away from the egg.

'I'm too weak. Pemba is too close. I need more time.'

Samuel studies the egg, recognising that something has changed.

'Where's the map?' he asks.

Faro places the cane and the basilarium on the table.

'Samuel, the egg showed you the map for a reason. It got you here. Now it's gone it's protecting me again. When you touched the egg something changed.'

'What do you mean?' He continues to stare at the object, but feels his temperature rise.

'When the bearer of the egg died I became its keeper once again. I was meant to guard the egg until I found it a new bearer. That's part of the reason why I needed it brought to me. Between bearers, it is at its most vulnerable. Samuel, the next person to touch the egg when it's in this state, becomes the bearer. It isn't something I, or anyone else can control.'

Samuel feels the explosion of blood pumping harder through his veins, circulating at extra speed around his tired body. He looks at Faro. The difference in his eye colour has become more prominent. He can feel his throat tightening, his breathing becoming shallower.

'Samuel,' Faro says. 'You are now the bearer.'

He can't respond; his mouth feels like someone has shoved it full of sawdust. Hysteria enters his bones, starting at his feet and working its way up through his body, making him feel like he can't breath. He clamps a hand to his chest, pulling his top away from his skin, wanting to be anywhere but here. He hadn't needed clarification, he'd understood.

'Here.' Faro holds a small bottle out to him. 'Drink this.'

Samuel knocks the vial out of Faro's hands, watching it slowly hit the ground. It doesn't break, but the liquid seeps out onto the floor. He stumbles over to the window that reaches right up to the ceiling. He needs air. He needs it now.

'How do I get out of here?' His voice sounds raspy and choked; nothing like his own.

'Samuel, you must get somewhere safe. I don't know if Pemba knows the egg has a new bearer. But as soon as he does, he will be after you.'

Samuel looks back, wondering whether to tell Faro of the dream he had, of Pemba attacking him. He wonders if it was a dream. He leans back, gripping hold of the railing that's running round the room.

'You wanted Pemba to come here. You wanted this to happen,' he says.

'No. It's true, I need to mend the egg, to trap Pemba again, but I didn't want any of this.'

'You made the egg. *You* created it. You must be able to change who its bearer is?'

Samuel sees the effect his words have on Faro; a look of utter despair is stretched across his face.

'I can't. Yes, I formed the egg, but the egg has written its own rules now. And I need time to try and fix it.'

Faro's voice is strained, like his throat has restricted. Samuel imagines the lump that has formed; he can feel it in his own throat. He turns to look back out of the window. Dark heavy clouds fly overhead, swirling rapidly, like the harpies' smoke. Below, Calder and Toko still stand guard. But in the distance, emerging from the forest are others. He's sure he can see Anka, and, he guesses, more Plain Seekers.

'They're coming.' He takes a deep breath and squeezes the rail. 'Faro, there's something else I should tell you. I think I saw who killed the bearer.' His fingers continue to grip the parapet. 'I think it was a Plain Seeker.' He doesn't turn round. 'If it was, if some of them have betrayed this world, betrayed you, then how do we defeat Pemba?'

No answer comes, just silence. Samuel finally turns around, but finds the room empty. Faro is gone, and so is the egg.

Chapter Forty Eight

'Faro!' he yells, searching the room.

He checks the bookshelf that he's sure he'd seen move earlier. Nothing seems out of place. He leaps down the stairs, glancing out the window as he goes. The others are still waiting, but just as he's about to cast his eyes away, something stops him. He grabs the railing, almost tripping and falling down the stairs. In the far distance is a black cloud rolling forward, towards them, and beneath it are dark shapes, riding the landscape of waves. He doesn't hesitate any longer, he continues down, taking two steps at a time, missing the last few altogether. As he regains his balance he makes for the door, taking a quick scan of the bottom floor to check for Faro. There's no sign of him. He forgot that the door doesn't have a handle, but as he approaches, he can see it's ajar. He slips his fingers through the gap and prises it open.

'Toko, Calder!' he shouts, stumbling out. They both turn round.

'Samuel. What is it?' Toko asks. 'Where's Irith?'

Samuel runs up to them.

'It's not what we thought. Irith is Faro.' He speaks before thinking.

'What?' Calder replies, looking up at the windmill. 'What are you talking about?'

'There's no time to explain, but he's gone and he took the egg with him. He didn't have the strength to mend it.'

Senta leads Paladin over to them.

'What is it? What's happened?' she asks.

'The army are coming,' Samuel says. 'I saw them, from the window. They must have followed us here. They're all coming.' He points into the distance. The others all turn to look.

'Gideon!' Toko shouts.

Gideon emerges from round the other side of the windmill, the mace solid in his hand. 'It looks like his army have found us. They're on their way.'

'There are too many of them. What about Faro? We've got to find him, and the egg...' Samuel trails off.

'There's no time. We must get word to the Davadores, let them know what's happening.'

'Toko, there's something else. Something I tried to tell Faro. I'm not sure who we can trust. I don't thin–'

'Samuel?' a strong, voice comes from behind him. He spins round.

'Anka!' he exclaims. 'You found us. Where are the others?'

'They're not far behind. Have you still got the egg?' He jumps down from his horse, landing neatly, then strides over to Samuel and the others.

'I had it. Then Irith took it.' Samuel glances at Toko, who looks confused. Samuel frowns, running his hand through his hair and looking back to the windmill. 'He's gone.'

'What do you mean gone?' Anka commands.

'He just disappeared.'

Anka clenches his fists, seemingly unable to speak.

'Anka, do you know where Alexis is? Did Mantel tell you she'd been taken?'

Anka's face softens. His grey eyes grow a little warmer. He parts his lips, then lowers his gaze.

'Yes, I know. But I don't know where she is, or how to find her.'

Anka's horse whinnies and Samuel looks to it, realising it's the same horse from the forest.

'It was you,' he says, turning to Anka. 'You were there, with Phoenix, then when Alexis got taken.'

Anka glares at him, his jaw tightening.

'I followed both of you, some of the way. I wanted to make sure Alexis was safe. But I failed. I lost sight of the harpy that took her.'

'How many of you are there?' Toko interrupts.

Anka raises his stare, but doesn't look at Toko. Instead he glares past him.

'There's my team and five other squadrons I managed to summon. More are on their way.'

'What about the Davadores, have you alerted them yet?'

Anka now stares at Toko, and Samuel watches his cheeks suck in as he bites his tongue.

'No, not yet.'

'Why not?' Calder urges.

'Who *are* you?' Anka asks.

'They're with me. They helped me get the egg to Irith. This is Toko, Calder, Senta and Gideon,' Samuel says, wanting to diffuse the tension. He takes a step closer to Calder, watching Anka's face redden as the colour works its way up from his neck to his cheeks.

'Anka, they took Calder's son.' Samuel softens his voice.

Anka stops still for a moment, the lines on his forehead disappearing. Seconds later his face settles back into a scowl.

'I'm sorry, Calder.' Anka turns to Toko. 'We hoped it wouldn't get this far. We had hoped we'd be able to stop it. I will get word to the Davadores.'

'Thank you,' Toko replies.

Samuel watches Calder and can almost see the rising worry leaking out of his pores.

'They must have been following us the whole time,' Samuel says.

'Anka!' a high-pitched voice sails through the air but Samuel can't see who it belongs to. A horse comes galloping out from the trees with a boy sitting on top, his hair bouncing about on his head.

'Sith. Where are the others?' Anka orders.

Sith, the name resounds in Samuel's head. The boy looks familiar but it takes a moment to place him. Then he recalls seeing the boy at Alexis'. He remembers Alexis speaking the name when talking about the gateway. The gateway that led him here. He resists all urges to speak to the boy, knowing they don't have time, and now not knowing who to trust.

'They're coming. I came on ahead,' Sith replies. His horse comes to an abrupt stop as he pulls tight on the reins. Dust flies up, covering both Samuel and Anka.

'Sorry,' Sith says. 'Is he here? Is Irith here?'

'No,' Anka replies, brushing the dust from his clothes.

'Oh.' The boy looks disappointed as he leaps down from the horse.

'Samuel, this is Sith.' Anka gestures to the boy.

'You're, you're the–'

'Not now, Sith,' Anka barks. The boy closes his mouth. 'I need you to do something for me. We need to alert the Davadores. Pemba's army are coming, it won't be long now. You must go and inform them. Tell them we're in danger and we no longer have the egg.'

'But I thought–'

'Sith, just do as I say.'

The boy nods and Samuel feels a pang of pity for him.

'How am I meant to–'

'You must open a portal. It's the quickest way to get to them.'

'But we're not meant to open portals.' Sith steals a glance at Samuel.

'I *know*,' Anka hisses. 'But none of that matters any more. Pemba's here, he knows we're after him. Just be careful, make sure no one follows you. Go *now*.'

Sith looks as though he's about to say something else, but changes his mind. Samuel watches him as he holds onto his horse's reins, tight. He closes his eyes, one arm out in front of him. Toko and Calder turn to watch. Samuel stays completely still, not wanting to break the boy's concentration. After a couple of minutes a small light appears between him and the boy. It sits in mid air, just like the one he'd seen back in the forest. He stands still, wanting to reach out to it, but knowing he shouldn't. The boy's palm faces the light, his fingers outstretched. He looks blurry through the light of the portal as it gets bigger. Samuel moves silently, stopping when he's standing facing the portal head on. As he looks into it he sees a large, familiar building, sitting on the edge of a cliff. Its walls are stone washed with reddy coloured roofs. There are lots of windows and bridges that look like they join one part of the building to another. Before he can say anything, Sith vaults onto his horse and with a final look at Anka, rides off into the gateway. As soon as the horse's tail is through, the portal shrinks until it's nothing but a tiny speck of light. A second later and the spark goes out altogether.

Chapter Forty Nine

'IT TAKES A LITTLE LONGER for the less experienced ones to open them,' Anka says, standing beside Samuel suddenly. Samuel acknowledges him with a nod, not knowing what to say. From where he'd been standing the boy seemed to do pretty well.

'The others should be here any minute.' Just as Anka speaks, Samuel hears hooves, thundering closer. He looks towards the forest and a whole herd of horses emerge, their riders guiding them. They slow when they see Anka, then bring their horses to a halt. The troops are a mixture of men and women of all ages.

'Anka,' a man says, now striding over to them. The rest remain on their horses, waiting for their orders. The man places a hand on Anka's shoulder and Anka looks pleased to see him. The guy can't be more than early thirties, but Samuel gets the impression he's a leader of another squad. As he turns he catches sight of the tattoo on the guy's neck. His features are strong, his eyes dark and his hair neatly cropped.

'Radis. They're close,' Anka says. 'This is Calder

and Toko, they're here to help. And Gideon and Senta?' Anka looks to Toko to see if he's got their names right. Toko nods. Samuel can tell from Toko's lack of words he doesn't think much of Anka.

Radis drops his hand from Anka's shoulder and strides over to them. He bows his head a little at them all, his eyes lingering slightly longer on Senta.

'We have over a hundred men and women here.' He turns to Toko. 'Hopefully more soon.'

Samuel stands back as Anka and Toko begin giving commands to the troops. He watches as they build a shield using their own bodies, at least six lines deep. Senta stands next to him, her spear upright, her hand clasped round it.

'Where do you think Irith went?' he asks her.

'I don't know. But I heard what you said.' She lowers her voice. 'About Irith, being Faro.' She glances sideways at him. 'He must have had good reason to leave and take the egg with him.'

Samuel hopes she's right.

'Samuel,' Toko says, turning to him. 'You and Senta go back to the forest with the horses, you'll be safe there.'

'But–'

'Don't argue, Samuel.'

Samuel looks at Anka. He's sure a slight smirk pulls at the corner of his mouth.

'I want to help. I want to find Alexis.'

'I'll find her,' Anka says.

'What about Irith and the egg?' Samuel urges.

'Hopefully he's taken it somewhere safe.'

'Samuel.' Calder places a hand on his arm and Samuel looks down at him. His hair looks a lot greyer than when he met him. 'I think it's best.'

Samuel clenches his jaw.

'Okay.'

'Senta,' Toko says, abruptly.

She nods, holding his gaze for a moment.

'Come on then, let's go,' she says, mounting Paladin.

'We'll see you both soon,' Toko says.

Samuel leaps onto Brawn, welcoming the familiar toughness of the saddle. Toko and Calder watch as they ride off, but Samuel notices Anka doesn't take a second glance.

Chapter Fifty

WHEN THEY'RE FAR ENOUGH AWAY, but still in sight of the windmill, Samuel turns back, hoping for a last look, but the doves are now all he can see.

'You alright?' Senta asks.

'Yeah. Where are we meant to go?'

'Far enough to be safe. I guess.' She seems to be concentrating on the forest path ahead. The horses gallop, but the wind rushing past him is still, dead almost.

'What are we meant to do, just hide, do nothing? I can't watch people die.' He strives to stifle his emotions, to force them back down to the place where he's held them for so long. But it's no use.

'We do what Toko asked.'

'Is that what you always do?' He tries to rile her and he sees her prickle slightly, but only for a second.

'I follow orders, but I believe this is the best thing. You cannot be put in danger. This isn't your fight, Samuel. You must be given a chance to get home.'

'I didn't think it was my fight, either. But things change.'

Senta doesn't reply and he makes no further attempt at trying to persuade her. He looks out across the plains, watching the dark cloud roll in.

'Look!' he exclaims, pulling on the reins and feeling the resistance from Brawn. 'Stop, Brawn, stop.'

'Samuel?' Senta slows her horse, turning it round to trot back to him.

'Look, over there. It's the harpies.' He stares into the sky, at the bird creatures. 'There must be hundreds of them. They'll never be able to fight them all, not as well as the army on the ground.'

Senta looks to the sky before replying.

'Others will come to help. The Davadores too.'

'What's that?' Samuel interrupts.

'What?'

'That, over there, on the top of that hill. It looks like a cage. Do you have any binoculars?'

'Binoculars?'

'You know, to see something that's far away.'

'Do you mean a voyaring?' Senta unclasps the top of a leather holder attached to her belt. Samuel hadn't taken much notice of the holder before now. She pulls out a small contraption. The bronzed metal object has a circular glass piece on each end, which she unfolds. The object goes over her fingers sitting on top of her knuckles. The glass piece nearest her is smaller than the one at the other end. The whole thing can only be about ten centimetres long but looks neat. She curls her hand into a fist before looking through the small piece of glass.

'Well, what do you see?'

'I'm not sure,' she says.

'Here, let me have a look.' He reaches out impatiently, brushing his hand against her arm. She twitches, moving her hand away from her face.

'Samuel I don't thin–'

'Please. Let me see.'

She sighs before removing the contraption from her hand and passing it to him.

'Slide it over your fingers so it rests below your knuckles. The second, larger glass-eye piece is the one that enlarges the image.'

He nods, slipping the voyaring over his fingers so it sits between his knuckles and finger joints, just like she said. Raising it to his eye, he inhales, then holds his breath. The glass has a sepia tint which makes the landscape look like an old painting. He tilts his hand upwards toward the sky. The harpies are flying in swarms. The ground beneath them is covered in orcs, orglins, and men.

'There must be hundreds of them,' he says, staring at the humans as they march forward, their guns held rigid in their hands.

'He's gathered quite an army.'

Samuel lowers the voyaring, wanting to tell her about the humans from his world.

'What if their weapons are better?' he asks.

'Our weaponry is strong. We can take them.'

Samuel feels encouraged by her optimism, but at the same time he wonders if they know what they're up against.

'Do you see the cage?' she asks. He looks through the voyaring again, trying to ignore the solid advances of the men and creatures. He swings his arm about, searching.

'There!' he exclaims. The cage sits on top of wheeled platforms, towering above the monsters. Two orcs are stationed at the front, towing on the large ropes that hang down.

'Can I make this any clearer?' he asks, studying the contraption.

'Just twist that cylinder and it should bring it more into focus.'

He does as she says before looking again. The cage appears empty, then he casts his gaze down. Two bodies are sprawled on the floor of the enclosure. He recognises the mass of auburn hair straight away.

'Alexis!'

'Where?'

'There. It's her, I'm sure.' He tosses the voyaring back to Senta. 'I think Phoenix might be in the cage with her. We've got to help them.'

'We can't. There are too many. You'll never get them out without…'

Samuel doesn't hear Senta's last words, he's already silently ordered Brawn to move. The horse has picked up his pace quickly and they're galloping in no time.

'We've got to get to them,' he says to Brawn.

'Samuel!' Senta's voice catches on the wind behind him, but he ignores her. All he can think about is Alexis. The stillness of her body has filled him with a heat he doesn't know how to control. He has to get to her.

Chapter Fifty One

'SAMUEL, WAIT UP!' SENTA CALLS, cantering behind on Paladin. Samuel doesn't reply, knowing she won't be able to catch him and Brawn.

'Come on boy, we've got to find her.' He leans forward, hovering above the saddle, like he's seen Alexis do, his head close to Brawn's neck. He can hear the horse's breathing, rough and heavy, but he doesn't show any signs of tiring. His hooves thunder against the ground and the trees begin to blur. Then, without warning, Brawn slows.

'What is it, boy, are we close?' The horse snorts and shakes his head from side to side, his mane flicking up and missing Samuel's face by inches. His front hooves dig into the ground and they come to an abrupt stop. Samuel jumps down, glancing back, but not seeing Senta anywhere.

'Stick close by me,' he says to Brawn, one hand lightly placed on the horse's side. He crouches, treading slowly towards the edge of the forest. The satchel on his side feels so light without the egg. He squats beside a large tree trunk, cursing as he nicks his arm on a thorn. The dark cloud has now descended and the army are no more than a few hundred yards away. Brawn stands right behind him as he peers out around the tree. The smell hits him first, forcing him to recoil. The rotten skin, the same as when Calder killed the orc, fills his nostrils. He sniffs, brushing his sleeve across his nose. The stench is a thousand times worse with all the other creatures hammering forward. He takes a deep breath, then peeks back out. The orcs' backs are arched, their heads down, spit dripping from their mouths. The orglins seem gathered together, clomping on. Every now and then one disappears, sometimes reappearing nearby, other times not appearing again at all, at least not where Samuel can see. His muscles tighten, preparing for them to materialise anywhere.

He ducks back as something runs past, waiting a moment before looking again. Men trudge by, all in line. Some carry guns, some have swords. Those that don't bear the familiar khaki army clothes are dressed all in black, with metal plates on their shoulders and chest. The harpies screech in the sky above them, their wings beating hard, causing a wind to help push the army forward. Fire escapes their mouths, igniting trees. Screams from those caught in the blaze and the smell of burning leaves, turn his stomach. A quiet whine comes from behind him.

'Shhh, it's okay boy,' he says, as he turns round to

comfort Brawn. Another pair of horse's legs stand solid in front of him.

'Samuel. *What* are you doing?' Senta hisses, leaning down from Paladin.

'Senta. What took you so long?' He notes her scowl as he turns back to look through the trees. 'We've got to be quiet. They're just through there.'

The smell of the monsters wafts over him; the scent of sweet vinegar, is masked for a few seconds, as Senta drops to her knees beside him. He can almost feel her skin touching his. He doesn't look at her, but concentrates on the army.

'What do you plan on doing now?' she murmurs.

'I don't know. But I couldn't just sit around doing nothing. Especially now I've seen her so close.'

Senta silently gets up and after a moment or so he turns around.

'What are you doing? Where are you going?' he asks, seeing she's mounted her horse again.

'If you're so intent on putting yourself in danger then I'm going to have to do something to help.'

'What do you mean?'

'Here, take this.' She slides the sabre out from her belt. Samuel takes the handle of the sword as she holds it out to him.

'But won't you–'

'I've got this,' she says, patting her spear. 'Remember what Gideon told you.'

He turns the sword over in his hands, the blade thick but ending in a sharp point. She tosses him a sheath, another to attach to his belt. He slips it on and slides the sword into its holder. He feels the pull of the weapons as they weigh him down.

'What are you going to do?' he asks again.

'I'm going to be the diversion. They're close to the others; if I distract them now, not only will it give you a chance to get to Alexis and Phoenix, but it also means that Toko and the others can use it to their advantage.'

'But that's suicide!' Samuel exclaims, stepping towards her.

'I'm quick,' she replies, then points down to a brown substance smeared in the grass. 'You'll want to cover yourself in some of that.'

'Mud?'

'Not quite.' Her mouth and eyebrows twitch. 'Smother some on Brawn too. Where his white parts show. You'll want to smell just like them.'

Samuel looks at Brawn, realising how much whiter he's become.

'If, *when*, you reach Alexis and get them out, she should be able to use her powers to get you and Phoenix away from there,' Senta says.

'Why wouldn't she have done that already?'

'I don't know, something must have stopped her. But that sword will cut through anything. It's made from a metal called lisson. Use the thin side to cut through objects, but when fighting use the thicker blade, so it doesn't break. You'll be able to get them out.'

'When will I see you again?' he asks, touching Paladin's nose.

'When it's safe.'

Samuel nods, patting the horse's side.

'Okay, well…'

'I'll see you soon, Samuel,' she says, a smile passing across her lips. He doesn't know whether it's the angle, or from what she's about to do, but her features seem even more striking. He takes a step forward, but with one prompt action she tugs on the reins and kicks her heels into Paladin's sides. The horse is off, passing through the trees without hesitation.

'Be ready!' she calls back.

He runs a hand through his hair and down the back of his neck. His hands tremble a little. A soft wetness nuzzles his shoulder as Brawn bows his head. Samuel raises his arm and runs his hand up the horse's muzzle.

'It's just you and me now, boy,' he says.

Chapter Fifty Two

ALEXIS STAYS LOW IN THE CAGE, trying to conserve her energy. She winces as the wheels hit a large rock, jangling the tight chains bound to her bloody ankles. The screech of the harpies whip around her and she turns to the boy who's lying a few feet away. He hasn't said a word since they tossed him in the enclosure with her. If it wasn't for his moans she would have thought he was dead.

'Where are they taking us?' she murmurs. Blood splatters onto the floor just in front of her. She looks up, but there's too much going on to see where, or who it has come from.

'Alexis!' a familiar voice calls. She looks round, trying to locate the voice. 'Alexis,' Anka repeats, riding up alongside the cage. She runs to the bars, her arms stretching through.

'Anka!'

He reaches out his hand and takes hold of hers. She grips back, relieved to see his face, but noticing that he looks a little older.

'You came for me,' she says.

'Of course,' he replies, his face relaxing as he smiles. 'Do you know where the egg is?'

'Samuel had it.'

'Not anymore.' Anka shakes his head. 'It seems Irith took it.'

'Look out!' Alexis screams, as an arrow flies past Anka, narrowly missing his ear. He ducks, letting go of her hand. The harpy fires again. Anka reaches down to his boot, pulling out a dagger. In one quick motion he looks up, takes aim, and throws the small knife into the air. A piercing screech reverberates as the dagger slices the creature's wing.

'We've got to get you out of this cage,' he says.

'It's these.' She jangles the necarsus chains. 'They – Anka behind you.'

Anka swings round, keeping his balance on top of the horse. An orc brings its axe down, but he deflects it with his sword. The clang of metal drills through Alexis' ears. She feels helpless in the cage, watching the attack on her friend. Anka veers the horse round, to face the enemy. He swings his weapon, blocking every attack, but not able to make his own. Moments later he gets swept up in the sea of creatures and Alexis loses sight of him.

'Anka!' she screams, pacing the few feet up and down the bars, but she can't see him. She's alone once more, among the mass of bodies.

Chapter Fifty Three

Samuel stands beside Brawn, holding onto his reins for reassurance, a steadiness more than anything. He hears the first signs of battle before he sees it. It's been only moments since Senta left him, but he knows she'll have reached the army. He closes his eyes and pictures her astride her horse, galloping along the edge of the forest, before venturing out into the sea of creatures. The shrieks from the harpies splinter down around him. Roars resound from the beasts on the ground. Their clashing weapons reverberate through his ear drums, as they clamber over one another, all wanting a piece of her. He can't bear it.

'Come on,' he says to Brawn, swinging his leg up and over the horse. The saddle feels softer beneath him, as though it's now moulding to him, or him to it. He grabs the reins once more and Brawn takes off, his trot turning into a speed like no other Samuel has experienced. He races on, the trees rushing past, then veers off through them and out the other side. Samuel keeps his head low as the fight greets him. Brawn instinctively takes him forward, swerving around the creatures. Samuel glances up towards Faro's windmill. Toko and the others race down, the fight almost having reached them. Gideon's panther paws spray up dust, his stride covering more ground than any of the others. Samuel casts his eyes to Calder, who is holding his sledge hammer with both hands, preparing to fight. He and Toko disappear into the billow of monsters and Samuel turns just in time to see Senta in the middle of the action. Her spear is held high, but the creatures wash over her, swallowing her up.

'No!' he screams, pulling on Brawn's reins. Dust flies up into his eyes as Brawn changes direction. Samuel draws his sword, his grip tight, though a little shaky.

'Get off her!' he yells, as he reaches the mound of creatures. Gideon's words of advice are only a whisper in his head as he slashes the sword down, slicing through an orc's arm. The monster's scream pierces his ears and the noise seems to alert the other creatures. One by one, they look up from their prey to Samuel. The deep-throated grunts and growls echo around him. Orglins manifest from every direction. An orc drags itself away from Senta, who's now lying on the ground. It reaches Samuel and Brawn and swings its axe backwards.

Move, move your arm, do something, Samuel thinks. He raises the sword above him, but before he can bring it down on the creature's head the orc is thrown back. He hits the ground so hard, Samuel feels it shake beneath Brawn. The large cat sinks its teeth into the orc's neck, spraying dark liquid. Its huge paws press down on the creature's chest. Samuel watches as it wrestles with the flesh, taking seconds to silence its victim. Once the orc is motionless the panther turns and looks up.

'I'll help Senta. You get Alexis,' Gideon growls.

Samuel stares at the orc beneath Gideon, the last bit of life seeping out of it.

'Go,' he snarls, swiping his paw at an orglin as it shimmers out of thin air.

Samuel brings back his right arm, pulling the reins, steering Brawn's head away. The horse complies immediately and makes off towards the cage again. As Samuel looks back, the monsters turn to Gideon. They scrabble over each other trying to get at him. Samuel swallows hard, the burning lump in his throat almost choking him. He squeezes his eyes shut, then turns round, trying to ignore the growls and yelps.

'Let's find her,' he says.

Brawn weaves in and out of the destruction. There's no order, just mayhem, men and monsters roaming everywhere.

'Where are you?' he murmurs, just as a shooting pain sears through his head. It lasts seconds, then everything goes black.

Chapter Fifty Four

'GET OFF ME,' HE SAYS, feeling a warm wetness on his cheek. Brawn stands tall above him, his tongue aiming again for his face. Samuel rolls onto his side, out of the way. He shakes his head, hoping the ringing in his ears will subside. 'Brawn, what are you doing?' A rush of air fills his ears, and the high-pitched sound is replaced with screams and metal against metal. He puts a hand to the back of his head. It's wet and sticky.

'Get up,' a voice flatly orders.

Samuel lifts his head and finds himself staring at a face that's smeared in green and black paint. The skinny man is close, and towers over him, but Samuel can see from his khaki clothes that he's from Earth. The man is holding the end of his rifle to Samuel's chest. His tiny dark eyes show no recognition that Samuel is from Earth too.

'Wait,' Samuel says. 'Don't shoot.'

The man sneers, as if enjoying the power he has over Samuel. He wipes the back of his hand across his sharp nose. Out of nowhere an altaira flies into the man's face, her wings beating hard. Samuel takes his chance and flings his arm across his chest, throwing the weapon away. The man's mouth drops open. Samuel doesn't hesitate and jumps up, grabbing the gun with both hands. He yanks it from the man's grasp and swings the butt of the rifle round hard, making contact with the side of the man's head. A deep-throated grunt escapes from the man, who collapses onto the solid ground. Samuel brings the rifle round, aiming it now at the man's chest as he stands over him. His finger trembles on the trigger, but the man's eyes don't open. He lies still, not even his eyelashes flicker. Samuel pushes the end of the rifle further into his chest, but there's no reaction. He breathes out heavily, waiting a few more seconds before lifting the gun away. When satisfied, he turns around and trudges off, his head pounding.

'Brawn?' His heart flutters. 'Brawn?' A gentle whine carries through the air. The horse stands a few metres away, his ears twitching. Samuel ploughs through the muddied earth towards the horse, keeping his focus on him the whole time. Brawn snorts loudly, rearing up, and Samuel spins round. The man is now standing, unsteady on his feet, but able to hold a small pistol and aim it. Samuel brings the rifle up, but he's too late. The pistol fires, narrowly missing him. He drops to the floor, but the man doesn't get a chance to fire again; Brawn has raced past him and trampled the man to the ground.

It's all over in seconds. Samuel stands, his knees slightly bent, the gun still shakily aimed forward. Brawn circles the man then returns to Samuel, nuzzling his nose into his chest, and breathing warm air over his head.

'Brawn. You, you saved my life.' He places a hand on the horse's mane, then leans into him, grateful for his strength. Inhaling deeply he waits for the tremor in his legs to subside, before hauling himself back up onto the saddle. He tucks the rifle into the strap and Brawn trots off, moving around the mounds of fallen bodies.

AS BRAWN SLOWS, blending in with the other horses, Samuel stares up at the cage that is now in front of them. With the push of the fight he feels as though they're caught in water, struggling to get upstream. He tries to ignore the constant rush and focus on the figure on the floor of the cage. The tension in his chest eases as he runs his eyes over her long hair.

'Alexis,' he says, her back facing them.

Her head turns slightly, hesitant. 'Samuel!' She leaps round, instantly throwing her arms out to the bars of the cage. He looks at her body that is now covered in blood and bruises. Her rich, green eyes are paler than the last time he looked into them.

'Samuel, what are you doing?' she says, as her eyes dart about.

'What do you think I'm doing? I've come to get you out of here.' His voice rises above the noise.

'But how? What–'

'Shhh, stay quiet.' He reaches behind him. 'Here, you'll be needing this back.' He hands her the crossbow through the bars. She smiles as she takes the weapon.

'Thanks.'

He looks at the gap between him and the cage door, then back to her. She's staring at him, her mouth moving, but he can't hear what she's saying.

'What?' he yells.

'You're going to have to jump!'

He wonders if he's heard her properly, and he studies her lips as they speak the words again, emphasising the word 'jump'. He nods, dropping Brawn's reins.

'Stay close,' he whispers to the horse, before digging his foot into the stirrup that's closest to Alexis, then swinging his other leg round. It's awkward, he's not really at the right angle, but with Brawn not able to stop, there's nothing he can do. *One, two, three.* He lunges forward. Cold metal smacks against his hand, as he curls his fingers, gripping one of the bars. Heat surges through his shoulder as he dangles from the railing, the tips of his shoes scraping along the ground. He reaches up with his other arm.

'Damn it,' he curses, unable to get a grip. Alexis reaches out, but the chains around her ankles pull her back.

'Come *on*,' he says. Swinging his arm back, he throws it against the cage, this time managing to get a firm hold. His shoulders burn as he pulls himself up, placing his feet on the edge of the cage, just between the gaps in the bars. He fumbles for the heavy sword Senta gave him, sliding it out of the sheath slowly, so as not to lose his balance. He doesn't have much room to manoeuvre, but he brings the sword up and back, then lowers it, a little clumsily, but hard enough to hit the chains holding the cage door shut. For a second nothing happens, then they melt apart, silently. The door creaks and falls inwards, clattering as it hits the floor. Samuel takes a quick look round, but the orcs pulling the cage don't falter; the noise of the battle has masked his break-in. He uses his arms to gain a little momentum, swinging out and through the opening, before tumbling inside.

Chapter Fifty Five

'WELL, I DIDN'T THINK IT would be that easy.' He grins, looking up at Alexis, trying to ignore the shooting pain in his injured shoulder. She returns his relief with a smile.

'Try it on these.' She rattles the chains.

Samuel looks down at the shackles bound around her ankles. He places a hand on her bare foot, rubbing some of the blood away.

'What have they done?' he murmurs, his jaw clenching. Alexis responds by placing a hand on his arm. He looks up at her and without thinking touches her face. It's so soft beneath his fingers, he feels as though his rough skin will damage it. He quickly draws back, but she grabs his wrist.

'Thank you,' she says.

'What for?'

'For not leaving me.'

Samuel holds her gaze for a few seconds before picking the sword up off the cage floor. Turning it over, he brings the thin blade down on the chains, slicing through them, even more easily than before. A light shoots through the metal as they break, then as they fall to the floor the colour drains, leaving behind dull, rusty shackles.

'Where did you get that?' she asks.

'Long story.'

'Did you see Anka out there? He was here just now. He tried to help me, but–'

'I didn't see him,' Samuel says. 'I'm sure he'll be okay.'

Alexis nods, looking out into the throng of people. A soft moan comes from behind him and Samuel turns.

'Phoenix!' The boy is on the other side of the cage, with his knees tucked into his chest as he slowly rocks back and forth. He drops next to the boy, but doesn't touch him.

'Phoenix, it's me, Samuel. Remember?'

The boy doesn't answer, and keeps his head buried in his arms.

'Is he hurt?' Samuel asks, turning to Alexis.

'I don't think so. He hasn't said anything, but I think he's scared. I tried to take a look at him, but every time I got close he groaned louder. How do you know his name?'

'He's the boy from the forest. But I met him properly in Kirkela.' Samuel turns back to him. 'Remember? We were there with your mum and dad. They're worried about you. Your dad isn't far away.'

Phoenix stops groaning.

'We've got to get out of here,' Alexis whispers. 'Can you get him up?'

Samuel reaches his hand out to place on the boy's shoulder, but at the last moment picks up some hay from the floor of the cage.

'That drawing you did of Brawn was really good. I hope you've still got the knife?'

Phoenix doesn't answer.

'Brawn is near,' Samuel continues. 'You could do another drawing of him.'

Again the boy doesn't reply. Samuel wants Phoenix to go with them of his own accord. If he has to force him, he knows it will bring unwanted attention.

'Okay,' Phoenix finally responds, through a mouthful of saliva. Samuel smiles up at Alexis, who looks unsure but relieved.

'Good. Tie your boots up. You don't want to be tripping over them.' Samuel stands, taking his eyes off the boy. 'Alexis, there's something I need to ask you. Actually, there's a lot I need to ask you.'

'We don't have time.' She moves away from him, gently brushing his hand aside.

'I know, but it's important.' He glances at Phoenix, who's doing as he asked. His careful looping of the laces reminds Samuel of a toddler.

'I've *got* to ask,' he says, facing Alexis again. 'Did you know you shouldn't touch the Egg of Darkness between bearers?'

Alexis narrows her eyes and stands very still.

'What are you talking about?'

'Don't lie to me,' he says.

'I'm not lying.' Alexis' voice rises. 'The egg has never switched bearers. At least not in my lifetime.'

Samuel regrets his accusatory tone. He can see from the quizzical look on her face that she has no idea what he's talking about.

'Samuel, what's going on?'

He ignores the question, wondering how to tell her.

'You've never met Faro have you?' he says.

Alexis looks at him, questionably.

'No. No one has met Faro. How could they? He doesn't stay in one place long enough. And it's too dangerous.'

'What about Irith? You've never seen him before?'

'No,' Alexis replies, the strain in her voice showing her increasing frustration.

'Well, I have. Both of them, actually.' He takes hold of her pale fingers; she doesn't pull away. 'Irith and Faro, they're the same person. Irith is Faro, or Faro is Irith. Either way, they are the same. And now Faro has the egg.'

Alexis' gaze falls from his face, down to his chest.

'He couldn't mend it,' Samuel continues. 'I don't know if he took the egg to get it away from me, to keep me safe, or to get it further from Pemba, so he could try and fix it. Whatever the reason, we need to find him. We need to help him defeat Pemba.'

Alexis seems to have entered a daze. Her stare is fixed, her body rigid.

'Alexis?' Just as he takes hold of her shoulders, shaking her a little, an arrow twangs against the cage bars. 'Get down,' he says, dragging her to the floor with him. He looks past her to the harpy in the sky. 'You've got to open a gateway,' he says, watching as the harpy pulls back another arrow in her bow string, preparing to fire. *'Now!'*

Chapter Fifty Six

ALEXIS NODS, SEEMING TO HAVE REGAINED her focus. She shoves her boots back on as another arrow descends. Its been over-shot, or misfired, and it soars through the cage, and out the other side. It hits the ground, splintering among the trampled feet.

'*Come on*, let's get out of here!' Samuel yells.

Alexis nods again, as her eyes dart about the cage. Phoenix is still crouched on the floor as close to the bars and as far from the exit as possible. Samuel bends next to him as Alexis stands in the middle of the cage. Her eyes glaze over, her arm outstretched, everything about her still. Her skin is smooth of any creases it had. A spark of light flickers in mid air, just as a groan escapes Phoenix.

'Shhh, it's okay,' Samuel murmurs.

Alexis breaks her concentration, looking to her left.

'What is it?' he asks.

'I don't know. It's an odd feeling. Something I've felt before.'

'Just hurry.' He watches the orcs surrounding the cage.

'I'm trying. I can't do it if you kee–'

'Get down!' Samuel lunges forward, seizing her and forcing them both to the ground. His hand wraps underneath her head, to stop it hitting the floor. His fingers crack as he takes her weight and instantly his hand goes numb. He doesn't hesitate. Leaping up, he pulls the sabre from his belt, thrusting his arm forward and slicing it through the air. It meets the oncoming target, carving straight through the orc, cutting its body in half. Its head and torso fall into the cage, whilst its legs drop backwards. The bodiless legs make their way down the battle line and it isn't long before another orc turns to see where they came from. Its eyes narrow as it focuses on Samuel and Alexis. Samuel's heart pounds.

'Open the portal. Open one, *now*.'

She raises her arm out like before, as if trying to get the gateway open under command. Samuel ignores the gunshots, the flying arrows and the grunts from the monsters.

'Grab hold of me,' Alexis urges, as the new portal flickers open.

Samuel slips his hand into hers.

'Phoenix, you're gonna have to hold on to me,' he says.

The boy doesn't answer, or look up, but after a few seconds he grabs hold of Samuel's t-shirt.

'Ready?' Alexis asks.

Samuel nods, his insides twisting. Alexis takes a step forward and he follows. The heat surrounding the gateway draws him in, just like before. He feels a sharp tug on his shirt and looks to Phoenix. Panic is smeared across the boy's face. Samuel looks down at his feet and watches the fingers grip tight around Phoenix's ankles. Samuel's gaze follows the hands and arms attached to them. At the edge of the cage, straining to hold his head to see, is an orglin. Samuel lets go of Alexis and grabs hold of Phoenix by the shoulders.

'I've got you,' he says to the boy. 'Alexis, grab my waist!'

He feels her arms wrap around his stomach.

'Pull!' He tightens his muscles, preparing for the tension. They manage to scramble backwards, closer to the portal, but Phoenix struggles beneath the creature's grasp.

'Pull!' Samuel yells again. He feels the monster give way a little more. The drag from the gateway behind them is strong. Phoenix finally wriggles free and Samuel feels the release from the orglin as they tumble backwards into the portal, the gushing wind drowning out the sound of any screams.

Chapter Fifty Seven

'SAMUEL?' ALEXIS SAYS, STARING DOWN AT HIM. She wonders if the bad passing through the gateway has affected him. He's sprawled on the floor, but his dark eyes look up at her.

'I'm okay. Didn't hurt as much as before.'

'It shouldn't have hurt at all. It wouldn't have, if it weren't for that stupid creature.'

She stares at where the portal was. Nothing is left behind, except a few dust particles.

'Where are we?' Samuel asks, checking on Phoenix, who is next to him, shaking.

Alexis looks round at the ruins and everything that has been blanketed by dust.

'It's a small town called Lorin. It's eastward, a little way from Iriths. It was the only place I could think of in a hurry.' She glances up at the sky. 'I knew Pemba and his army had already been here,' she adds.

Samuel nods, looking round. 'We should move away from here.'

Alexis notes the waver in his voice. 'We should be safe, for the moment.'

He looks up and down the street, before running a hand through his hair.

'Not if a gateway is opened.'

Alexis feels an unease. 'Samuel, is there something you're not telling me?'

His eyebrows twitch as he scans her face.

'Someone might open a gateway. They might try and follow us.'

'Only a Plain Seeker could open a gateway and they wouldn't.'

Samuel is silent, still staring at her. She notices his pupils shrink, then widen and shrink again. She hears Phoenix shuffle his feet behind her and a quiet moan leaves his mouth.

'You trust the Davadores, I know that,' Samuel says. 'But I'm just not sure who we can trust at the moment.'

She listens as he tells her about re-entering Nekton. She's aware of her breathing becoming shallower as she watches his lips move. His mouth twitches uncertainly as he describes the bearer and the marks of the Plain Seekers. His words echo through her skull, getting louder until she feels as though she'll never be able to fill her ears with anything else.

'Did you know?' he finally says. His change in tone jars her thoughts.

'Did I know what?'

'Any of it? About Faro, the Davadores, the betrayal of Plain Seekers.'

She fiddles with the strap across her chest, until the haze of confusion disperses.

'No, of course I didn't. I had no idea. And I'm not sure I believe it. How can we be certain? Maybe the egg was tricking you into seeing things?'

Samuel opens his mouth but pauses before speaking.

'Irith *is* Faro – that's no trick. When the Davadores gave you the Egg of Darkness, did they say how they got it?'

The realisation of what he's asking smacks into her like a violent wind.

'They've got nothing to do with this. They were trying to protect Faro's identity, like *you* said. They entrusted me with the egg. Perhaps they knew other Plain Seekers might not have been so worthy.' She realises with those words that she has admitted the possibility of treachery among her kind.

'I know about the Davadores' rule,' Samuel says. 'About the third child. Tertias.'

Alexis looks at him sharply.

'That rule is in place for a reason. White Plains may seem like Earth, in many ways, but it is very different. We'll do anything to stop our planet from being destroyed.' She drops her gaze as soon as the words spill out of her. She feels a lurch in her stomach. 'I'm sorry,' she says, after a heavy sigh.

'I know it's hard to admit that certain Plain Seekers have been disloyal.' He wraps his strong fingers around her wrist, trying to get her to look at him. 'People from my world. They're here. They've joined Pemba's army too.'

Alexis recoils. She can see the hurt in his face.

'So that's why the gateway was open; the one you travelled through, from your world. It was opened for them to come here. So they could fight with Pemba,' she says.

Samuel shrugs. 'Does that mean that boy, Sith, he's–'

'No. He wouldn't have. He's too young. He's harmless. All he wants is to help.'

Samuel replies with a nod, but Alexis doesn't know if it's a nod of agreement or to appease her.

'We need to move away from here. We'll find somewhere that is sheltered and I'll open up another gateway.' She lifts a hand to place on Phoenix's shoulder, but a twitch from him warns her not to.

'A gateway to where? Where are we gonna go?' Samuel asks.

Alexis reaches behind her, grabbing her crossbow. She feels complete again with it in her grasp.

'Back there. Back to Irith ... Faro.'

She stares down at Phoenix. If it weren't for his big frame she would think he was just a small boy. His face is stained with dirt and dried tears. She bends next to him. All the time she'd spent with him in the cage he'd barely lifted his head, and it isn't until she's eye level with him, that she notices his sparkling blonde eyes.

'Phoenix. We're safe now. You're safe.' She looks to Samuel, who's watching her and the boy. 'We'll get you back to your family.'

Samuel looks grave as he bends next to Phoenix.

'She's right. Come on now. Come with us. We'll get you home,' he says.

PHOENIX FOLLOWS THEM AS THEY HURRY through the deserted streets, his feet dragging along. Alexis looks down at her shoes. They're covered in dust from the dirty tracks. She looks at the ruined buildings: people's lives gone in seconds.

'What are we gonna do when we get back there?' Samuel asks.

'We must find the others. Try and find Faro. Or…'

'Or what?'

'I could take you home. It's still not safe, but I've already opened one gateway. I could try to take you back to your family.' She stares at the path ahead of them, not able to look at him. She feels her heart rate quicken, as she waits for his reply. There's silence. Eventually she looks at him, but his gaze is set forward. She wonders if he heard her.

'Samuel?'

'Don't ask me again. I can't leave you now. You still need help, and like you said before, my world could be in danger too. Especially now we know Pemba's recruiting from Earth. I have to help you finish this. But please, don't ask me again.' He strides past her, his body stiff.

She inhales slowly, then opens her mouth to speak. Her lips waver for a few seconds before she snaps them shut. She shakes her head and continues on, now following his footsteps.

Chapter Fifty Eight

ALEXIS LOOKS AT THEIR COLOURLESS SURROUNDINGS. The trees and plants are grey and dead, and the particles of debris from what were once the town's buildings, catch in her throat, making her cough.

'Do you hear that?' Samuel asks.

'What?'

'Nothing. There's no sound at all.'

Alexis nods. 'The rest of my world will turn into this, if he and his army take hold. It's what every world will be like he if he wins.'

'Do you think the people from here fled before the army attacked?'

'I don't know,' she replies, noticing him tense. 'Hopefully they managed to get away, get into hiding somewhere.' His shoulders loosen and she knows that's what he wanted to hear. A groan comes from behind them and Alexis turns back to Phoenix. He's not shaking anymore, but his body is hunched over.

'It's alright, Phoenix,' Samuel says, bending near to the boy.

'I must open a portal soon,' she says.

'Where were you thinking of taking us back to?'

'Faro's windmill. I saw it from the cage, on top of the hill.'

Samuel stands and faces her. 'But that's where they all are.'

Alexis glances at him. 'I know. But sometimes it's best to hide in plain sight.'

Samuel doesn't reply, but pulls gently on her wrist, then reaches up to her face. She feels her whole body stiffen as he pinches a strand of her hair.

'A piece of ash,' he says, as it disintegrates between his fingers. His eyes are warm and surprisingly full of life. She remembers the touch of his hand on her face back in the cage. It takes every ounce of her strength not to tremble.

'So, you can open portals inside buildings as well?' he asks.

'Yes, but it's a little tricky. And it means it's better if we're inside somewhere this end.' She looks around at the rubble.

'We better find somewhere then,' he says. His eyes hold her gaze fiercely, as though he can't look away. She drops her head, feeling her face flush.

THE CLOSENESS OF THE AIR IS STIFLING, and as they jog on through the ruined streets she daydreams about splashing cold water over her face. She tries to ignore the throbbing from her ankles – pain left behind from the chains. None of this stops her, as she knows every moment that passes someone is dying at the hands of Pemba and his army. She keeps a firm grip on her weapon, holding it close to her chest, just in case.

'What about there?' Samuel asks, pointing. She follows his finger and can just make out a thin spike reaching up into the sky, behind partly demolished houses.

'Let's take a look,' she says, turning her jog into a run. She hears Samuel's footsteps thud behind her.

She looks back at Phoenix, who is struggling along. Samuel's hand hovers by his arm, not touching it, but an invisible force willing him forward.

'Down here,' she says, taking a sharp left into a narrow street. She stops as iron railings loom in front of her. Samuel and Phoenix catch up a few seconds later.

'This is perfect,' Samuel says, grinning.

She stares up at the structure. Its grey stone slabs have been left untouched. The point they saw from a distance was the tip of the steeple. A silver cross sits just under the arch of the roof, almost hidden. Windows run all the way around the building, each one tall and rounded at the top, all except for one, underneath the cross. This one is a large circle with an image etched into the glass, though from here she can't make out what it is.

'Come on,' Samuel says, making his way to the door.

Alexis stares up at the grand opening. It must be at least seven foot high, maybe even taller, as it goes into a point at the top. She looks at the round wrought iron handles which are placed low, the same height as her stomach. Samuel's already taken one in his hand, slowly twisting it.

'Wait. Let's do it together at the same time,' she says, taking hold of the smooth iron handle.

'One, two, three.'

They twist and pull. The heavy door creaks but doesn't budge.

'It must be locked.'

'Try again,' she commands. She pushes her feet into the ground, making sure her stance is solid. His side moves first and a small slither of light breaks through the doorway. Her side gives way and they heave the doors apart, just wide enough for them to slip inside. She looks behind her as Samuel and Phoenix enter, then she heaves the doors shut behind them.

Chapter Fifty Nine

'WOW, IT'S MASSIVE,' SAMUEL SAYS, his voice echoing around the church interior. Alexis allows her gaze to roam around. The windows seem even larger from the inside and have a golden tint to them. She watches Samuel as he guides Phoenix to a bench. The boy obediently sits down, as she makes her way up the aisle to the pulpit, running her fingers along the wooden pews as she goes.

'It looks just like the churches back home,' Samuel says.

'It would,' Alexis replies, continuing to make her way forward, but flicking her head back to look at him. 'Where do you think Earth got the idea of churches from?'

'Really?'

'We don't just gain knowledge and ideas from other worlds. We have been known to spread a concept as well.' She raises her voice as she nears the end of the aisle. 'Some take, others, not so much.' She watches him as his gaze follows the large stone slabs up to the arched beams. The beams sink into the walls, held snug, then break free as they reach across the ceiling. They create a sturdy web-like structure, that she knows has held the building steady for hundreds of years.

'Isn't it a bit weird?' he asks, now looking back at her.

'What?'

'That this hasn't been touched. It doesn't look like they destroyed a single part of it.' Samuel's voice gets lost as it reaches up to the high ceiling.

Alexis doesn't reply, but leaves him engrossed in the colourful window, as she makes her way towards the pulpit. As she reaches it she can see the intricate carvings wrapped around it. A large bird protrudes from the front, casting its wise gaze out over the church. She looks back at Phoenix, who seems so small sitting there, slowly rocking back and forth.

'Are you ready?' she says, raising her arm.

'Yeah, I guess so.' Samuel has walked up the outside and is now close to her.

'What's wrong?'

He shrugs. 'It just feels weird, being here.' He lowers his voice. 'It's so silent, so still. I've not been in a church since...'

'Since your brother?'

'Yeah.' Samuel doesn't look at her. 'The car accident, he was driving. It wasn't his fault, but...'

Alexis edges a little closer, her action prompting

him.

'I left him. I went to try and get help, but I was too late, the car exploded. When I dream about it I just keep seeing his face, and the flames, over and over.'

Alexis drops her arm, the gateway just a speck in the air.

'Were you badly hurt?'

'No. Just some cuts and bruises, and a bit of whip-lash.' He places a hand on the back of his neck. 'I know it wasn't my fault, but I left him there.'

'You left him to get help. And if you hadn't, you wouldn't be here now.'

'But why him?' He finally looks to her.

'It must have been awful,' she says, not knowing what to say to make him feel better.

'We were twins. We did pretty much everything together. It's weird. I think everyone finds it weird; he's gone but I'm still here. I feel like, like my mum and dad, in some way they…'

'I'm sure they don't blame you.'

He looks at her, as though bemused that she knew what he was thinking.

'I dunno. I think they did for a bit. Maybe not now. But I know they find it hard, because we looked so alike. Sometimes I wonder if they'd find it easier if we both…' His voice cracks again and he swallows hard.

'I can't imagine anyone would think that.' She places her hand on his arm and he tenses.

'Sorry, I shouldn't have said that. You're right. I've never told anyone all that before. I couldn't face telling my mum and dad the details. They just think I was pulled out of the car, unconscious. How can I tell them I left him?'

Alexis pauses. 'You don't have to tell them. At least you've told someone. And I don't think you did the wrong thing.' She squeezes his arm.

'Thanks.'

'It's true. And I'm glad you told me. I wish we had more time, but–'

'It's alright,' he says, releasing himself from her grasp. 'I'll get Phoenix.'

She nods, then turns to the back of the church. The window that she'd seen outside with the stained glass image, looms above her. The herd of horses etched on it are now clear, and she can almost see the movement of their hooves. She turns away from it, needing all her concentration if she's to open a gateway somewhere so specific. She recalls the windmill that she briefly saw, and remembers everything she's been told about Irith. Gradually the light grows, and when the portal is fully open she drops her arm to her side and looks through the gateway. It's as clear as if she were in the same room. The chairs are empty and books are spread out on the table – there's no sign of an invasion.

'It's ready,' she calls back. Her voice resonates,

louder than she intended.

'Come on, it's alright.' She can hear Samuel murmuring to Phoenix as he entices him up the gangway.

'You ready?' she asks, as he stands by her side.

He nods, taking her hand again just like before. His fingers gently squeeze around hers. She squeezes back.

'Come on Phoenix,' he says. The boy takes hold of his t-shirt once again, though his eyes are cast elsewhere. Just as she's about to take the first step she suddenly remembers what Samuel said before.

'Why would anyone have come after us? Even if we have been betrayed; you don't have the egg.'

'Huh?'

'Neither of us has the egg, so what would be the point in them trying to track us down? Is it to do with you touching the egg, and the bearer? Is there something else you've not told me?' She glares at him, ignoring the pull from the gateway. He holds her gaze, though she spots a drop of sweat gather on his forehead.

'Maybe it's best if we get back there first.' He nods at the portal, then flicks his head towards the boy. Alexis tames her desire to disagree. Instead she returns his gesture with a curt nod of her own. She digs her nails into the back of his hand and he grimaces, but doesn't say a word. She takes the first step, her foot disappearing from the wooden church floor and entering into non-existence. The energy of the gateway always grips her, giving her a rush like nothing else. As the last bit of her disappears through, she embraces the heat and the few seconds of nothing, before emerging on the other side.

Chapter Sixty

'WE MADE IT,' SAMUEL SAYS, looking relieved to have walked through the gateway without any trouble this time. Phoenix is still gripping his top, playing with the material between his fingers.

'Of course we did,' Alexis replies. 'Now, tell me what's going on.' She drops his hand, but instead of answering her he rushes over to a table.

'It wasn't like this before,' he says. 'It was more ordered. Someone's been here.'

'Keep watch over Phoenix,' Alexis says. 'I'll go check upstairs.' As she makes her way up the staircase, she observes Phoenix wander over to the edge of the room and squeeze himself in between two bookcases. Samuel mumbles something to him but she doesn't hear what.

Just before she reaches the top of the stairs she draws her crossbow. The action is unnecessary, as the space is empty; no person or creature in sight. The movement of the fight outside catches her eye through the large window, and with the windmill so silent, the army of Plain Seekers seem to dance against the rhythm of the creatures in the battle below.

'Pemba's army look strong. They're advancing,' she calls down.

'Any sign of Faro or the egg up there?' Samuel's voice floats back.

'No.'

'What about the Orbis? Do you think he still has it?'

'I don't know,' she replies, beginning her descent. Samuel turns to look at her, having been staring out the window.

'I'm sorry,' he says, as she reaches the bottom step.

'What for?'

'I've really messed up.' He grips hold of the bannister with one hand. 'When I met Faro, he told me something. Something about the bearer.' Samuel looks back to Phoenix, who is still huddled on the floor, staring at nothing it seems.

'Samuel, what is it?' she urges, gently.

He brings his gaze up to meet hers, and she feels a force from it, like before.

'When I touched the egg, I became the new bearer.'

A slight gurgle escapes her throat, and she forcefully swallows some air.

'I had no idea,' she says, flopping down onto the step, before her legs give way. She scrapes her fingers through her hair, as if pulling it tight will ease the sudden pain in her head. 'What have I done? I was meant to protect you, take you home.'

Samuel bends next to her. 'It's not your fault.'

'Can it be undone?'

'Apparently not.' He wraps his hands around hers and unclasps them from her head.

'Do you feel any different?' she asks, now looking at him.

He shakes his head from side to side.

'No, not really. A little clearer up here, perhaps.' He taps the side of his head and the corners of his mouth twitch. His pupils shrink, as though a bright light has shone on them. Then, they enlarge as a shadow blankets the stairs above. Alexis leaps up, and pushes him aside, away from the steps and out of view. She throws her arm forward and places her finger carefully on the trigger of the crossbow.

Chapter Sixty One

'YOU DON'T HAVE ANY SPECIAL POWERS, I'm afraid, not superhuman ones, anyway.' Samuel recognises Faro's deep voice instantly as it bounces down the curved walls. He jumps in front of Alexis, the tip of the bolt almost touching his chest.

'It's alright,' he says, placing a hand on her arm. 'It's Faro.'

She doesn't drop her weapon, but her finger relaxes from the trigger.

'Alexis. I'm glad you're safe,' Faro says, still at the top of the stairs, not attempting to descend. 'You must come with me, both of you. *Quickly.*'

Samuel stares up at Faro's thin face.

'Where is the Egg of Darkness?' he asks.

'It is safe, as is the Orbis. For now. Please, you must come with me.'

Samuel looks to Alexis and then to Phoenix.

'He might be safer here,' Alexis says.

Samuel nods, hurrying over to the boy.

'Phoenix, wait here. We'll be right back, okay?' The boy stops his low humming and nods.

Samuel follows Alexis up the stairs. He wonders how close the egg is – he's felt strange ever since Faro took it from him, like something is missing. He concentrates on Alexis and her clothes as they stretch over her skin as she climbs the stairs. When they reach the top, he sees Faro waiting for them by a bookcase.

'What did you mean about superhuman powers?' Samuel asks.

Faro turns away from him, to the shelving. 'You will be stronger, but more mentally than physically,' he replies, fiddling with a book on the shelf. 'It is this mental strength that you will need as a bearer to the egg.'

'Why?'

He raises one eyebrow. 'The egg is strong, you know that.'

Samuel feels himself tense.

'And so too is Pemba. You will need great mental strength to keep the egg safe, but also not give in to what it holds, or what it will hold again – my brother.'

Alexis makes a slight noise as if to say something, but then seems to change her mind. A vibration shudders through the building. Samuel watches the books as they tremble.

'We're safe here, we're still protected. For the time being,' Faro says, as the bookshelf swings open. 'Follow me.'

Samuel looks to Alexis who appears just as bewildered. She treads behind Faro, with her crossbow still in hand. He follows them both, the bookcase creaking shut behind him. The heat hits him the most, not the darkness. His eyes adjust after a few seconds, with a little help from the large burning candles that surround the room. In the middle is a circular wooden table and around it are six wooden chairs, with high backs. Now sitting at one end, facing Samuel, is Faro. Beside him are two tall round tables, each displaying a basilarium; he immediately feels drawn to the one on the left. Four of the other chairs are occupied by people with cloaked hoods. Everyone is silent. He can hear Alexis breathing, she's standing so close to him. The hairs on his neck prickle with each breath that hits his skin.

'Mantel?' Alexis says.

The Davadore slips his hood to the side as he turns his head.

'Alexis. You're okay,' the Davadore replies.

Samuel edges around the room. None of the other Davadores have shifted in their chairs. Their faces remain draped in shadow. Mantel's face looks just as pinched as the last time Samuel saw him, in Kirkela.

'Mantel is the head of the Davadores,' Alexis explains, without taking her eyes off him. 'Quisan, Lahon and Nidel are second in command,' she continues, gesturing to the cloaked figures.

Samuel frowns, unnerved by the stiltedness of her

introduction.

'Mantel, why didn't you tell me about the egg, about the bearer and Faro?' Alexis asks.

Mantel is the first to lift back his hood. The other three follow. Three men and one woman–Nidel, if Samuel remembers the introduction correctly.

'Alexis, why don't you sit?' Faro asks.

'No, it's okay, I'd prefer to stand.'

'You did well, my child,' Mantel says, turning his face fully to her.

Samuel continues to move round the table, wanting to get a better look at the other Davadores. Shadows are cast across Nidel's face. She looks up sharply as he passes. Her stare is crisp. Quisan and Lahon have the same colourless skin and bony features. Their hair is smoothed back over their sharp round skulls. Quisan's is a little longer, reaching down just past his ears. His dark eyes are deep set and Samuel can see shadow in the recesses of them as he follows his movements around the room.

'I'm sorry, Alexis,' Faro says. 'Don't blame the Davadores. These secrets had to be kept. What matters is that the egg is safe, but we *must* capture Pemba again.'

'How can we do that if the egg is still fractured?' Samuel says, directing his words at no one in particular. He spots a glance between Faro and Mantel.

'What's going on? What aren't you telling us?

Why are you all up here when the fight is out there?' Alexis asks.

'Samuel,' Faro begins, clasping his cane. 'I explained to you that once the new bearer is chosen it is final, but I wanted to be completely sure. I searched through every book I had, every scroll of information I've ever gathered, to see if I could change what has happened. And to see how I could mend the egg.'

Samuel notices all eyes are on him. He feels torn, a part of him wanting to turn and run, another part desperately wanting to grab the basilarium; the invisible force from it is now even stronger than before.

'What does all this mean?' he asks.

'It means, Samuel, that my brother's betrayal has weakened me more than I realised, and with him being so close I cannot repair the egg. The only way for me to seal it, it seems, is if he is trapped in the egg, far from me.'

Samuel tries to take a deeper breath, wanting to slow his heart rate. Everyone in the room is quiet.

'Samuel,' Faro continues, 'now that you are the bearer, only you can take Pemba back into the Darkness and try to trap him once again.'

Chapter Sixty Two

SAMUEL CAN FEEL THE PULSE in his fingers as he squeezes his hands together. It throbs, alarmingly fast. He can feel his tongue sticking to the sides of his teeth; he desperately needs a drink.

'But how, how can I do that? I'm not even from here. I didn't know anything about other worlds, about other creatures, *or* Pemba until just a few days ago.' He doesn't hesitate, knowing the Davadores must realise by now he's not from this world. 'Pemba knows I'm the bearer doesn't he? That's why he showed himself to me in Kirkela. And that's why they took Phoenix,' Samuel continues. 'They thought he was me. They thought he'd have the Egg of Darkness.'

Faro stares at him, his brow furrowed, his lips pursed.

'Why do we need to trap Pemba? Can't we destroy him here?' Samuel says, asking the question that's been plaguing him ever since Alexis was taken. He avoids Faro's gaze, aware he's talking of killing his brother. The room is quiet and he turns to Alexis, but she won't return his stare.

'I can't,' Faro says. 'That's why I built this prison.' He gestures to one of the basilariums. 'When we became the bearers of the Orbis we gained immortality. The only way to destroy Pemba is to keep him prisoner. He must be sent back into the Darkness once more. There, he will become weak and we can make sure the egg is kept safe, so he never escapes again.'

Samuel feels a shiver run through his body. A clammy sweat radiates off every part of him. He feels like he's in the grips of a high fever.

'We'll help, Samuel. We're all here to help,' Faro says.

'We can't be sure of that.' Alexis moves out of the shadows.

Mantel turns to her. His movements are slow but assured.

'Samuel.' She turns to him. 'I think you should tell them what you saw.'

Samuel feels the Davadores' eyes lock back onto him. Their silence sends a cold air out into the room and he focuses on Alexis, not wanting to look at their pallid faces.

'Samuel, what did you see?' Faro's voice is soft. He's nothing like the Davadores, or his brother.

'I...I think I saw who killed the bearer. Not exactly who, but I saw the mark of two Plain Seekers.' He risks a glance around the room and hears the murmurings of the others.

'Samuel, are you sure?' Faro asks.

'I didn't *see* them attack the bearer but I heard it, and I did see their mark.'

Faro scrapes back his chair and with a low grunt hauls himself up on his cane. He looks weaker with every moment that passes.

'This changes everything,' he says. 'Did you not have any idea there were traitors among your elite?' Faro poses the question at Mantel and for the first time, Samuel sees a flash of colour cross the Davadore's face. He sees the skin tighten over his jaw as he clenches; any tighter and Samuel is sure it will crack.

'We had no idea,' Mantel replies, recovering quickly. 'But perhaps what you saw, Samuel, isn't quite what happened. We know how scared you must be, being so far from home. Home,' Mantel repeats. 'Where is that exactly?'

Samuel feels the anger bubble inside him, starting in his stomach and making its way up into his chest and throat. Mantel's face is blank, but his stare is intense.

'I know what I saw,' he says, ignoring Mantel's question.

'He's right,' a voice emerges from the doorway.

Samuel turns to find Anka, now standing just inside the door. Blood is slowly making its way down his nose from a gash on his forehead. His clothes are ripped and muddied, but he still looks strong. His sword is in its sheath, but Samuel can see the remnants of bodily fluids on the handle.

'Anka,' Alexis says, rushing forward and throwing her arms around him. Samuel feels his shoulders tense.

'Anka? What's happening out there?' Mantel asks.

'We're struggling to keep them back. We need to do something and soon.' He gently pulls away from Alexis. 'Samuel's right. There *are* some who have betrayed us. It's hard to believe but it's true.'

Samuel feels a slight lightness in his chest hearing Anka agreeing with him.

'But who?' Alexis asks. Samuel focuses on the top of her head, where her soft, shiny hair sits neatly.

'You won't like it, but I believe Sith is among those who have betrayed us. I think he is the one that opened the gateway that led Samuel here, and he did it to let more of Pemba's army through.'

'No!' Alexis cries. 'No, he wouldn't do that.'

'I'm sorry, Alexis,' Anka replies, taking hold of her hand. 'Sith has betrayed us. I don't know for certain, but it could have been him that killed the bearer.'

The words are barely audible, a quiet hiss from Anka's mouth. Samuel struggles to believe that the lanky boy he saw on the battlefield had anything to do with the murder.

'We must get the Orbis and the Egg of Darkness away from here,' Faro says. 'If Plain Seekers have betrayed us, then no world will be safe.'

Alexis stares at Mantel, looking for a response from her elder.

Mantel clears his throat before speaking.

'You're right, Faro. Plain Seekers will be able to open a gateway and follow you anywhere. With your brother draining your strength, why don't you let Anka take the Orbis somewhere safe? He can keep moving, travelling through plains. And you can help Samuel trap Pemba in the Darkness, whilst we track down those who have gone against us.'

Samuel shifts his weight from one foot to the other. The action grabs Anka's attention. He glares at Samuel as if he hadn't realised he was there until now.

'How can we trust him?' Samuel asks, talking to Mantel but not taking his eyes from Anka.

Anka snorts and raises his hand. 'There is no doubt of their trust in me.'

Samuel looks at each of the Davadores. Nidel seems calm, her long nail tapping rhythmically on the table as she purses her lips. Quisan and Lahon look towards Mantel, quietly awaiting his response.

'I wouldn't be here if I was betraying them,' Anka continues.

Samuel feels a chill run through him again, this time it seems to freeze the blood in his veins. He watches as Faro nods, picking up the basilarium to his right. His actions seem unusually slow. The whole room feels as though it's entered some sort of time delay. Samuel wonders if everything has slowed, or if it's just in his head. He watches Faro hand the basilarium that holds the Orbis over to Anka. Something doesn't feel right. He can feel his heartbeat lag, thudding against his chest, but his pulse pumps hard, as though the blood is trapped in his ears and is throbbing to escape. Anka reaches up, but just before he takes the box from Faro his eyes flit to Mantel. A nod comes from the Davadore. Anka sees the acknowledgement and slowly accepts the box. *I wouldn't be here if I was betraying them. Them. Them.* The words resound in Samuel's head.

Time reverts to its usual pace as Anka lifts the basilarium away from Faro and holds it high in the air. A drop of blood from Anka's hand drips to the floor. Samuel looks down at Anka's shoes. He sees the tear in his left boot. It's like a laceration that cuts right through Samuel. Now it's clear. Now he knows who killed the bearer.

Chapter Sixty Three

'WAIT! STOP!' SAMUEL YELLS, grappling with his dagger. 'It was him! He killed the bearer.' Alexis watches as Samuel aims the weapon at her friend. Instinctively she throws herself between them.

'No!' She holds her hands up, realising the crossbow in her left is directed at Samuel. The anger in his eyes turns to confusion and her arm lowers just a little.

'It was *him*,' Samuel insists, risking a glimpse from Alexis to Faro.

Alexis turns to Anka, expecting to be confronted with a look of shock. Instead he appears calm, almost relieved.

'You're not as stupid as I thought,' Anka says. 'But what you say doesn't matter anymore. Does it Mantel?'

Alexis feels the saliva in her mouth shrivel. Her throat is so dry, when she swallows she feels as though a thousand tiny blades are scratching her gullet. She stares at Anka, all familiarity about him now gone.

'Mantel?' Faro's voice is soft, broken, as if all his trust has leaked out in that one word. 'Mantel, please tell me you didn't have anything to do with this?'

The Davadore remains silent, his gaze firmly on Anka. Nidel stands, the chair scraping along the floor, making Alexis' teeth clench.

'You cretin,' Nidel says. 'You have the Orbis, why did you admit to anything?'

'I knew we should have done something when he let Alexis carry on without him,' Lahon interrupts. 'You were meant to be with her at *all* times.'

Anka lowers the basilarium, unable to hide his surprise at the Davadores' harsh words.

'She would have been suspicious if I'd insisted,' he says, his voice droning. 'But I stayed close.'

'I thought you had been following us to protect Alexis and the egg,' Samuel says. 'But all you wanted was to make sure she led you to Faro, and the Egg of Darkness reached him.'

With their attention elsewhere, Alexis watches Faro dive forward, but Lahon is fast, and he hurls his arm out, throwing Faro into the corner of the table. Quisan is on his feet and on top of Faro before Alexis can move. Lahon kicks Faro's cane from his grasp, sending it across the floor to the other side of the room. Alexis swings her arm up, positioning her crossbow on Quisan, at the same time pulling the knife from her boot and focusing it on Anka. Her hand shakes just a little. Samuel trains his own dagger on Lahon. A deep chuckle comes from Mantel as he stays seated.

'It wasn't meant to happen quite like this,' he says.

'What are you talking about?' Alexis asks. 'Anka, what's going on?' She ignores the intense burning that is emanating from the back of her neck – wondering if Anka and the Davadore's have betrayed her, why her mark hasn't alerted her before now.

Anka's face drops and for a moment he looks young again. She sees the boy she grew up with, the one she played and trained with. Then, as he turns back to Mantel his stare goes cold.

'Anka? Is it true? *Did* you kill the bearer?'

Anka doesn't reply. He doesn't look at her. His face is as vacant as the Davadores'.

'Let's all just calm down. Try not to get too excited,' Mantel says.

Alexis feels the sick rise up, burning the back of her throat.

'What wasn't meant to happen like this?' she demands from her elder. He doesn't respond, so she continues. 'You made Anka kill the bearer. Didn't you? You wanted the Egg of Darkness. You wanted to capture Faro in it, with his brother, so you could get the Orbis.'

Chapter Sixty Four

ALEXIS ALLOWS THE REALISATION TO FLOOD her mind. All her thoughts, doubts, the niggling things that she's kept hidden, she lets them go. She accepts them. She feels her blood running freer through her, and realises this is why her mark hadn't warned her of them – she hadn't let it. But she feels clearer now, more certain, more able, and from Samuel's stare she feels his gained strength and she soaks it up.

'How many years did you search for the bearer?' she asks.

'Too many,' Mantel replies.

'Is that what you had Orlo doing? Did you stop him because he betrayed you? My father–'

'Your father is weak. He has no ambition, no desire to be better. You're lucky we didn't kill him.'

Alexis feels her muscles tighten, every inch of her skin tingles.

'You killed Orlo, didn't you?'

'The past is the past,' Nidel says.

'How can you say that?' Alexis never liked her, but never realised she was this cold. 'How many more have you killed? How many Plain Seekers have you conditioned into thinking like you?' Alexis realises her efforts are now empty. She could have questioned their methods, but she thought what they were doing, their training, was to help her world, not destroy or control it.

'Alexis,' Anka says. 'Don't you see? Don't you see what we could be? People will look up to us. We won't be different anymore. We'll be treasured, respected.' Anka reaches out to her, but she recoils.

'No. People respect us now, Anka.'

'No they don't. It's like Pemba's army. They all wanted to be accepted. They didn't want to be pushed aside anymore. Well, neither do I.'

'You're comparing yourself to Pemba's army!' Alexis yells. 'They've destroyed hundreds of homes. They've killed so many people. What's happened to you?' She holds her arms up, not wanting him to touch her.

'I want you to see our way of thinking,' Anka replies.

'It's not *your* way of thinking. It's *theirs*.' She points to the Davadores. 'I thought you trusted us, trusted *me* to get the egg somewhere safe.' She spits her words at Anka and the Davadores. 'You're cowards, all of you.' She takes a deep breath, unable to say any more.

'Alexis.' Anka tries again, holding his hand out. 'Please, you have to see. This is for the best. It will help us, and our world.'

'You're helping no one,' Samuel says.

Anka spins to face Samuel, and Alexis is sure if he wasn't holding the Orbis, he'd have a weapon pointed directly at Samuel's head. The speed at which he changes scares her.

'Sith has nothing to do with this, does he?' she asks.

Anka sniggers, wiping some of the blood that's trickled onto his nose.

'Sith, stupid Sith. You're still worried about him. He might not have killed the bearer, but he's the one who started this whole war.'

Alexis blinks hard. She's trying to focus on him and everyone else in the room, but her mark is throbbing and the burning tingle is now travelling up and down her spine.

'What are you talking about?'

'He followed me and Radis when we made our visit to the bearer. He got into such a state, seeing what we'd done. That's when the egg got damaged. We tried to make him believe the death of the bearer was an accident. It took a while for us to calm him down, but eventually he did. He'll believe anything.'

'But he looked up to you, Anka. He would have done anything for you and you know it. How could you do this? You've betrayed us all.'

Anka's eyebrow twitches. His hands grip the basilarium a little tighter.

'We didn't know the egg was damaged, that it was letting light in.' His scowl softens and Alexis knows that he wants to tell her what happened.

'We didn't know Pemba was growing stronger, not before it was too late. We never wanted him to escape.' Anka briefly looks to Mantel, but the Davadore doesn't say a word, so he continues. 'What we wanted was for the discovery of the Egg of Darkness, and the death of the bearer, to lure Faro out of hiding. Then we would have been in a better position to trap him in his own creation, and like you said, take control of the Orbis. It didn't work out to plan, but the Davadores, they worked it to their advantage.'

Samuel turns to Mantel, swinging the dagger to point at the Davadore's neck.

'Why didn't *you* touch it?' he asks. 'Why didn't you touch the egg when they brought it to you? *You* would have become the bearer, and then you could have trapped Faro in it with his brother.'

Nidel steps forward, slicing her long thin sword through the air, coming to rest just inches from Samuel's arm.

Faro, who's been quiet until now, with weapons aimed at him, clears his throat.

'He knew he couldn't touch it,' he says. 'He knew if he did, he would get sucked into the Darkness.'

Chapter Sixty Five

MANTEL'S LIP CURLS AND HE LEANS BACK a little, away from the point of Samuel's dagger. Alexis watches Samuel as his forehead creases and his gaze drops from Mantel to the old man.

'But Samuel touched it. He entered Nekton, not the Darkness,' she says.

Faro shirks free of Quisan's grasp. The Davadore doesn't try to restrain him, knowing there's nowhere for Faro to go.

'Only those of good intent can touch the egg and not get drawn in,' Faro says.

'That's why you needed Alexis.' Samuel turns to Mantel. 'That's why you let *me* bring the egg here. The map wouldn't have shown itself to you.'

Alexis feels the room start to spin. She keeps her focus on the table, something stationary. The shame washes over her, as realisation kicks in. The feeling runs through her entire body, even sinking to her feet, stopping her from moving them. Pemba's words echo in her head. *You have no idea. They're just using you.* She tightens her grip on the crossbow.

'You had to change your plans, once Pemba had escaped. I got it all wrong. I thought you needed me to find the way to Irith, to Faro, to *protect* the egg. But you wanted Pemba to follow me,' she says. Her voice sounds odd, higher and more strained, but she keeps talking. 'You banned gateways, not to stop people from getting in, or to protect our world, but to keep *us* trapped. You wanted Pemba and his army to work their way through White Plains, destroying it and us. You wanted him to track me. All that time I was doing the one thing I thought I was preventing.'

Mantel clicks his tongue against the roof of his mouth. The noise creates a violence in Alexis which makes her shake internally. She imagines throwing herself across the room and slamming her hand into his jaw. The brutal thought surprises her and she inhales deeply.

'Alexis. We had great confidence in you. You're loyal and you're very strong. We trusted you to risk your life for what you thought was right. You did everything that we asked. It actually worked out well,' Mantel says, drawing everyone's attention back to him. 'Pemba's escape wasn't what we planned, but his rampage through worlds to find his brother, gave us an advantage. It made people lean on us more, with little persuasion needed. They wanted our help. Alexis, we can be the saviours in all this. People need a leader. They need someone to help rebuild their world, their lives. All we ever wanted was the Orbis, but now we have more, we have both. Now we can rule anywhere.'

Nidel stares at her leader, looking so smug, Alexis almost loses control of herself.

'He said *a* leader, not leaders,' Samuel says, also having been watching the female Davadore. All the Davadores edge towards him, but Mantel holds his hand up. Faro thrusts forward again, but Quisan and Lahon draw their long thin swords, the same weapon as Nidel and Mantel's. They force him back and he stumbles against a chair, before sinking into it.

'I won't let you control the people in this world any more.' Faro's words ring with vigour but his head hangs low.

'We've done what we must, to make sure everyone has the best life.' Mantel raises his voice. 'We know not everyone has liked us, but now they have no choice. Besides, how do you think everyone here has survived so well? How do you think this planet is so strong? No subtle ruling and too many people, it would get out of hand, become uncontrollable. This world has served its purpose for us, for many years. But we always knew we could do better. We strive to be better. Plain Seekers are one of the greatest things we've ever found, but there always has to be change. Maybe now it's time to move on.' Mantel brushes the creases from his cloak before he stands. 'You could move on with us.'

Alexis feels her breathing shallow as he glares at her. Her stomach tenses as she tries to keep her anger from erupting.

'Mantel. Mantel, what are you talking about?' Faro asks. He lifts his head, his long hair falling from his face. 'What do you mean, too many people?'

'Faro, come now, you must have realised,' Mantel replies. 'You don't honestly think that people can be trusted, that they can uphold what you ask? Accidents happen, but these accidents must be taken care of. The rule of two children per household was put in place for a reason. We do not take rule-breaking lightly.'

'You can't be serious?' Faro croaks. 'You mean, you killed innocents, just because they didn't fit in with your ruling?' Faro's face is full of colour, the crimson almost looking out of place among the pallidness in the room. 'What have you done?' he yells.

'Mantel?' The word is gentle on Alexis' tongue, as if that one word holds all the answers. She looks to Anka, whose brow is creased.

'Mantel, is this true?' Anka asks.

Mantel doesn't respond, but turns to Alexis.

'You've been lucky, my child, but I'm afraid everybody's luck must run out some time.'

'What are you talking about?' Alexis screams, now unable to control her emotions.

The Davadore moves away from the table, slowly running one finger along the dark wood. He sighs heavily, as though tired of explaining.

'My dear child, you're a tertia. *You* are a third child. But I see now I made a mistake in not killing you when you were born. We were told your powers would be greater than most, and I thought we could use that to our advantage. But I should have killed you when I had the chance, just like the others.'

Alexis watches as the walls appear to move. The ground sways beneath her. It takes all her strength not to collapse to the floor.

'She's a tertia?' Anka says.

'No,' Alexis mumbles. 'No, you're lying!' She dives forward but Anka blocks her attack. In her peripheral she sees Faro fly between Quisan and Lahon, the action so sudden they react a moment too late.

'The Orbis!' Faro yells, as he sprawls across the floor, reaching out for his cane. Alexis takes her chance. She swipes her dagger at Anka, catching his arm. She feels it scratch through material, then make contact with skin. It slices through with ease, finding its way deep into the flesh. Anka jerks back, dropping the basilarium, clearly shocked by her attack. The thud as the box hits the ground feels like the loudest sound that's ever entered Alexis' ears. She reaches for it, before Anka can bend and take it from her. In one swoop she has the box in her grip. She continues to move, rolling onto the balls of her feet and propelling herself to the safety of the wall. She spins so her back is against it, then she takes a moment to survey the room. Quisan and Lahon have reached Faro, his fingertips inches from his cane. Anka is squeezing his arm to stop the blood, which is already dripping onto his hand. The most surprising sight is Samuel. He's standing behind Mantel, his dagger at the Davadore's throat, his other wrapped round his waist. Nidel is half a metre away. She holds her sword, aiming it at Samuel, with a sudden uncertainty. The smirk that had seemed printed on Mantel has been replaced with a grimace. For the first time, Alexis sees his skin look damp, a little shiny, as the sweat creeps from his swollen pores.

Chapter Sixty Six

'STOP,' ALEXIS SAYS, the word ricocheting off every corner of the room. The struggle between Quisan, Lahon and Faro ceases, and everyone turns to her. Now she has everybody's attention she isn't sure what to do. They're outnumbered, five to three. She has the Orbis, but they could just as easily take it back. Then she sees it, the snake, wrapping itself around Faro's cane. She hadn't noticed it slither into the room. Its skin is dark purple, smudged with brown, and all but its blonde eyes blend into the wooden staff. Its tongue flicks out, as if trying to tell her something. She listens to her mark and feels no danger towards the reptile.

'You won't get what you want,' she says, hoping the others don't turn and see the snake. 'You'll never be able to control the Orbis, like you have us. How do you expect to stop Pemba?'

Mantel strains to look at her, Samuel still holding the blade against his throat.

'We,' Mantel struggles to speak, 'we don't expect to stop him. There are plenty of others who are willing to risk their lives to do that.'

Alexis chances a glimpse back at the snake. It's inching along the floor, closer to Faro, dragging the cane with it. She feels her pulse quicken as it gets nearer, only inches from Lahon and Quisan. If they turn now they'd be able to reach out and grab it. She waits just a few seconds more.

'Now!' she screams, as Faro closes his fingers around the cane and the snake unwraps itself. A light shoots out from the end of the staff, spreading across the entire room. It's so bright she has trouble seeing her own hands, but she doesn't let go of the basilarium. She watches the snake-like shape through the brightness, growing, transforming back into its human form.

Moments later and the light fades. The room now looks very different. Faro is standing at one end, his cane in his hand, aiming it forward, daring anyone to go near. A man and woman stand either side of him. Quisan and Lahon are still on the floor, and Phoenix is crouched, quivering in a corner of the room, his tongue flicking out one more time before it transforms completely.

'Gideon, Senta,' Samuel says, staring at the man and woman who are next to Faro. Mantel uses Samuel's distraction by ducking and slipping through his grasp. The knife nicks his throat. Alexis watches Samuel draw the sabre from his belt and swing it round. As he spins, the weapon finds a target: Nidel screams as the blade slashes her side. Alexis releases the bolt that's been waiting in her crossbow and it sinks its way into Mantel's chest. She reloads. Gideon and Senta pounce on Quisan and Lahon, grabbing them by their arms. She watches Anka reach for his sword, but before he can unsheathe it she aims her crossbow at his head. She slowly pulls on the trigger, stopping just before the sear releases. The familiar creak of the string as it tightens makes Anka stop. He looks at the heavy bolt, then to her. Her breath shudders as his grey eyes widen, then narrow, as a streak of lightning attacks his arm. He falls backward, his hands reaching out.

'Anka!' She tries to rush forward but is pulled back. Nidel's fingers dig deep into her arms. Anka writhes on the floor, making his way over to Mantel, the impact having only winded him.

'Mantel,' he rasps, holding his arm and grabbing the Davadore. Mantel is clutching his chest, Alexis' bolt still lodged securely.

'Anka, no!' Alexis screams, as Anka struggles over to the door leading to the balcony. She searches round for Samuel and sees him on the floor, blood leaking from his arm: she hadn't seen him get hurt. She wriggles in Nidel's grasp, but the Davadore reaches round and grabs hold of the basilarium. Alexis holds on, her wrist twisting back, her tendons stretching, but Nidel shows no sign of letting go. Twisting her body round, and dropping her crossbow to get a better grip on the basilarium, she finds herself staring into Nidel's eyes. Slowly, the Davadore smiles. Alexis feels the agony before she realises what's happened. At first her mind can't tell where she's hurting. All she can feel is a burning, stabbing pain. She looks down at her stomach and sees the blood already soaking her top. Her fingers weaken at the sight and Nidel pulls the box from her, almost stumbling backwards as Alexis involuntarily lets go.

'Nidel! *Come on.*' Anka's voice is distant, but clear. Alexis turns to see him standing in front of a gateway. With his arm damaged the portal flickers far more than it should, but Mantel has already disappeared through. Gideon and Senta are still struggling with Quisan and Lahon. Alexis looks for Faro, but can't see him in the bright light that's now spanning the room once again. The room begins to spin, and she crumbles to the floor, the blood gurgling in her ears. Feet pound past her, but she still can't see anything through the light. As she lies there the shine of a metal bolt catches her eye. She reaches out for her crossbow, wrapping her fingers around the wooden frame. She shoots aimlessly, with the hope she has shot in the right direction. The light begins to shrink again. She watches as the Davadores make for the gateway. She fires more ammunition, and a bolt finds its way into Quisan's leg. An arrow flies from somewhere, scraping across Lahon's arm. They tumble into the gateway. She watches Anka, struggling to keep the portal open. He looks at her, his face unreadable, as she loads her final bolt and takes aim. Her finger releases the trigger. The bolt hurtles forward, desperate to reach Anka, but the gateway starts to shrink and he dives through. Seconds later, it closes completely and the bolt sails past, connecting with the wall an instant later.

Chapter Sixty Seven

'ALEXIS,' SAMUEL SAYS, SLIDING ACROSS the floor on his knees. 'Alexis. It's alright, I'm here.' Her blood is seeping out onto the floor, staining the wood. If he lifts her top he's worried it will pour even faster. He takes hold of her hand. Her pale skin is tinged yellow and he can see the veins running through it.

'I'm sorry,' she says. 'I had no idea they were, that Anka–'

'Samuel, step back,' Faro says, kneeling beside them. He lowers the tip of his cane so the dove rests gently on Alexis' stomach. 'Step back,' he repeats. Samuel does as he's asked, moving to the side, but keeping hold of her hand.

'Where's Phoenix?' she asks, straining to turn her head. 'He was right here. He helped–'

Faro places a finger gently on her lips.

'Faro, the Orbis. I had it–'

'I must concentrate,' he says, waiting for her to nod before continuing. Samuel watches the wings of the dove flutter as Faro moves the cane over the laceration. A thin streak of light shines down on her, spreading across her body, concentrating on her middle. She closes her eyes and lays her head down on the hard surface. Samuel studies her, letting his gaze follow the contours of her face, down her neck to her chest, which expands heavily as she struggles to breath.

'There,' Faro says, moments later. The light evaporates as he moves the cane away. Samuel looks at her top which is still a dark scarlet, but a dry crust has now formed around the edges. He squeezes her hand and she opens her eyes, blinking away the tears that had formed but not fallen. She sits bolt upright and yanks her top up over her stomach.

'Not a mark,' she murmurs. Her skin returns to its usual smooth paleness as she smiles.

'Good as new,' Samuel says.

Faro runs a finger over the dove and it seems to respond, moving its head towards his finger.

'Thank you,' Alexis says, throwing her arms around the old man. The embrace takes him by surprise and he falters, before finally patting her on the back.

'But the Orbis, they've got it. Nidel took it.'

Faro pulls away from her.

'It's not always easier to see in the light,' he says, his mouth twitching as he withdraws both basilariums from his tunic.

Samuel can feel the tension ease a little in the

room. Senta and Gideon hover over them, not saying a word.

'Can you fix anything?' Samuel asks, looking to Faro's cane.

Faro laughs, a gentle sound that echoes around the room.

'No, unfortunately not. But let me take a look at that arm.'

Samuel rubs his shoulder, his head thumping.

'It's okay, it's nothing.'

Faro leans forward, but as he does, Samuel notices a shadow flicker on the wall near the door.

'Phoenix,' he says, seeing the boy now standing there, rigid.

At the sound of his name the boy seems to panic, and he turns and flees the room. Samuel leaps to his feet, ignoring the pain in his arm.

'Phoenix!'

He shoves the door open, the bookcase having swung back as Phoenix fled. His eyes scan the landing, but the boy's already gone. Samuel looks over the banister and sees him at the bottom of the stairs, looking about wildly, before spotting the door.

'Phoenix, no! Don't go outside!'

The boy doesn't listen, he's already clawing at the exit, trying to break out. Samuel dashes to the top of the stairs, then hurtles down them two at a time. When he gets to the bottom the door is half open. He charges for it, not thinking about anything other than the boy.

The air outside almost chokes him; it feels dense in his lungs, unlike before. The shrieks and screams from the fight hit him forcefully, causing him to hesitate. A white shape catches his eye on the ground: a dove has fallen from its position. Small red droplets tarnish its wings. As he looks around he notices at least another half a dozen birds lying on the ground, lifeless. He turns away from them.

'Phoenix!' Calder's voice slams into him as both he and Toko run up the hill towards them. 'Phoenix! No, go back, stay inside!' Calder shouts again to his son. The tension in Samuel's chest eases a little as he spies Phoenix hovering at the side of the windmill, the noise clearly having dazed him. Just as he starts to make his way over, a dark shape drops from the balcony, landing soundlessly in front of the boy. The bony fingers peek out from the long sleeved robe and wrap themselves around him.

'No! Pemba, leave him alone!' Samuel yells.

Pemba glares at him, pausing for just a second, before disappearing. Phoenix is left standing there, an odd expression on his face. Before Samuel, or the others can reach him, he collapses to the ground.

'My boy,' Calder says, as he gets to the top of the hill, making straight for his son. He falls to his knees, grabbing Phoenix's shoulders before he slumps completely in a heap.

'What happened? What *was* that?' Alexis says, now beside Samuel.

The boy's deep crimson blood oozes out from his stomach and onto the ground, mixing with the dirt and grass.

'No. Come on son, you're alright.' Calder sobs. He holds the boy in his arms, scraping his hair back from his eyes.

'Papa. You're here,' Phoenix says, not shrugging his father away this time.

'Yes, son. I'm here. Of course I'm here.' Every now and then he pulls the boy in close, hugging him to his chest. 'Do something! Someone!' he screams.

Samuel watches as the life seeps out of the boy. He rubs his eyes, tears stinging his face. *This can't be happening.* Flames rise, then he sees Ethan. His mouth is wide, his silent screams wrapping around him.

'No,' Samuel murmurs. 'No!' He sinks down on the grass. 'Calder, let me see, let me see him.' The man holds the boy to his chest, not letting go. 'Help! Faro! Help us!' Samuel screams as Alexis drops to the ground next to him.

'He saved us,' she murmurs. Her grip is firm on his arm but he can feel the quiver from her.

The boy's eyes flicker, before finally closing. A groan escapes him, his mouth partly open. A tear squeezes from the corner of his eye and runs down his cheek. He looks even younger than before.

'He's just a boy,' Samuel mumbles. Toko bends, gently taking hold of the boy's wrist. He feels for a pulse. Calder looks to him, his eyes swollen, his mouth open in anguish as Toko shakes his head.

Chapter Sixty Eight

A LOUD HOWL ECHOES AROUND THE TOP of the hill, muffled only when Calder buries his face into his son's chest. Samuel feels his stomach tighten. The black hole inside him, left from his brother's death, suddenly grows again; he tries not to let his energy get sucked back in.

'*No.* I won't let this happen,' he says.

'Samuel,' Alexis murmurs. 'It's happened. He's gone.'

'*No*, we can stop it. We can stop him.' He looks back at the windmill. 'Where's Faro? He can help him.' He feels a strong grip on his shoulder and he looks round to find Gideon. His eyes are misty, but his expression is blank.

It feels like hours they've been standing, still, listening to the sobs coming from Calder, a ruined man. Then, Samuel feels the helplessness seep away and anger creep in to take its place.

'Someone's got to stop him,' he says, taking one last look at Phoenix, before turning to Alexis. Her cheeks are stained with tears, and every now and then one drops onto her bloodied top. He forces his legs to move, running past them all, unable to look at Calder sobbing into his son's back. Inside the windmill he takes a quick look round, but there's no sign of Faro. He races up the winding staircase, his legs a little weak and his heart pounding as he reaches the summit. He stops instantly as he notices the gap in the bookshelf.

'Faro?' The word escapes him as he makes his way over to the wall. He peers into the secret room, but it's too dark to see anything. Taking one last glance back, he walks through, and the bookcase creaks shut behind him. The room is as he left it moments before, only now just one candle burns. It takes a moment for his eyes to adjust, but when they do, he sees the furniture still knocked over, and a gathering of Alexis' blood staining the floor. He looks to the round tables and sighs with relief as both hold a basilarium. His relief doesn't last long as he spots Faro curled up on the ground by the wall on the far side.

'Faro!' He rushes over to him.

'He's weak.' A voice leaks from the shadows.

Samuel spins round, almost feeling his heart hit his ribcage.

'Pemba? What have you done to him?'

'Which one are you going to go for?' Pemba asks.

Samuel casts his gaze around the room but is unable to work out where the warlord is.

'Why don't you just pick one?'

A slither of light glistens on the far side of the room and Samuel looks back to the basilariums – he knows he won't have a chance to take both boxes. A familiar pull emanates from the one on the left and he dives forward, grabbing the box and swerving round the table, heading for the light. He slips his fingers in between the gap and yanks it open. Light streams into the room, but he doesn't look back.

Standing on the top of the windmill the fields are splayed out below. The bodies are still, limp, like lifeless dolls, and the blood covers the fields like poppies. The wind lashes around him, harsh at this height.

'Give it here, boy.'

Samuel spins round, clasping the box to his chest with one hand and clutching on to his dagger with the other. Pemba now stands in the light, between him and the doorway. He looks even stronger than before, the freedom and killings seeming to have restored him.

'What you have in your hands won't do you any good. Not if you don't have this.' He gestures to the basilarium that's hovering above his palm, the Orbis safe inside. 'I can destroy all worlds, all life, in seconds.'

'No, Pemba. If you do that you'll be gone too.' Samuel looks around for something that might help him, but the balcony is empty.

'But I have that.' He nods at the basilarium in Samuel's hands. 'That may have been my prison, but it can be my safe haven when everywhere else is in ruins.'

'But what would be the point?'

Pemba sneers, as if Samuel understands nothing.

'I would be safe in that, until the time came, when I could emerge again, with my army of followers, and take my pick of whatever world I desire. Now give me the egg and this can all be over. You can be with your brother again.'

Samuel feels an invisible force attack his chest, then his stomach. He feels the acid build, making its way to his mouth, its taste rancid. Silence fills him and his vision blurs, all his senses abandoning him.

'You want to see him again, don't you?'

The words sound like they're in his own head. He tries to focus on Pemba, watching his mouth, but it doesn't move.

'Give me the egg.'

'Don't give it to him, Samuel.' Faro's voice is loud and strong. Samuel looks to him in the doorway. He's hunched but his eyes are alive with a fire burning in them.

Pemba whips round, moving away from the door, closer to the edge of the balcony. It takes a few seconds for Samuel to realise the burning pain in his hand. The basilarium is red hot. He takes his chance, working his hands quickly around the box until it quietly clicks, his eyes flitting between Pemba and Faro the whole time.

'Come now, brother,' Pemba says, his voice wavering a little. 'He's an innocent. We can settle this, just me and you.'

'I agree he's innocent, but unfortunately for you, Pemba, he's also your ruination.'

Pemba laughs, a deep rumble in his throat, but Samuel can see his hesitation. As Faro moves forward, his stride now strong, Alexis appears behind him. Pemba covers the basilarium with his robe, but Samuel can see he's fumbling to open it.

'No!' he yells, diving forward, ramming into Pemba and knocking the basilarium from his grasp. Faro doesn't hesitate; a quick circle of his cane and the box flies over to him, landing neatly in his hand. Samuel tumbles backwards with Pemba, twisting the lid off his own basilarium, just as Pemba takes the brunt of the railing. A second later and they fall off the edge of the windmill together.

'Samuel!' Alexis screams down after him.

As they flail through the air he struggles to know which way is up. Flashes of colour circle him as the altaira soars down with them. Pemba's robes wrap around him, almost choking him. Samuel wrestles his hands free, the basilarium still open and the egg remaining clasped in its claw. The ground is coming up fast. He stretches his finger until it finds the egg. *I just need to touch it.* A bright light propels out, and all he can do is grip the basilarium in one hand and Pemba in the other, as they both get sucked into the Darkness.

Chapter Sixty Nine

Pemba's fingers claw at his wrists, but Samuel holds on. The warlord's tongue flicks out, his cursing soundless as they spin round, making their way to the Darkness. Closing his eyes, Samuel concentrates on the pull of the egg, blocking everything else out. The rushing air pulls at his clothes, then suddenly it stops. He opens his eyes, tearing his hand from the egg, the heat from it marking his fingers.

The landscape around him is empty of everything but perished trees. The air is foggy, the ash raining down on him, as he scrambles to his feet.

'Pemba!' he yells as he fumbles with the lid of the box. It proves difficult with his fingerprints almost singed off, but after a few seconds the lid locks into place. He stumbles across the arid ground, the rush from entering the Darkness tearing its way through his body. As he makes his way over dead branches he notices a stillness that he's never experienced before. There's no sound, no wind, nothing but complete silence. If there was ever any life here, there isn't now.

'It's just me and you, Pemba!'

No answer comes. There is no sign of the war-lord's existence.

'Samuel!' The silence ends instantly.

'Alexis?' he exclaims, spinning round to find her emerging from a gateway, with Toko, Senta, Gideon, and Calder just behind.

'Samuel,' she says again, throwing her arms around him.

'What are you doing here?' he asks.

'What are *you* doing? He'll kill you,' Alexis replies, breaking away.

'I had to do *something*. How did you find this place without the egg?'

'I followed you. But there's no time to explain. Where is he?'

'I don't know. I opened my eyes and he was gone.' Samuel takes another look round. 'What are you all doing here? What about the army? Where's Faro?'

'Faro is safe, with the Orbis,' Toko says. 'It's too dangerous for him to be here. If he gets trapped in the Darkness then we have no hope.'

'We've got to find Pemba,' Calder says, forcefully.

'No. We've got to leave, *now*,' Alexis replies, the gateway shrinking behind her.

'I came here to destroy my son's killer. I'm not leaving until I find him.'

'Calder,' Alexis says, softening her voice.

'I'm sorry, Calder.' Samuel cuts in. 'I'm sorry

about Phoenix. But Pemba can't be killed. He can only be kept here.' He watches the confused look on Calder's face turn to anger. His eyes narrow, his breathing becomes heavier through his nostrils, and he tightens his grip on his sledge hammer.

'Calder, it's true,' Alexis says. 'Pemba is immortal.'

Toko places a hand on his friend's arm, but Calder doesn't respond. Samuel turns to the others. Other than some cuts and bruises they look okay.

'You alright?' he asks Senta, glad to see her.

She nods. 'A big black cat came to my rescue.' She glances at Gideon, who barely responds, other than with a twitch of the eyebrows.

'We've got to get back, so Faro can mend the egg,' Alexis interrupts. The gateway behind them is now closed. 'Put that in your bag.' She nods at the egg. 'Pemba won't be far, he'll be watching, waiting for us to leave, so he can try and return.'

'Senta, you fly up, see if you can spot him, while Alexis opens another gateway,' Toko orders.

Samuel watches her as she leaps into the air, transforming in a second. She flies off without looking back.

'I'll take a look down here,' Gideon says, his last words a growl as his hands become paws and he bounds off through the dead forest.

Samuel can hear the continuous smacking of Calder's sledge hammer into his palm. He can't imagine how it must feel, knowing you can't seek revenge on the person who killed your son. He tightens his hold on the bag as he places the basilarium inside.

'Keep watch, while I concentrate,' Alexis says to him and Toko. She turns from them, preparing to open another portal. It isn't long before a small hole reveals itself in the air.

'Toko!' Senta's voice sails down from the mist as she swoops back to the ground. 'Toko, it's difficult to see anything. There's too much fog up there, he could be anywhere.' She transforms before she touches the land, her legs running on air the last few metres.

'Look out!' Senta yells, dashing forward to shield Samuel and Alexis, her spear held solid in front of her. She swipes it, batting away the sphere of electricity that was heading for them both. Samuel slides the sabre from its sheath, feeling the shiver of nerves run through his body. The gateway is almost fully open.

'Samuel, come on, go through,' Alexis says.

'Not without all of you.'

'Alexis, Samuel, get back!' Toko shouts, as more sparks fly from the mist.

Alexis drops her hand from the gateway and draws her crossbow, a bolt already loaded. They all inch round, creating a circle, their backs together, each one holding their weapon out in front, ready. A dark shape weaves through the fog and Senta fires an arrow.

'Attack!' Toko yells.

Samuel feels a bolt from Alexis' crossbow splinter out into the air. Arrows fly past his ears from Senta's bow. They all shield him, moving forward and pushing him back, towards the gateway. He grips his sword, feeling strong. He doesn't want their protection, he wants to fight.

Now, through the fog he sees Pemba, standing tall, his hands held high, drawing the mist into them. Sparks fly from his long fingers, as black orbs of electricity grow. His fingers twitch, sending currents to deflect the arrows and bolts that are fired at him. The arrows fall to the ground like matchsticks.

'What do we do?' Senta yells.

'Keep tight,' Toko replies. 'Hold your ground and keep blocking.'

His voice fades as he moves forward, away from the group into the fog. He raises his sword reaching to the sky, ready to slice down.

Chapter Seventy

'TOKO, NO!' ALEXIS SHOUTS. 'He'll kill you!'

'Listen to her!' Pemba bellows. 'Give me the egg, Samuel.'

Samuel glares at him, his sabre held out, just like Gideon showed him, though his feet don't feel so grounded. The bag strap sitting across his chest feels heavy, as though compressing his lungs. He looks round to the gateway but without Alexis' attention it's dwindling once more.

'There's nothing you can do, Pemba,' Samuel says. 'Just answer me one thing: how many men have you taken from my world?'

'Taken?' Pemba snarls. 'None. Those who have joined me, every man, every creature, wants the same thing I do. They want something better than what their world has given them.'

'But you would betray them in an instant. Just like you abandoned your brother. Betraying others, people you don't know, *maybe* I could understand. But your own brother.'

'It was easy. Perhaps you would have done the

same one day, if you'd have had the chance.' Pemba sneers.

An explosion erupts in Samuel's head. He sprints forward, his feet pounding over the rough terrain, heading directly for the aggressor.

'Samuel, no!' Alexis yells, behind him.

A second later and he's forced to the ground. He can't breathe, and he can't see anything except red. Commotion surrounds him, screams shuddering through him.

'Samuel!' Alexis says, bending next to him, her hand on his leg.

'I'm alright,' he murmurs, rubbing his arm. 'What happened?'

'Senta threw off his aim a little.'

'You can't protect him anymore.' Pemba stares down at Alexis, metres from them. Alexis stands, shifting her weight from one foot to the other, her crossbow in her hands, ready, as Samuel struggles to his feet.

'You won't win, Pemba,' she says. 'Your army. They've probably been destroyed already. And those that haven't will flee. You'll be all on your own, again.'

Pemba's body convulses. It takes Samuel a moment to realise he's laughing.

'I'm better on my own.' His laughter rings out, as he blows the ash from his deathly lungs.

'Look!' Senta says, pointing. The ash behind Pemba flickers white as it swirls in the air. Auburn smoke rises from the ground, working its way around him.

'Pemba,' Faro says, his voice drifting through the smog. 'My brother. These people have done nothing to you. It's not them you want, it's me.'

Pemba turns his head, searching.

'Faro?' A sphere of dark current grows between his hands. 'You're wrong, Faro. For years it *was* about you. I wanted you to suffer, for what you did to me, for leaving me here. But my thirst for suffering has grown. All the time I've spent here, watching, waiting, knowing all the life that was still going on, it's left me bitter, but hungry. I've seen other worlds, I've watched them make stupid mistakes. They need a leader. Someone who can show them where they've gone wrong.'

'You don't want to lead,' Faro replies, finally coming into view. 'You want to rule. Killing people is not leading. Everyone has their own choices.' He's standing behind Pemba, his cane pointed at him, the dove's wings still, as if caught in mid flight. His tunic flutters from an invisible wind and his eyes are bright, the differing colours even clearer than before.

'We should take him down now, while he's distracted,' Samuel whispers to Alexis. 'There are more of us than him.'

'Wait,' she replies.

'What *for*?' Calder says. 'He looks weaker just being back here. We can take him.'

Samuel nods, also having noticed the sudden change in Pemba. His skin looks thinner, similar to how he was before.

'Enough!' Pemba shouts at his brother. 'Enough of your talking. It should be *you* here, Faro. If I can't kill you, then keeping you here will have to be enough.' Pemba spits his words, and sparks fly from his hands.

'Don't make me do it again, Pemba. You made your choice,' Faro bellows.

'I know not to trust you. I'm stronger now.'

'You sure about that?' Calder yells, charging towards him, his sledge hammer held high.

'Calder, no!'

'Come *on*,' Gideon growls, leaping forward, with Toko and Senta not far behind, their weapons poised, ready.

'Samuel, stay back,' Alexis says, turning to him.

'Come on,' he replies, ignoring her and running towards Pemba, gripping the sabre with both hands.

Chapter Seventy One

PEMBA HOLDS HIS HANDS HIGH, gathering power from the dark clouds above. In one swift movement he brings his arms down and propels the ball of lightning. It strikes Calder, exploding on impact, throwing him backwards.

Gideon sprints on his four cat legs, then leaps up, sailing through the air, his claws out ready to slice. Pemba hurls another ball of force at them. The panther howls as it hits him and fiery particles attack his body. He whimpers as he falls to the ground. Samuel watches as the panther slowly disappears and Gideon's human form returns. As he reaches him he drops to his knees. A warm sticky substance touches his hand and he looks down to find blood leaking from Gideon's body.

'Gideon? Come on, get up.'

A groan comes from the man and his chest rises and falls heavily.

'Pemba!' Faro yells.

Samuel looks up and watches as he soars from the ground, his arms held high in the air, just like before.

White sparks fly out from his cane as he lowers it towards Pemba. A rush of electricity pours from it, hitting his brother directly in the chest. Samuel waits for the scream, for the howl of pain. There's nothing but silence. Pemba's clothes light up, flames engulfing him for a few seconds before dissipating. A deep cackle comes from him, and Samuel sees what little damage Faro has caused. There's no blood, no broken limbs, just a little smoulder rising from Pemba's clothes as they flutter in the invisible wind.

'What the hell?' Samuel clambers to his feet, but stays next to Gideon.

'I told you, I'm stronger now, *brother*,' Pemba says, sneering.

'No,' Faro mutters, staring intently at his cane.

'Keep together,' Toko murmurs.

Samuel feels his strong presence and is grateful. They form around the fallen Gideon and Calder. Samuel watches as Faro shoots again and again at Pemba, but his laughter continues to echo out.

'Now my turn!' Pemba says, throwing his arms forward and launching his attack on his brother. Black lightning streaks through the air, hitting Faro time and time again.

'No!' Samuel screams. He watches as Faro falls to the ground, his cane flying out of his grasp.

'Fire!' Toko yells.

The bolts and arrows swipe past Samuel, finding

their target, but have no effect on their victim. Toko throws a multitude of daggers, aiming for every inch of his body. But Pemba continues to advance in on his brother.

Samuel can feel the energy in the air. Every part of him feels alert; his skin is tingling and he can feel the pulse in his neck. He blocks out the shouting and allows his eyes to focus in on Faro's cane. As the others continue their barrage of ammunition he makes his decision.

Keeping low he darts across the dry ground, the cane his only target. *Almost there.* He reaches out, but lightning strikes him, ricocheting from elsewhere. He ignores the searing pain that's attacking his arm. With the cane metres away he dives forward, grabs it and tumbles onto his side, taking cover behind a rock. He stares at the dove; one of its wings has been taken clean off. The wooden cane darkens beneath his palm. It's a lot lighter than he thought it would be.

'Please work,' he murmurs, peering out from behind the rock and seeing Pemba almost on top of Faro. Above him the clouds are thick, closing in. Samuel checks the satchel, the basilarium still intact inside. He swings it round onto his back, then grips the cane in his left hand, his right arm hanging by his side, weak and bleeding. A final glance at the others tells him they haven't got much ammunition left. With one last deep intake of breath he stands and steps out in clear view.

Chapter Seventy Two

'PEMBA,' HE SAYS. His voice is deep. He almost doesn't recognise it. Pemba falters before turning to him, his mouth twisting upwards.

'Samuel!' Alexis shouts. Out of the corner of his eye he sees Toko grab her.

'Get back!' he yells, before turning to Faro, who's lying still on the ground, his hair draped over his face. As he raises his arm, aiming the cane at Pemba, he feels it shudder in his hand. After a few seconds a bright light shines out, spanning across everything.

'Don't be stupid, boy,' Pemba says.

Samuel doesn't lower the cane, but stands firm. The light begins to change colour, settling into a deep purple. He focuses on Pemba, imagining the attack, then without warning the light begins to move, creating ripples. After a few moments the cane shakes and a current projects from it, moving through the light and hitting its target. Pemba cries out, the force pushing him backwards. Instantly the bright light disappears, sucking back into the cane. Samuel stares at Pemba, the smoke still rising from him. It takes a second to clear and then he sees the damage he's done. A neat circle, a few centimeters wide, has appeared on the warlord's stomach. As Samuel strains to look closer he realises it isn't a circle but a hole, a hole that has burnt right through him. He looks down at the cane, turning it over in his hands.

'He's strong, Pemba,' Faro says, staring up at his brother from the ground.

'How? How?' Pemba stammers, somehow still standing.

Samuel looks to Toko and the others. They're focused on Pemba and Faro, all except Alexis, who's staring intently at him.

'You underestimated him,' Faro says. 'You thought he wasn't a part of this. Well you were wrong. He's the bearer now. He's the bearer of the egg, the Egg of Darkness. He's the bearer of *you* now, brother.'

Samuel feels the cane tremble in his hand once more, and the dove's wing flutters. He aims it again at Pemba, whose face is now contorted. He can't take his eyes from him. Pemba rises up, hovering above them; his arms splayed at his sides remind Samuel of an angel. His fingers, still bony and pointed, stretch towards the ground. His dark hair swirls around him, and his once hanging clothes flow, like a loose suit of armour. He lifts his arms higher, his hands together. The hole in his stomach is miraculously shrinking, but he's weak, the electricity between his hands flickering.

Samuel wills the cane to fire and it does, this time hitting Pemba in the shoulder. Samuel holds it steady, shooting again and again, making impact every time. His legs, his arms, his head. With each blow, Pemba gets weaker, until, finally, he collapses to the ground. His veins return to the surface of his skin, but no blood leaks from his wounds.

Samuel can feel the heat from the cane; he can feel its potential, and it fills him with a sense of power. He's never felt so in control.

'Samuel!' Alexis shouts. 'Samuel, come on!'

He looks over to her, not even realising she'd been calling to him. A gateway is now open and Senta and Toko are helping Gideon and Calder through. Samuel stares at Alexis. Her eyes are wide, her mouth open, screaming his name, but he can't hear her. All he can hear, all he can feel is the heat. The rage rises inside of him, his blood coursing through his body so fast he feels as though it's going to spill out.

'Samuel, look out!' Alexis screams.

He spins round to find Pemba now standing, his arms thrown forward. Samuel dives behind a fallen tree. As he hits the ground something drops from his pocket. He looks down and sees Alexis' necklace; the silver feather lying in the dirt. The shiny surface of the sabre catches his attention. He stares at it, seeing his face, his brother's face, in the reflection. However, the face isn't like before, this time it looks strong, *he* looks strong. Grabbing Alexis' necklace, he stands to face Pemba.

He takes one last look at him, watching the smoke floating from his clothes, then squeezes the necklace in his palm and aims the cane. This time his hand and the staff are completely steady. The cane's power hits Pemba in the leg, then again at his waist and arms. Finally it hits him directly in his chest, right where his heart should be. The force propels Samuel backwards. He hits the ground hard but doesn't feel it; his body feels strangely light, as if indestructible.

'Samuel.'

Someone tugs on his arm and he looks up to find Faro hunched next to him.

'Come. Come now,' he says, going to take the cane from him. The man suddenly doesn't look so weak. He reluctantly releases his grip on the cane. As soon as he does, he feels his pulse slow, his blood settling.

'We must leave, now,' Faro repeats.

Samuel clambers to his feet. He takes one last look at the writhing Pemba, before following Faro over to the others. Senta, Gideon and Calder have already passed through the gateway. Samuel can see White Plains through the portal.

'Are you alright?' Alexis asks him.

'Yeah, I'm fine.'

'Come on you two, you go,' Toko says, as Faro disappears through.

Alexis takes his hand, gripping it tightly. She steps ahead of him and they enter the vacuum.

'No! Don't leave me here!' Pemba screeches. Samuel turns to see him, still on the ground with the marks from the cane burning his skin. A dark orb is alive in his hand.

'Toko, watch out!' Samuel shouts, as the ball of light leaves Pemba and heads towards them. They're too far into the portal to go back. Samuel falls, watching as the light hits Toko, then everything goes black.

Chapter Seventy Three

SAMUEL FEELS A HAND ON HIS SHOULDER and he realises he's kneeling on the forest floor. He can hear Alexis saying his name but his thoughts are screaming so loudly in his head he can't form any words to speak.

'Samuel, you're hurt. Let me help you,' she says. He feels a tug and looks down to see her wrapping a piece of cloth around his bloody arm.

'Where is he?' he croaks. 'Where's Toko?' He staggers to his feet. The forest is quiet, no noise of war.

'He's right...' Alexis falters, turning back to where the gateway had been. Samuel turns too. There's no sign that a portal had been there, not even a speck of dust shows where they came through. His eyes scan the forest, then he spots Toko lying face down in the grass. He runs to him, dropping to his knees before placing a hand on the man's shoulder and gently rolling him over. A groan comes from Toko, and Samuel feels the warm blood seep onto his hands, as it leaks from his chest.

'Don't worry about me,' Toko gasps, clutching his

wound. 'You've got to repair the egg, now, before Pemba regains his strength.'

'Samuel.' Faro is standing over them. 'Samuel, give me the egg.' He holds his creased fingers out, waiting.

'Help him first,' Samuel urges. 'Heal him.'

Toko grabs his wrist. 'Give him the egg.'

Samuel's eyes drop to his bag, then to Alexis, who gently nods. He pulls the basilarium out from the satchel, relinquishing it to Faro. The man swiftly undoes the lid, his movements faster than before. He whispers something to the one-winged dove, before holding it over the egg. The dove glows, and its wing flutters as it's moved back and forth, an inch from the egg's surface. The dark clouds on the egg swirl, away from the fissure, as if scared by the light. Faro's stance is much steadier than before, and as the crack slowly begins to shrink, so does his agedness – his face softening and his back straightening.

'It's done,' he says, handing the basilarium back to Samuel. Samuel takes a look at the egg before replacing the lid: though its surface is shiny and splinter-free, the black fog still billows, and Samuel is sure he can hear Pemba's screams beneath it. He carefully places the egg back in his satchel, then turns to Faro.

'Please, you have to help Toko.'

Toko doesn't resist, his breathing becoming shallower as Faro bends beside him. Calder is now knelt the other side of his friend, clutching his own chest, badly wounded from Pemba's hit. Toko turns to him, the building sweat on his forehead now dripping down his face.

'I should never have let them push you and your family out,' he splutters, blood trickling from his mouth. 'I'm sorry.'

Calder grips his hand tighter and shakes his head, reassuring his friend.

'Faro?' Samuel says, softly.

Faro turns to them, away from Toko.

'The wound is too deep, too close to his heart. I don't kno–'

'Please,' Alexis says. 'You have to try.'

Faro nods gravely, then places his cane on the man's chest. The dove's light shines again, only this time it's just a glimmer. Faro moves the cane over Toko's chest in a figure of eight. Samuel isn't sure how long it takes, but finally he begins to see the wound shrivel at the edges. Seconds later and Toko coughs, spluttering blood across the forest floor. Faro sits back heavily, the cane clasped in his hand, but the dove no longer moving.

'It's not completely healed, but it's sealed the worst,' he says.

Samuel listens to Toko's heavy breathing for a few moments, then stands. As soon as he does, Alexis throws her arms around his waist and buries her head in his chest. He wraps his arms around her, holding her firm, ignoring the burning tightness in his shoulder. Her honey scent fills his nostrils, as he breathes in deeply, clinging to her as much as she does to him. After a few moments she pulls back.

'Sorry, I, I…'

'Don't apologise,' he says, looking into her eyes and brushing his hand against her cheek. She holds his gaze for a moment, before letting go. The others are lost in their own worlds: Senta, is murmuring to Gideon and checking his injured arm. Toko is lying still, peaceful, with his eyes closed. Calder and Faro are next to him, but Samuel can see Faro has healed Calder's lesion.

'Are you okay?' Samuel asks Gideon, whose arm is hanging lifelessly by his side.

'Yeah. It's fine, just dislocated, I think.' Gideon's voice is hoarse. Without saying a word, Faro gets up and runs the cane over his arm. A moment later and the shifter is able to raise it and roll his shoulder, seemingly with ease. He nods his thanks.

'Samuel,' Faro says. 'Let me heal your arm too.'

Samuel looks down at the dark material that's now saturated with his blood. The light from the dove is warm as it spreads over his arm and shoulder. Once finished, he can move freely again, without pain.

'We should go and see if the others still need our help,' Senta says. Her eyes are blurry, but her voice sounds strong.

'Gideon, Calder, you take Toko somewhere safe. He needs to rest,' Faro says.

Gideon nods at the man, then looks to his friends.

'Take this.' Senta holds out a flask of water. Samuel notices the way Gideon stares at her, and the small glance between them as she goes to leave. He places a hand on Calder's shoulder.

'See you soon,' he says, but the lurch in his stomach tells him he may not. As he pulls away, Calder grabs his hand, squeezing it briefly.

'Be careful, kid,' he replies gruffly, without looking up.

As they leave the cluster of trees, Samuel glances back at the three men. Gideon has edged closer to Toko and Calder, and he watches as he holds out his flask. He's glad to see Calder accept the token.

Alexis' stomach rumbles and she claps a hand to it.

'It's alright, you must be hungry. We've not eaten in hours,' Samuel says.

She looks at him and smiles briefly, allowing her hair to fall and cover her face.

'We're not far,' she replies. 'I didn't want to open the gateway too close, I didn't know what danger would be there; if any of Pemba's army are still alive, then they'll be weaker, from Pemba being trapped. It shouldn't take us long to get back, then we'll see what destruction has been left behind.'

Chapter Seventy Four

ONCE ON THE OUTSKIRTS OF THE FOREST, Alexis recognises the shimmering dove wings, still surrounding the windmill. The sight below them shows the remainders of the battle. The once empty plains are now full of flesh and bones. Creatures are sprawled everywhere, limbs separated from their bodies. The trees are gone, burnt to the ground, but ash still floats in the sky. The only other movement is made by rags of clothing flailing in the wind. The acrid scent of decaying bodies sweeps with the gentle breeze. She tries to shake the unsettled feeling in her chest, but it persists. She's desperate to find her family, to learn the truth, but she knows she must return Samuel home and help track down the Davadores.

'They were already rotten before they were killed,' she mutters, staring at the monsters.

'Not all of them,' Samuel replies, his focus on the soldiers. 'Do you think they're all dead?'

'If not, they'll have probably fled back into the shadows.'

Alexis watches Samuel as they walk up the hill.

He's clutching tightly to the bag and she wonders if he can feel something from the egg.

'Samuel? Are you alright?' she asks, as he turns back to the plains below.

'Yeah. Sorry I just…'

'Just what?'

'I don't know. Nothing.' He looks at her and smiles while running a hand through his dirty hair. 'I really need a wash,' he says, changing the subject as he turns back round to carry on.

'You and me both.'

As they reach Faro's windmill, a sound carries on the wind. It's a familiar voice, and one she's sure is calling her name. She turns and sees Sith, running up the hill towards them.

'Alexis!'

'Sith!' She wraps her arms around the boy, squeezing her body around his bony shoulders. 'You're safe.' She takes a step back. His gaunt cheeks flush and he breaks into a toothy grin. His smile fades as he looks around and sees the sparse group.

'Where are the other Plain Seekers?' Alexis asks him.

'Most have gone to help villagers. Where's Anka?'

'He's gone, with the Davadores. I need to explain some things to you,' Alexis says. 'But not now, later.'

The boy nods, gravely.

'How will you know who to trust now?' Samuel

asks, directing his question at Faro.

Faro clears his throat. 'We'll find out. Whoever has betrayed us, will have surely fled by now, so those who are left will be the ones to trust, I hope.'

Alexis places a hand on the man's arm.

'It's my fault,' Sith says, hanging his head. 'I should never have trusted Anka, what he told me–'

Faro takes a step towards him.

'No. *I* let the Davadores get away with so much, for so long. They've ruined this world. We *must* find them, before they settle somewhere else and rebuild their army. They won't give up. They'll still want the Orbis, and the Egg of Darkness.' Faro's eyes focus on Alexis.

'We must set this right,' she says.

'Yes,' Faro replies, nodding. 'The main thing now, is that they are both safe and so, Samuel, are you. And it needs to stay that way.'

'But Faro, we have no idea where Anka has taken the Davadores,' Alexis urges.

'Maybe they've gone back to the Lyceum?' Senta suggests.

Faro doesn't respond. He rubs his thumb and forefinger together, as if in thought.

'If they do, it will only be briefly. He'll have taken them somewhere safe, be it on this world or another. We'll find them. Like I said, what's important now is that we have both the Orbis and the Egg of Darkness.

And we must get you home.' He turns to Samuel.

'I can look after him,' Alexis says.

'I know you can, child, but he can't stay here. You must think, were the Davadores or Anka ever told where he was from?'

'I never told Anka where he'd come from, just that he'd travelled through a gateway which shouldn't have been open. Now I realise there were probably gateways from other worlds, letting warriors in, so Anka couldn't have known which one it had been. Sith?' Alexis asks, turning to the boy.

Sith scrunches his brow.

'No. I don't think they know. The portal that was open from Earth, to let some of Pemba's army through, was only left open because of me, because I disturbed it. I don't even think it was Anka that opened the gateway.'

'I'm the only one that saw Samuel come through,' Alexis says. 'I'm the one who eventually closed it. Even the army that hunted us back to Rythe wouldn't have known; the portal was closed long enough before they came for them to have seen any trace, any essence of Earth.'

Faro pauses then turns to Samuel.

'This means, Alexis, that you're going to have to take him back there, back to Earth.'

Chapter Seventy Five

'WHOA, WAIT, HANG ON,' SAMUEL SAYS, stepping forward. 'What will happen about the Davadores and Anka? And all the other people that are helping them?'

'We'll find them, Samuel,' Faro says. 'But the Egg of Darkness should be separated from the Orbis, as it was before. The further apart they are the better. As the bearer of the Egg of Darkness I'm afraid it will have to stay with you. Sending you back home will be the safest thing. The egg wasn't on Earth before,' Faro continues. 'And, like I've said, sometimes things are better in plain sight.'

'But, but...' Alexis stutters, a heaviness in her chest.

'Alexis, it's for the best.' Faro places a hand on her arm. 'For everyone.'

She wants to argue but stops herself, knowing he's right.

'I can't go,' Samuel says. 'What if me going home puts my mum and dad in danger? What about the people that joined Pemba's army from my world?

What if there are more of them back on Earth?'

'Pemba will have brought his entire army here to fight. They will have entered through many different gateways, I'm sure,' Faro says.

'But you don't know that for certain. You don't know if some have gone back home.'

'No, Samuel, I don't. But if there are people back on your world that were a part of his army, they no longer have a leader. And they won't know about you. We will have people watch you, make sure you and your family stay safe.'

Alexis turns to Samuel, realising Faro's right.

'I promised I'd get you home, Samuel, and I will. Now I can, I'll take you back.'

Samuel looks defeated. He glances at Senta, but she doesn't return his gaze.

'Samuel, you've helped us more than we could have ever asked for,' Faro says.

'But what am I meant to do with the egg?'

'Keep it safe until we can find the Davadores.'

'And then what?'

'I don't have all the answers yet, but you will be safe, Samuel.'

'What about all of you? Can I ever come back?'

'Let's concentrate on getting you home first, back to your family.'

Alexis places a hand on Samuel's arm and he turns his attention to her. She sees the strength in his eyes, a light that was there before but is now brighter. She stares at him until finally, she sees his acceptance.

SAMUEL STANDS JUST OUTSIDE THE DOORWAY to Faro's windmill. He looks round at everyone, standing, waiting for him and Alexis to leave.

'Say goodbye to the others for me,' he says, turning to Senta.

'I will,' she replies, leaning forward and kissing him briefly on the cheek, before throwing her arms around his neck. He stumbles backwards slightly, then after a second or two squeezes back. She pulls away, not saying anything else. Out of the corner of his eye he notices Alexis staring.

'Here,' he says, handing her her sabre. 'Take this back, it's yours after all. And I don't think having something like this at home would go down too well.'

'What about that?' She nods to his dagger. 'You're keeping that one, then?'

'Well, that one I can hide a little more easily.' He grins at her. 'And it sort of feels a part of me now. I think I'll feel safer with it.' As he speaks a pang of realisation hits him. 'Hey, where are Brawn and Paladin?'

'They're safe. I left Paladin in the forest. She's out of harm's way.'

'Samuel, take care of yourself and that,' Faro says, tapping the satchel with his cane. 'I'll be keeping an eye on it, and you. I'm sure we'll see each other again soon.' His stare falters on the bag for a few moments, as if he's having a difficult time letting it go. Eventually he drops his cane back to the ground.

'I'm sorry,' Samuel says, then continues before Faro can ask why. 'I'm sorry about your brother. Being twins…I know how it feels. I know if my brother had ever betrayed me, I'd still want to stick by him, somehow.'

'Well, in a way I have. Keeping him in the Darkness is protecting him as well as others.'

'Yeah. I guess so.'

'You'll always have Ethan, Samuel,' Faro says.

Samuel sighs, feeling the weight in his chest ease.

'Can I see it?' he asks. 'The Orbis?'

Faro's mouth twitches. He reaches inside his tunic and from almost out of nowhere produces the basilarium. He takes the lid off with great speed, then tilts the box slightly, so Samuel can see inside. Samuel takes a closer look at the egg he'd only been able to get a glimpse at before. It sits in a similar clasp to the Egg of Darkness, but the egg is in no way the same. Small, pale yellow shapes, which look like islands, are dotted around its sun-like centre. He moves closer, but Faro slides the box back over it, clicking it into place.

'You mustn't look for too long, it's complexity

starts to play with the mind,' he says.

Samuel doesn't know what to say. The pull isn't like the one from the Egg of Darkness; it's strong, but in a different way. He feels a desire to look again, but he doesn't ask.

'What will you do now? Now some people know who you are.'

Faro's smile wanes.

'It will be okay.'

'Come on then,' Alexis says, running a hand down his arm.

Samuel frowns. 'Where are we going? Can't you open a gateway here?'

'There's something I want to show you first.' She smiles at the others before turning and making off. He looks at Faro, Senta and Sith one last time, then tilts his head before hurrying after her.

Once they're a few hundred yards away he looks back. He raises his hand to give a slight wave, but notices Faro huddled close to Senta, appearing to be in deep conversation. He's too far to hear anything, so he turns and jogs a little, to catch up with Alexis, wondering what it is she wants to show him.

Chapter Seventy Six

'WHAT DO YOU WANT TO SHOW ME?' Samuel asks, as they make their way down the hill, the other side from where the battle took place.

'You'll see,' Alexis replies.

They continue on, until they come to a small cluster of trees.

'I wanted you to see someone before I take you home.'

A short sharp whistle escapes her lips, and Samuel watches as a white horse trots out from behind a tree.

'Brawn?' The horse canters over to him, then nuzzles into his chest. 'Brawn, look at you,' Samuel exclaims. 'You're white, there's not a black hair on you.'

'It's amazing, isn't it?'

'I don't understand.' Samuel runs his hand up the horse's nose.

'I think he's finally back to his old self, now Pemba's no longer a threat and his army gone. Like I said before, all the horses on his world, Fortis, are white, but I think the shock of being taken and what Pemba's army did to him, made his coat turn dark.'

Samuel looks into Brawn's eyes. He's never felt a creature understand him as much before, and he can't bear the thought of leaving him.

'I will see you again, won't I?'

Alexis smiles. 'Are you talking to me or Brawn?'

'Both of you,' Samuel says, turning to her.

'You're the bearer, Samuel. I have to protect the bearer.'

He smiles, then slowly the corners of his mouth drop.

'I'm sorry,' he says.

'What for?'

'What Mantel said. About you.'

Alexis' smiles fades. 'I just need to find my family. I need to find out what happened. I've only ever known my brother, and if I really am a tertia, a third child, then what happened to our other sibling? Does this mean *they* were killed? All because they thought my powers were greater?'

He looks at her mouth. It wavers into a sad smile.

'I have so many questions. But the only people I'm going to get answers from are my parents.'

'You'll find them. I know you will. You'll get the answers you deserve. But whatever they are, being a tertia doesn't make you bad. You've brought no dishonour to your family.'

Without thinking he leans forward, placing his lips

on hers. They feel soft, softer than her cheeks. He closes his eyes and instinctively places his hands on the small of her back. She doesn't move, then after a few seconds he feels the pressure of her lips against his.

Something whacks his arm but he ignores it, enjoying being lost in Alexis' scent, his nose buried in her hair as he hugs her. Another blow comes to his left shoulder.

'Ow!' he exclaims, pulling back. 'Brawn, stop it.'

The horse stares at him.

'I think he's jealous.' Alexis laughs. 'Come on, climb up.'

'Where are we going?'

'You'll see.'

He jumps up on Brawn, and Alexis gets on behind him.

'Shouldn't you be in front? I don't know where we're going.'

'Don't worry, I'll guide you.' She wraps her arms around his waist and clasps her hands together in front of him. Brawn takes off, trotting calmly out of the forest.

THEY'VE NOT BEEN RIDING LONG, but Samuel can't keep quiet any longer.

'How did you follow me into the Darkness without the egg?'

Alexis is quiet, but he can feel her stiffen. He fidgets round in the saddle to see her. She's smiling, her head lightly resting on his back.

'In all honesty I don't know. I've only ever been able to locate people if I have something of theirs, like I said. But…'

'But what?'

She lifts her head and it comes to rest closer to his ear.

'But with you, I just knew. I didn't need to have anything of yours, I just felt you. It was like you were a part of me.' She laughs a little. 'I didn't even think I could open a gateway there.'

He feels the skin on his neck tremble as her breath seeps into his pores and he welcomes it, his body feeling stronger than it has done in months.

'WE CAN STOP HERE,' Alexis says.

He hadn't realised it but he'd closed his eyes, enjoying the rhythmic motion of Brawn's hooves clipping the ground and Alexis' body close to his. He opens his eyes and the sunlight hits his pupils.

'Where are we?'

'Just over there is the most amazing sight you'll

ever see. No matter how many worlds I've entered, nothing ever compares to this,' Alexis replies, jumping down from Brawn. Samuel follows, and they walk up the last stretch of the mountain, leaving Brawn munching on some grass. As they approach the peak, Samuel feels the air change; it thins out, giving energy to his body.

'It's called White Plains for a reason, you know,' Alexis says, grabbing his hand and giggling. After a few metres she comes to a halt and he collides with her. He laughs, then stops when he sees the sight in front of them. He'd thought the view from Faro's windmill was good, the land laid out below so similar to the waves of the sea, but this is something else entirely. The world beneath them stretches for miles. There is nothing but pure white land.

'It's almost too bright to look at,' he says.

'I know. It's untouchable. This spot here is the purest air you'll ever find. I always come here if I feel I need to recharge myself.'

Samuel enjoys the warmth of the air on his skin and a sense of freedom, a feeling he hasn't felt in a long time. He shuts his eyes and the light of the land almost penetrates his eyelids. He relishes it all, not wanting to be anywhere else.

Chapter Seventy Seven

A CLOUD DRIFTS ACROSS THE SKY and its shadow awakens Samuel. The ball of anxiousness moves in his stomach once more.

'What am I going to say to my mum and dad? How can I explain any of this?'

'You don't,' Alexis replies. 'You can't tell them anything.'

'But they're going to want to know where I've been. They'll have been going through hell.'

'I know.' Alexis turns to him. 'But you can't tell anyone from your world about this. I'm sorry, you just can't.'

He sighs, breathing out heavily through his nose.

'Come on, it's time,' she says, turning from the view and heading back towards Brawn.

'Where are you going to open it up?'

'Somewhere close to your house. There's no point in sending you back to the forest, your friends will be long gone and you'll only have to make your way home.'

She stops beside Brawn, the horse now standing

still, staring at them both. Samuel watches as Alexis settles into her familiar stance, her feet slightly apart, her body tilted a little to the left.

'Take my hand,' she says. 'Imagine home.' She slips his hand into hers, then with her other reaches out. Her pupils dilate, as the gateway in front of her grows.

'Wait,' he says, tugging her back. The portal wavers.

'What is it? What's wrong?'

'You're a Plain Seeker.'

'You've just noticed?'

He pulls a face at her.

'What I mean is, can't you show me some other worlds, before you take me back?'

She smiles, seeming enlivened by the thought.

'Where do you want to see?'

'I don't know. Where's the best place you've been?'

'There are so many,' she muses.

'Wait. What about Mar, Mari,'

'Do you mean Maris? How do you know about that world?'

'Faro. I saw a globe at his.'

She moves her hand in the air, her fingers making gentle shapes.

'Maris it is then.'

The gateway that was there snaps shut, then opens

again, as a small window.

'Have a look,' she says, taking a step back.

He feels the rush in his stomach as he inches closer.

'Can we enter?'

'I wouldn't if I were you.' She motions to the window.

He looks through and can see why. It's just like Faro described. All he can see is water, a deep blue mass of ocean.

'Is the *whole* world like this?'

'Pretty much. There are some areas of land. *Look* over there.' She grabs his arm forcing his focus. He follows her eye line, scanning the calm waters. A few metres away he spots a ripple.

'What is it?' he whispers, not sure if his voice will carry through the portal.

'Just wait, keep watching.'

He does as she says. The ripples get larger, then out of the water a dark shape begins to rise.

'What the hell is that?' he says, as the creature continues to soar. Its head looks to be at least triple the size of his own, its neck dark grey and its body seeming endless.

'It's a dracone. Watch, this bit's special.'

He gapes at the dracone as its body emerges from the water. He expects its under belly to be smooth, like the rest of it, but it's covered in glistening scales. The water runs off its back, leaving a colourful shine. It opens its wings, that until now Samuel hadn't even noticed, they'd blended so well. They stretch out, spanning metres, then begin to beat slowly, gathering air underneath them. Samuel can almost feel the wind rush at his face as the creature leaves the sea and takes flight.

'It's rare for dracones to leave the water. They hunt only once a month. You're lucky,' Alexis says.

Samuel continues to watch the creature as it flies further upwards, its body long, like a snake, but with four small legs that tuck up close as it soars.

'They look so peaceful,' he says, turning to her.

She smiles but doesn't return his gaze. Instead she grips his hand tighter. When he looks back to the small portal he notices the world is blurry. The sea is drying up, the sky is growing darker, and the gateway is getting larger. After a few moments he sees land, trees, grass and houses. It takes him a few more seconds to realise it's home. He lets go of her and takes a step forward, to get a better look.

'It looks weird,' he says, staring at the road, his road. He can see his house, his dad's car sitting in the drive. The neighbour's cat prowling about the street, doesn't even turn its head towards them. The street lights flicker on as night-time settles in.

'It looks different.'

'Everything will probably look different now.'

Alexis grabs his hand again.

'Wait,' he says, turning round. 'Brawn.' The horse trots up to him and nuzzles into his shoulder. 'Brawn, you be good. Make sure you keep this nice new coat white. I'll see you soon.' The horse whines, his nostrils flared and his hoof kicking dust up from the ground.

'Wait here, boy,' Alexis says to the horse.

Samuel rubs the bridge of Brawn's nose, then turns away, unable to look into his dark eyes any longer.

Chapter Seventy Eight

SAMUEL IS USED TO THE FEELING of the gateway now, he barely even notices the tingling heat, working its way into his body. Holding Alexis' hand and walking through, he feels calm. He focuses on her long hair that is caught, frozen, floating around her face as they pass through. After a moment they step out of the gateway and onto his road.

He doesn't let go of her hand and she still grips his. He looks about him but the road is quiet, even the cat seems to have sloped off.

'Which house is yours?'

'That one.' Samuel points to a red-bricked end of terrace. One light is on in the downstairs room, the rest of the house is dark. 'It all looks a bit bland now.'

'It's home though, isn't it?'

'Yeah, it's home.'

Alexis slips her hand out from his.

'I never asked before, but do you have anything from Earth?'

'No, not yet.'

'Then I guess you'll have to come back,' he says,

smiling.

She grins at him, then her face turns serious.

'Samuel, you must keep the egg with you at *all* times. Don't take it out of the basilarium. Do you still have the pouch I kept it in?'

Samuel produces the small bag from the bottom of the satchel. He watches as Alexis pulls out the rope she'd cut and loops back through some leather lace.

'If you don't have the satchel with you then tie this to you.'

Samuel places the basilarium back inside the pouch, then puts it all into the satchel.

'We'll watch over you until everything is resolved with the Davadores and Anka,' she says. 'You won't be on your own. But I have to leave you now.'

'Already? But what if I need you?'

'Like I said, someone will be watching out for you.'

'But what if I need *you*,' he urges.

She smiles at him then drops her head. Her hair falls across her face and he reaches out a hand to tuck it back behind her ear.

'I'll know if you need me,' she says, a grin spreading across her face.

He stares into her eyes, the green flecked with brown enticing him in. He kisses her again, wanting to savour everything about her.

Moments later she pulls away. He rubs the back of

her neck, watching the skin on her collar bone flush, as she smiles at him.

'Here, this is yours,' he says, holding out his hand to reveal her necklace.

'It gave you strength?'

He nods and she wraps her hand around his, closing his palm.

'Then keep it.'

Samuel feels the breeze tickle his arms.

'I really can't go with you?' he asks. 'What if I check my mum and dad are okay and then leave again? I could lie, make something up. It could work,' he says, seeing Alexis' eyebrows rise.

The gateway hovers behind her. He can see Brawn, a blurry image, standing strong, waiting for her to come back through. He turns around to face his house.

'I'm not looking forward to this conversation.'

'You'll be okay, I know you will.'

Samuel grips the bag and fumbles with his sheath, tucking it, and the dagger into the satchel.

'Yeah but…' He turns back to her. 'Alexis?'

The portal is shrinking and he can just make out the back of her, disappearing through.

'Alexis!' He runs forward, diving for the gateway, but he's too late. He flails through the air and lands on the grass verge with a thud. Jumping to his feet he spins round, but the gateway is gone.

'I'll miss you,' he whispers.

ALEXIS WATCHES HIM FROM ANOTHER GATEWAY, just out of sight.

'I had to leave, Brawn. If I hadn't left then I don't think I would have been able to.' She watches Samuel walk up to his house. He takes his time, trudging slowly up the path, his hand clasped to the strap of his satchel. He hesitates outside the front door, then after a few minutes he knocks.

'I can't watch him anymore.' She lowers her hand and the gateway shrinks, just as the door opens.

'I'll miss you too,' she says, turning away from the portal as remnants of Earth dance across her skin.

The End

Read on for a sneak preview of *Origins,*
Rebecca's next novel.

ORIGINS

Rebecca Perkin

Chapter One

I THOUGHT I KNEW MY FAMILY. That was the only thing that had been going through my head all day, and continued to as I stared out of the classroom window. The teachings of Mr Norton were just a hum, like an annoying wasp. There were only two more weeks of school and then I was done for good. I should be concentrating on my exams, but all I could think about was last night and what I'd found in the loft. The photograph was still in my blazer pocket, where I'd carefully folded and placed it. I desperately wanted to look at it again, but I couldn't take it out in lesson. A bit of screwed up paper landed on my desk and I looked up to find Megan staring at me.

'Eva, what were you just daydreaming about?' she whispered.

I didn't want to tell her about the photograph just yet.

'Prince,' I replied. The singer's name popped into my head, as he'd been the last thing I'd listened to on my iPod.

'Which one, Will or Harry?'

I rolled my eyes at her.

'Neither. I meant Prince. You know, 'Purple Rain'?'

I watched Meg's mouth as it formed a silent circle of realisation.

'Is Chorlie picking you up later?' she asked, twirling a strand of blonde hair around her pencil.

I smiled at the affectionate term my friend had adopted for my brother.

'Yeah, you want a lift?'

'Will you two stop muttering,' Mr Norton cut in. 'You may be days away from leaving this place, but I've got years left, so do me the courtesy of listening.' He glared at us for a few seconds before turning back to the whiteboard. Meg grinned, then scribbled something in her notebook before holding it out for me to read: *A lift would be great. Will we be stopping at Aladdin's cave?*

I nodded, knowing she meant my dad's DIY shop, also the place where my brother worked.

'Not for long,' I muttered quickly, before turning my attention to the front of the class. I tried not to think about the photo that felt like it was burning a hole in my jacket. There was an hour left of school and I needed to focus.

'HEY LOOK, THERE'S JOSH,' Meg said, elbowing me in the ribs. I turned to see our friend in his running gear, jogging towards the school track, his dark hair bouncing up and down. 'Hey, Josh!' Meg yelled, thrusting her hand in the air. Josh turned then, seeing us, began jogging backwards whilst sticking two arms up and waving them about frantically. I laughed at his goofiness.

'Why hasn't he asked you out yet?' Meg murmured, her mouth close to my ear.

'We're just friends,' I replied, but I couldn't take my eyes off him as he made his way onto the field. Meg wrapped her arm through mine.

'You want to be more than that though, don't you?'

Before I could answer, my brother's familiar red pickup truck crawled up the school's driveway. I watched a group of girls turn and stare as he came to a stop. That happened a lot. He was a tall, toned nineteen-year-old with golden brown, dishevelled hair. That was Meg's description of him, not mine, though I still hadn't figured out why, in the three years since we'd moved to the New Forest, he hadn't had a girlfriend. Meg had suggested that he did but he kept her a secret.

'Hey you,' Charlie said as I climbed up into the cab next to him.

'It's okay if we give Meg a lift, isn't it?' I asked, as

she got in next to me.

Charlie smiled and his grey eyes lit up. 'Sure.'

Twenty minutes later, we pulled up on the pavement outside a parade of shops.

'Won't be long,' Charlie said, leaping down from the truck.

I looked up at the shop sign – *Seswick DIY*. I liked that Dad had put our family name on it.

'He really doesn't say much, does he,' Meg said as we followed Charlie into the store. I didn't reply because it was true, Charlie never spoke just for the sake of it, but I liked that about him.

'It always smells like a hamster's cage in here,' Meg continued as we entered the organised chaos that was Dad's shop.

'It's wood chipping,' I replied, taking a couple of lollipops out of the tub, Dad kept on the counter.

'Your brother's truck smells of it too.'

'Are you gonna keep insulting my family or do you want this?' I said, holding a green lollipop out to her. I loved my friend but sometimes she didn't know when to shut up, and since I'd found the photograph in the loft it was all I kept thinking about. Anything else seemed like an annoying chatter in my ear.

'I'm not insulting them,' she said. 'I like hamsters. I was thinking of getting one actually.' She took the sweet. 'Green, your favourite colour.'

'I know,' I said, stuffing the sweet into my cheek.

'They're the colour of Josh's eyes too,' she added and grinned.

BACK HOME, AFTER DROPPING MEG OFF, I watched Dad as he took his dinner plate over to the deep ceramic sink, where Mum was washing up. He gently placed a hand on the small of her back, kissed her on the cheek, then whispered something in her ear. She laughed and I looked to my brother who was engrossed in his dinner. He lifted his head, as though he sensed my gaze. After a quick glance at Mum and Dad, he returned my look with a grin. I thought again about the photo in my pocket. Did he know? Had I missed it for the last fifteen years?

'Charlie boy, do you want to come and help me in the workshop?' Dad said, resting his large hands on a dining chair.

'Sure.'

'Don't be too long out there tonight, Scott,' Mum said, with a hint of playfulness.

Dad winked at me, and lines creased around his eyes.

'Do you think they just go and drink beer and watch football in the shed?' I said to Mum once they'd gone.

She laughed and continued washing up. 'Don't let

them hear you call it a shed.'

I scraped some of the salad dressing off my plate then licked my fork. Now would be a good time to talk to Mum about what I'd found, but I didn't know how to start. I opened my mouth a few times, willing the words to come out, but they procrastinated.

'You okay, sweetheart?' she said.

'Yeah, fine. Why?'

'You were quiet through dinner.'

I could feel the redness creep up my neck. I felt as though I was going to cry but I had no idea why. I pulled the folded photo out of my jeans pocket and placed it carefully on the kitchen table. The image was of two teenage girls, one a little older than the other. Both had pale skin and green eyes but the younger had bright auburn hair, whilst the other's was dark black. It was clear that they were sisters, that had been affirmed by the writing on the back: *Me and my sister – 1984.* I looked to Mum and her wavy auburn hair that draped down her back.

'How come you never told me you had a sister?' One moment the words wouldn't come, the next they tripped out of me, stumbling over themselves as though they were running to be free. Mum stopped washing the plate and let it fall back into the soapy water, her shoulders hunching forward. I felt a sudden surge of guilt, a need to run and put my arms around her, but I didn't.

'That was a long time ago,' she finally said. Her voice sounded tight, like the damp tea towel that she was twisting round her hands.

'How can you say that? You've got a sister and you never told me.' I didn't want to keep blurting the words out, but I couldn't stop them.

Mum sighed, still not turning to face me. 'Aoife died, long before you were born. Not long after Grammy and Grandpop. I was only sixteen.'

I swallowed, struggling with the lump that had lodged in my throat. I'd had no idea that she'd lost a sister as well as her mum and dad. I pushed my chair back and made my way around the solid oak table.

'That's why we called you Eva,' she continued. 'It's an anglicised version of Aoife.'

'I'm sorry, Mum,' I said, putting my hand on her back. 'I shouldn't have asked.'

She tossed the tea towel onto the kitchen worktop then turned to me and smiled.

'She was family. You deserve to know. I guess I'm just still so angry about it.' She turned back to the window.

I was desperate to ask her more questions, but I didn't want to make her feel worse.

'I was just so lucky to meet your dad shortly after,' she said.

I smiled, knowing how much she loved Dad, just by the tone of her voice.

'I thought you met him when you left Ireland, when you were twenty?'

She picked up the dishcloth and began scraping an oily tray.

'You must have some exams to study for?' she said.

I dropped my hand from her back.

'We'll talk more about Aoife another time.' Her voice had softened but she didn't look at me again.

I GLANCED AT THE CLOCK on my bedside table: 9.57pm. The only glow was coming from that and the laptop on my desk. I'd been lying on my bed staring at the photograph of Mum and Aunt Aoife for the past hour. I thought how young my aunt had been when she'd died. The thought made my head spin a little. Both her and Mum had the same small dimples when they smiled. I didn't know what I was trying to get from staring at the photo, maybe the answers I'd wanted from Mum. I'd never felt she, or Dad, had lied to me before. They'd always spoken openly about both their parents dying, but right now I felt weird, like my world had spun a little off kilter. I needed something comforting, something that would make me feel better. I looked at my guitar; it was too late to play, I needed something else. I hauled myself off the bed

376

and went downstairs to the kitchen.

I shut the freezer door, disappointed and annoyed that there was no ice cream. I looked at the kitchen clock. The small shop down by the harbour would still be open for another half an hour. If I ran, I could be there and back in under twenty minutes. As I threw a hoody on over my t-shirt I could hear my brother's voice in my head – *Lymington might be a lot quieter than Brighton, but there's still plenty to be wary of.* That was what he'd said to me not long after we moved here. I remembered it clearly as we'd been on a bus at the time, and every passenger, aside from us, had been at least seventy.

THE SUMMER EVENING AIR WAS COOL, especially near the harbour, but it felt fresh and was something I liked about living here. I'd been resentful when we'd left Brighton, not wanting to leave my friends, but the forest and its surroundings had grown on me.

As I walked into the newsagents the door set off the gentle ping of the bell. The fluorescent glow of the strip lights was a little bright after the dimly lit streets. The cashier barely lifted his head from his magazine as I made my way to the back of the shop. Apart from a radio playing heavy metal, the only other sound in the shop was the gentle buzz of the freezers.

I placed the tub of cookie dough ice cream on the counter and handed over a screwed up fiver. The boy's dirty fingers hovered over the money whilst he finished reading an article. I stared at the top of his greasy head, wondering whether to ask him to hurry up.

A few minutes later I walked back out into the cool air clutching my ice cream. The brisk walk had helped clear my head and I realised Mum must have had good reason not to mention her sister, and would probably speak about her when she was ready.

As I traipsed up the cobbled road, past the colourful shop buildings, I noticed a man stumble out of the pub. He looked about fifty and had a round belly, that was clearly full of alcohol. I side-stepped into one of the shop doorways, but he walked up the hill, away from me. As I watched him, I noticed another figure in the shadows further up the road. My heart fluttered and I tucked the tub of ice cream into my hoody so I had both hands free.

The street was quiet, apart from the odd laughter that came from the pub. The round-bellied man made his way slowly up the street, then swayed down an alley. The other figure, that had been draped in shadow, now seemed to find its feet and briskly walked after him. The figure's gait was familiar. Suddenly I was glad for the ice cream – I could feel the dampness through my t-shirt.

As the shadowy figure turned into the alley it glanced out at the road. I almost called out as I realised the solid jawline was that of my brother, Charlie. But the way he looked back, as though checking to see no-one was watching, made me stop. *What the hell is he doing*? I hadn't realised it but I'd started walking towards him.

I stopped by the jewellers next to the passageway. Something dripped onto my foot and I looked down at my flip flops. The ice cream was starting to melt against my increasing body heat. I placed a hand on the cool brickwork and peered round the corner. A security light had come on at the other end of the alley and I could make out the heavily-built man and my brother close behind him. I watched as my brother speedily pulled something from his belt. I couldn't quite make out what it was, but he slipped the instrument over his fingers. As he made a fist, something twinkled in the light. It was a blade.

Now, just a step behind the drunken man, he brought his arm up swiftly and sliced the man's back. As he brought his arm down he caught the guy again, then a second later he put his other arm round the man's head and brought the blade to his neck.

I stepped back, turning away from the alley. I could almost hear the skin being torn as I imagined my brother cutting through him. An involuntary motion of my muscles forced me to silently wretch, but nothing came up.

I had to run. I forced my heavy legs to move, going back the way I'd come. It was much easier to run down hill, with gravity propelling me forward. My only fear was of tripping over my own feet. Something wasn't right. It couldn't have been my brother. But even as the tub of ice cream slid out from under my jumper, making its melted way down my jeans and onto the street, I knew what I'd seen was real.

Acknowledgements

I was very lucky to have a mum and dad who encouraged my reading at an early age. It helped that I loved reading, but without their support and ability to make reading fun, I may not have formed such a close relationship with books. I have many people to thank for the editing of the book, both professionals and friends. It took a lot of time and energy getting it to a publishable state and I couldn't have done that without my partner, Kate, who re-read the book so many times she ended up dreaming about it. Many of the made-up words in *White Plains* are linked with Latin and a combination of existing words in the English language, but I have Kate to thank for *Davadores*. Great thanks goes to my sister, Laura, who was the perfect reader of this genre and who gave invaluable feedback. Thanks also to John who gave *White Plains* its final edit before publication; his funny margin comments made any changes bearable! I'm fortunate to have people who support me in becoming an author and I give thanks to those, friends and family, who bought my book even when they had read it for free!